Caroline Stickland was born in 1955. With a degree in English and American Literature from the University of East Anglia she became involved in adult literacy tutoring. Her first novel, *The Standing Hills*, was runner up for the 1986 Betty Trask Award and the Georgette Heyer Historical Novel Prize. Her second novel was *A House of Clay*. Caroline Stickland is married and lives in Dorset.

Acclaim for *The Standing Hills*:

'Finely written . . . special and different'
Daily Mail

'Elegantly written . . . a wealth of lovingly recreated detail'
Times Literary Supplement

THE DARKNESS OF CORN

Caroline Stickland

CORGI BOOKS

THE DARKNESS OF CORN
A CORGI BOOK 0 552 13834 7

Originally published in Great Britain
by Victor Gollancz Ltd

PRINTING HISTORY
Gollancz edition published 1990
Corgi edition published 1992

This book is set in 10/12pt Plantin by
County Typesetters, Margate, Kent

Corgi Books are published by Transworld Publishers Ltd,
61–63 Uxbridge Road, Ealing, London W5 5SA, in Australia
by Transworld Publishers (Australia) Pty Ltd, 15–23 Helles
Avenue, Moorebank, NSW 2170, and in New Zealand by
Transworld Publishers (N.Z.) Ltd, Cnr Moselle and Waipareira
Avenues, Henderson, Auckland.

Printed and bound in Great Britain by
Cox & Wyman Ltd, Reading, Berks.

To my mother
Jeannie Sadler

CHAPTER ONE

Every second Tuesday Beatrice Fayerdon drove out to visit her sister. Her way ran over twelve miles of lonely downs and valleys between Wynford Tarrent and Bridport and, though the countryside was quiet, it was not a road whose isolation gave any sense of safety. Many husbands, looking on Beatrice's bold and secretive eyes, would have thought that if such a young woman did not fall into one kind of trouble, she would fall into another; but Daniel Fayerdon was fond of his purse. He had been married three years and the son, who was one of the reasons which prompted him to take that particular wife, having not yet appeared, was growing less cautious of harm coming to Beatrice and more sensitive to the expense of sending one of his men with her. On a clear spring day in April 1824, she made the journey alone. She liked it.

For the first four miles, as she climbed the long, slow incline out of the hollow where her husband ground the ripe corn in the old rooms above the millrace, she was too occupied in guiding the trap to feel her freedom. It was more than six months since she had had reins in her hands. Jos Everett, who carted Fayerdon grain since the overseers had apprenticed him fifty years before, had been directed to drive her from the time of her marriage. He had grown almost beyond work and it hurt Daniel less in lost hours to send him than any of his stronger men.

It was an arrangement that suited both the old man and Beatrice. The time spent jaunting to and from the market town, with long afternoons in a warm and well-stocked kitchen, was a holiday to Jos and the company of his lively young mistress was, as he told her, as good as three penn'orth of ale. For her part Beatrice could relax with Jos as she could not do at home and it was her pleasure to coax him into tales of the past and snatches of cracked and reedy song as they jolted through the lanes. It was mischief that had first made her persuade him to teach her to drive but as he became more feeble she drove to let him rest and gave back the whip only when they were in sight of towns.

Their happy excursions ended when an attack of rheumatism in late October forced Jos to keep to his bed. It was the first bout of the complaint which had prevented him from giving any ghost of labour and Daniel, considering his age and the approaching winter, realized that he was beyond productive work. Against Beatrice's wishes he turned the old man off, pointing out to her that it was the responsibility of the parish, not himself, to care for the infirm. He did not take her protestations seriously; she was his wife and he paid no more attention to her pleas than to the groaning of the corn beneath his millstones. Indeed, he felt himself proved right in his decision by Jos's death some five weeks later and told Beatrice so on several occasions. His mother agreed with him.

The episode left Beatrice without a regular chaperone on her visits to Bridport. If Daniel had not been eager for her to continue her custom he would have forbidden her to go, rather than be obliged to put his mind to who best could accompany her, but he was determined to have her constantly appearing in her sister's house. To this end he tried sending his apprentice-lad, despite a proven lack of ability as a driver. Beatrice endured the strangled silence of this youth twice before demanding a replacement, saying that should they meet any rogues upon the road the boy could distract them from her only by fainting at their feet. Daniel thought of the benefits to him from a connection with her family and sent an assortment of his older men, but this caused discontent amongst the workers' wives and plain-spoken comments to Beatrice from her mother-in-law. At this Beatrice revealed her talent as a coachman, insisting that she was capable of making the journey alone, and Daniel, weary of pretending a deep interest in her welfare, gave his permission for the venture.

The cause of Daniel's keenness for the visits, and the other reason for his having chosen Beatrice as his wife, was her sister's husband. Thirza Randall, whose friendly, sensible intelligence had steered a civilized and peace-making course through life, had never shown herself so wise as in her choice of who to love. When Henry Lamford had inherited his family's thriving corn-merchant's business and had shown himself to be his father's equal in the profession, he had felt free to make an offer to the woman he admired above all others and Thirza had accepted him. She considered herself supremely lucky in an uncertain world to marry where she loved and now, six years later, she saw nothing in her life to make her think her decision wrong. At twenty-five, with a husband three years older who was open and affectionate in his nature, straightforward and talented in his flourishing trade, with two sons and an infant daughter all sturdy and well-mannered, she was almost content.

What dissatisfaction she suffered was caused by worry and guilt over her sister. It was at her home that Beatrice had met Daniel and, at first, it was her hospitality which had fostered their meetings. Neither she nor Henry knew the Fayerdons well. Wynford Mill was on the edge of the district with which Henry traded and had previously given its business to the Dorchester Corn Exchange, but Daniel, searching for grain that was cheaper and better, had sought out other sources and was negotiating the terms for wheat in the back parlour of Arland House when Beatrice had run in, looking for her sister. Daniel knew more of her family than she of his and he saw at once in this vivid girl a means of binding himself to a rising enterprise.

She was above him in class but not so much as to put her out of his reach. The younger daughter of a distressed gentlewoman who had been left an impoverished widow with two girls just after the birth of the second was not beyond his grasp. She was attached by her constrained and dignified upbringing to the gentry and, by her sister, to monied merchants, but in one aspect he felt himself her superior. Her father had been born to wealth and land but had squandered his inheritance in the life of a charming wastrel, leaving his wife with only the small annuity that came to her from an aunt; his father had been the tenant of a small-holding, whose mean industriousness and snatching at opportunity had left his wife and son in comfort and full possession of a mill. Daniel considered himself to be the future but a residual awkwardness with his social superiors soured him and his immediate calculation of Beatrice's potential worth to him was spiced by the knowledge that a lady would be his to order and humiliate. He needed a commercial advantage and a son and this glowing creature with the ready laugh, so obviously ripe for marriage, could hardly be more useful. He had added when relating this to his mother that she was lovely, but it was an afterthought.

He began to visit the cornyard at times when he was likely to be invited into the house and, over the glasses of dark currant wine and dishes of intoxicating green tea, his interest in Beatrice was delicately displayed. He had a reputation as a sound and honest man of business and his behaviour was impeccable. Beatrice was eighteen years old and eager to love whoever seemed to love her. There was a perverse, obstinate streak in her character which often led her astray, so that when rumours of Daniel being a hard master – of acting roughly to his workers and penny-pinching where spending would have improved his mill – began to worry her relations, she refused to believe them. Nothing of what was said against him was unusual in an employer, nor could anything definite be brought to her attention, but her family gradually came to feel that he was wrong for Beatrice and tried to discourage their companionship.

It was too late. Although social invitations were no longer sent by Thirza to Daniel she could not prevent him coming to the cornyard on business, and when Beatrice went out to him there it was inevitable that he should be invited in. Thirza, Henry and Mrs Randall all tried to dissuade her from committing herself to Daniel but without success. To Beatrice,

Thirza and Henry were her contemporaries and no wiser than she and she had not yet outgrown a wish to annoy her mother. She did listen with more seriousness to Henry's uncle, George Lamford, a clever, cultivated man with a true concern for the Randall women. It was with sadness that she had to disappoint him but she was unwilling to fight against what she was convinced was real love and George, as the local solicitor, was obliged to comfort himself by weighing up what was said of Daniel and admitting that he could put his finger on nothing substantial that was not in his favour.

Beatrice and Daniel were married in St Mary's Church, Bridport and went to live with his mother, Bella Fayerdon, in the house attached to Wynford Mill. Before the month was out Beatrice realized she had made a bitter and irredeemable mistake. For three years she had struggled, with great courage, to hide this from her family but, despite something secretive within her, she was not the kind of woman who could conceal her unhappiness from those who cared about her and their concern for her welfare made the Lamfords keep an interest in Daniel's trade.

Today Beatrice was feeling freer and more happy than she had done since she married. She had climbed out of the valley and made her way over the awkward bridge and narrow street of Toller Porcorum without faltering and was enjoying the sun and breeze and sight of the pony's fat, bouncing rump as it drew her up on to the high, lonely ridge of down that curved in long, solitary miles towards Bridport.

There was an orchard to her right and the bright snow-blossom of the cherry trees, the cream-white of the pears and the pink-tipped petals of the gnarled old apples were brilliant against the clear blue sky. There were daffodils amongst the grass with heads too heavy to be stirred by such a slight wind and on the verges primroses flowered. She had three young wood anemones, picked from the copse by the millstream, at her breast and swallows were darting here and there above the brook in the meadow to the left of the lane. All was fresh and growing and filled Beatrice with a bitter-sweet longing that was part light-heartedness and part a yearning for what she knew she could not have.

As she reached the ridge-top and was brought suddenly into the wide views of the high country – the depths and shadows of the downs and valleys, the woods and pools that went beyond and beyond out towards the sea – she shut her eyes for pain of what she did not choose to name. She felt herself drenched in the chill scents of spring and a burgeoning that was not hers. She had a delight in sensual things. It was natural to her to express all her emotions physically and the constant restraint and repression she was forced to exercise in her life warped and frustrated her. The affection that she would pour joyfully on whoever claimed it was asked for nowhere but in her sister's house and on this bright day the years stretched before her, carrying a fear of her whole life being without love, without passion, without children.

She had long since given up the hope of making Daniel care for her but that there might be no new lives to need her love was becoming an increasing worry. It was not only as a friend that Daniel paid no attention to her. At first the novelty of having a woman regularly in his bed, with a legal right to do as he pleased with her, was an excitement but when this had no longer been new and when months of conscientious effort had not implanted a son he lost interest. If he had thought on the matter he would have found that for him physical union had none of the zest and satisfaction he derived from the adventure of making money. It did not cross his mind that his behaviour hurt and distressed his wife and he would not have cared if it had. She had sworn to love, honour and obey and to him these vows on a woman's part were absolute and made her personal wishes immaterial compared with his own.

To Beatrice his touch had soon become repugnant but the early weeks of her marriage, before she realized that it was her husband and not the strangeness of the act that repelled her, had taught her that she could have flowered as a lover if she had been treated with kindness. The yearning for a man who desired her and the desperate craving for a child of her own in her arms had led her again and again into the humiliation of trying to entice Daniel into wanting her. It shamed her to have to coax her own husband into the performance of what she was sure other men were eager to do. She would have preferred the strength of mind to accept her unloved and barren position in his house but she knew that this feeling of spring would once more drag her down into an attempt to seduce him. Already a voice was whispering to her that Daniel knew he needed a son and surely, surely a little persuasion . . . ?

Briskly, she opened her eyes and began to busy herself by shaking off the sick longing that had replaced her rare happiness. With one hand she smoothed the skirts of her high-waisted gown, then loosened the fastening of her fine woollen cloak and pulled it off her shoulders so that it fell on to the seat about her. The cloak and the ribbons in her bonnet were a rich, dark green; the gown, with its starched, white collar, was a paler green, sprigged with yellow ears of barley. She was herself as like spring as her surroundings and anyone watching her would have found Daniel's indifference hard to understand.

Images of fruit and ripeness came into the minds of those who saw Beatrice. She had a figure that was both sleek and full and her movements were those of a cat which is roundly languorous at one moment, swiftly graceful at the next. She had a still and charming face surrounded by the braids and twists of her waist-long, dark-corn hair but in the serenity of this deceptive face her eyes were those of a hunter. Those who could see beyond appearances would have recognized that she was strong. There was a strength in the landscape that comforted her now. The downs to her left were smooth, long and treeless – a pale, tender green raised up to a stark, watery sky where a few streamers of bright cloud were being driven inland. Far out over the softer woods and hollows the sky merged into a deeper blue and from here, on this height, Beatrice thought she drew in the bitter tang of the sea. It exhilarated her. She loved this country. It was part of her routine life but today, pulled hither and thither as she was by her emotions, she was determined to do what she had longed to do so often before.

The broad plateau of Tarrendon Hill was ahead of her, standing out in mighty isolation from the ridge. An Iron-Age fortress, ditched and ramped against its enemies, it rose from the valley like the walls of a keep. The winds here in winter could force men to their knees and the cold, stern beauty of its face was a temptation to Beatrice.

She had never walked on it alone; she would do so now. Friends had brought her here to admire the August views and twice she had asked Jos to go with her as far as the ramparts. To have lived so close to her desire and tasted it only three times. Today she would have her fill. It was too lonely a place for her to have much fear of being seen. Parties did come on pleasure-jaunts but they were rare except in high summer and there was no village nearby. Nevertheless, she was aware how quickly the smallest piece of news travelled and how much it is exaggerated and so, to prevent any chance passerby giving Daniel a report of her diversion, she decided to screen the trap while she walked.

There were two rough gates at the entrance to the green lane that led to Tarrendon, one barred the way to the hill, the other – just beyond the first – led into the meadow that fell down into the valley. There was a hollow in this meadow before the ground sloped away which was large enough for a cart to turn in and was hidden from the road by the thick bloom of a hawthorn hedge.

Beatrice reined in her pony and after glancing all around, climbed down to open both gates. When they were wide she grasped the bridle and led the pony down into the hollow. He was a placid animal and showed no surprise or hesitation at this unusual manoeuvre but contentedly lowered his grey head and began feeling over the new grass with soft, pink lips. Beatrice lashed the reins out of the way of his legs and put the brake on firmly, so that pony and trap were held where they were, before she closed the gates. Looking from the first gate she could tell that nothing could be seen of them from the lane and, with some satisfaction at this innocent secret, she began to walk out to the hill.

The lane was barely wide enough for a vehicle but was an easy path for those on foot. The unworn turf showed how little the path was travelled and this, and the knowledge that the farm it lay on was tenantless, gave her confidence and a renewal of her sense of freedom. She began to walk with longer strides, sometimes almost dancing as she swept her feet through the tangled grass. There was an excitement in doing something unknown by others. A lark, startled by her approach, rose up out of the meadow and hung singing over the abyss beside her. She followed it to a gap in the bramble hedge and looked down.

Beyond the briars the ground fell sharply to such a depth it made her hold her breath. She shut her eyes for the pleasure of finding the sight there when she opened them. Ridged from side to side by the paths the sheep had taken as they cropped its precipitous sides, the coombe dropped away to a wood far below where the roof of the empty farmhouse was a darker shade amongst the trees. To her left the humped promontory of Tarrendon stood out into the vale. To her right along the hill-top and down into the valleys she saw her road as thin as the first stroke of the blade in the corn. She raised her hands and untied her bonnet, throwing it round behind the brambles. Then she drew out her combs and her heavy gold hair uncoiled, unravelling with slow weight down her back. Lifting her face to the sky, she pushed her fingers through it and it fanned and separated, hanging to her hips. She walked on.

The ditches were deeper than she remembered them. She climbed up on to the topmost ramp and moved along it at peace with herself. To one side the plateau, with its shallow depressions that had been homes millennia before, stretched away; to the other the earthworks dipped and reared. The breeze was stiffer here, blowing back her hair and bending last year's yellow grasses that bristled above the new growth.

With her heart beating quickly, she stood at the edge of the ramp and, holding her skirts in both hands, jumped. When her feet hit the steep turf, she ran as fast as she was falling so that her speed carried her up over the next rise and down into its hollow before she tripped and lay laughing among bright fronds of thyme.

She rested on her back with her arms behind her head, enjoying this sudden reversion to childhood and gradually, as the moments passed and her pulse slowed, she grew calmer and for a while she was unaware of the world.

She was roused by the sound of voices and was immediately alert and panic-stricken. How long had others been here? Had they seen her shameless behaviour? The prospect of disgrace at home and the end of solitary driving tightened her throat. She felt foolish and guilty like a boy caught with his fingers in the jam. The voices were behind her but she could not make out the words nor tell from which side they came. One of the few stunted thorns that grew on the hill was beyond her with a tangle of blackberry about its trunk. With her hair down and uncovered she could not make herself look respectable – it would be better to try to stay concealed. She rolled over and crawled to the thorn, dragging her awkward skirts with one hand. The tree, with the young leaves pricking the black branches, was high on the slope of the second ramp so that if she sat upright she would be seen by anyone on the other side of its ridge. She lay on her stomach between the thorn and the crest of the ramp and thought how ridiculous she would look if she were discovered.

She could no longer hear the voices and the hope that the speakers were walking away from her encouraged her to inch upwards and spy from behind a tussock of dead grasses. Camouflaged by the colour of her hair and clothing, she hoped to be able to creep to whichever side of the rise would hide her best.

As soon as she saw the strangers she knew theirs was no common visit to the hill. A man and girl, with work-worn faces, were climbing the last of the third ramp. At first Beatrice could see only their heads and shoulders but as they struggled up the painful slope from the valley, helping themselves with their hands, she saw that they were poorly dressed and the young woman was pulling a full sack with her. They were staggering and gasping from the exhaustion of the climb and whenever the girl paused for breath the man pulled viciously on a rope he had tied about her neck. There was a second man standing further along the ridge, watching as if he had agreed to meet them and had been impatient for them to come. He was dark and thick-set, dressed with careful, shabby smartness as if for a poor man's wedding, and each time he saw the first man wrench the girl's neck he rocked forward as though he wanted to knock him down the hillside but thought it would be unwise. As she climbed on to the ridge and stood with one hand holding her sack and the other pressed to her side, the girl looked at him with eagerness and shame.

A few sharp words passed between the two men but Beatrice could not make them out. The man holding the rope was small and wiry and despite his thinness and poverty had something flashy about him that made him look as if he would be at home on a race-course. It was an aspect, Beatrice thought, that would make him attractive to a certain kind of woman but it was obvious that the girl he led was not one of them. He appeared to have some sort of power over his companions for though the second man, larger and stronger than the first, had walked over to join the others and was plainly in a state of repressed anger, he did nothing to end the girl's humiliation.

From his stance Beatrice could see that the first man was enjoying his position. He appeared to be making joking remarks at which no-one laughed but himself and as he looked from one to the other he fingered the rope and weighed it in his hands. He seemed to be several times on the point of offering it to the other man before changing his mind.

At last the smarter of the two made a short, curt speech and the first shrugged and dropped his teasing manner as if it suddenly bored him. The second reached into his pocket and took out a cloth packet which he untied. He shook something out and there was a glint and gleam in the sunlight. Beatrice saw that he was holding sovereigns in his free hand; she had never seen a working man with so much gold before. The dead grasses chafed her but she did not move.

The first man, still holding the rope, put out his palm and the second counted the coins into it. There were five. Once they were in his possession the first tossed them slightly, then grasped them in his fist. He turned to the girl and rubbed the fist under her chin but this time she jerked her head away and the man who had paid over the coins put a hand on his shoulder and pushed him enough to make him stumble backwards. The second man said something roughly and the first, seeming to have lost whatever hold he had over the pair, shrank as if he expected violence and then, recovering himself, said something to the girl. She began a movement Beatrice could not make out but in a moment she saw that the girl was forcing a ring off her wedding-finger. There was a dark, greenish tinge where the copper band had been. The girl drew it off firmly and, looking into the first man's face with undisguised hatred, threw it at his feet. He laughed as he felt amongst the grass for it, then putting the ring into his waistcoat pocket he held out the rope. The man and the girl looked at each other and as he took the rope a tremor seemed to run through them both, which made the first laugh louder. The second made a threatening move towards him and he shrugged again and began to climb down the hill, still holding the sovereigns in his outstretched fist. When he was almost out of sight below the ridge he turned to call something back but the pair he had left did not acknowledge him.

The man now holding the rope led the girl down the bank into the hollow between the third and second rampart and closer to Beatrice. They walked along the bottom of the fosse until they were almost beneath her and stopped at another bundle wrapped in a brown blanket with a pale, hessian tool-bag at its side. From her vantage point Beatrice could look straight down upon them, impeded only by the dry stems of the tussock that hid her. She pressed her body into the earthwork, willing herself not to be seen. Her heart was beating powerfully.

A wife-sale – she had heard of them amongst the working people but never witnessed one. It was imperative now not to be discovered – no longer for any fear for herself but because she would not intrude on this pair's privacy. All sellings of which she had heard had been at fairs or markets – sites crowded with onlookers – but these people had chosen a place where nothing could be more exposed yet more safe from curious eyes. She wanted to leave them their dignity. She realized with surprise that she felt no disapproval. Staring down, she believed there was that about them which denied any tawdry reason for their action.

They were standing facing one another now. The girl was tall but a little beneath the man's height. She wore a russet gown and crimson shawl of the cheapest wool and long, brass earrings that swung as she walked. Her hair was thick and a vivid red, bound back from her face with a leather thong, but it was her manner that was most striking. She was perfectly straight-backed and at ease with herself physically and her unusual face with its broad features and wide eyes were lined with more cares than should have been suffered by one in her early twenties, yet it was disturbed by nothing but a calm joy at looking on this man. It was a face which had gazed on life's hardships and had been unafraid.

The man was older by a few years and, though

there was no grey in his rough, dark hair and he was well-fed, there were the marks of difficulties overcome on his face too. He had broad shoulders under his worsted jacket and his kerchief wrapped a thick neck. He looked strong and capable; a man who listened to many people's troubles. Now he had lifted his large hands to the knot in the rope that bound the girl. He tried to untie it but the strands had tangled too tightly and feeling in his bag of tools he drew out a knife and cut it away. The rope slithered over her back and down on to the turf behind her. Her neck was reddened where the halter had rubbed and he put both his hands softly on her skin and smoothed it. She put back her head and leant her body against his.

They were so close to her that Beatrice could hear some of what they were saying.

'Canader,' the man said, in time to the movement of his hands. 'Canader, Canader.'

The girl, with her eyes still fixed on his, said triumphantly, 'Canader Garth.'

'My own true wife.'

They smiled and he said, 'I have no ring to give you. He took all that I had.'

'I want none. Only you – and to be worth what you gave for me.'

He shook his head, saying, 'Above rubies,' and he slid his hands up into her hair and drew her face towards his. She clasped him with her arms and Beatrice, in her hiding-place, dug her fingers into the stony soil and forced back a moan of anguish that this was something strange to her. This beautiful, ardent thing was a practice of passionate love and no part of her life now or ever. Shamed by watching, she put her face down on the turf and when she raised it they had lifted their packs and were walking, with arms about each other's waists, towards the downs.

Beatrice waited for them to have left the ramparts before she sat up. She did not catch any glimpse of them through the hedge beside the green lane and thought that they must be crossing the meadow beside it and would not see her trap. Still she did not want them to suspect they had been overlooked. She opened the watch that was pinned in her pocket. It felt later but it was still before ten. The morning remained fresh and full of sunlight but now the shadows of the clouds were flitting over the valley, darkening the fields. She was sick and shaken after the events of the day. Closing her eyes, she raised her face to the sky, her hair fluttering in the breeze, and enfolded herself with one arm across her chest and shoulder. Pressing the other hand to her lips, she kissed the soft skin of her palm. Her longings and her loneliness seemed unendurable but beneath her distress there was a thought that strengthened her – she had seen a marriage ended and it had not been by death.

CHAPTER TWO

When Beatrice arrived at her sister's house late, flushed and excited no-one was surprised by her appearance. It was a mark against Daniel in the minds of all her family that he should be so complacent about her safety that he was unconcerned about her travelling alone. Although Beatrice had told them on her previous visit that the next time she would have no companion, none of her relatives had quite believed such a thing would occur until she had trotted up the wide expanse of East Street and drawn to a halt before the portico of Arland House.

Molly, the housemaid, had seen her arrival from the library window and, guessing that she would not feel confident in driving the trap around the corner into the crowded corn and stable yards, had run to give orders for a lad to take the pony and returned to the entrance, calling through the open back parlour door to her mistress and Mrs Randall that Mrs Fayerdon was arrived – all before Beatrice had gathered herself enough to face her family.

Thirza and her mother came out to greet her in time to see that she had truly been alone and amidst their exclamations Beatrice climbed down, crossed the swept cobbles and entered the hall just as the eight-day clock was striking eleven twenty minutes prematurely. As she stood on the flagstones having her cloak removed she thought sadly that it was here, as always, that she felt most at home, here that her megrims and frustrations were most calmed away.

There was a feeling of light and spaciousness about the whole house. It was a handsome family home and workplace, built eighty years before in the plainest Georgian style of hamstone that was a richer, darker honey than was usual. The façade, with its one sash-window to each side of the front door, its three on the two storeys above and the slate roof concealing the servants' quarters, fronted directly on to the main street and the side window of the drawing-room and the side and rear windows of the dining-room behind and bedrooms above looked out on to the busy cornyard so that private and business life mingled in the liveliest and most convenient fashion. The cornyard, which could be reached by a door at the end of the hall, was large enough to give no sensation of crowding or oppression to those watching its activities from the house and the barns, stables, yard-office and kitchens which enclosed the square gave some protection from the notorious Bridport winds.

The rooms themselves seemed designed to promote lightness of spirit, being of the dimensions and elegance to be comfortable and uncluttered without overawing their occupants by their size. Some were papered in patterns of flowers and birds but most had remained with their panelling painted white as was the style in the time of the house's completion. The drawing- and dining-rooms lay to the left of the hall and to the right the library, from which Beatrice had been seen, backed on to the parlour from which a door led on to a brick path running behind the kitchen, office and stables into a long, walled garden where the fruit-trees, roses, shrubs, lawns and vegetables were as entwined as the different strands of life in the house and grounds.

It was not only the property which was such a happy mix. The meals also wavered unselfconsciously between old and new customs and the varying demands of business and domestic needs and a hungry visitor was unlikely to arrive at any hour when food was not immediately available. The morning began early in the old-fashioned manner of several hours' activity on an empty stomach, followed by a substantial breakfast in the parlour at ten. If Henry expected to be away from the house at this time he would bolster himself with an earlier pot of mulled ale and slice of bread and would return for the modern indulgence of a midday meal. For this Thirza provided a variety of hot and cold dishes to accommodate the habits and traditions of her entourage. The older female generation ate a small luncheon, the younger took a larger luncheon and the men ate whatever was to hand and asked for pickles. Then, as Henry liked to spend the evenings with his family, he lengthened his working afternoon and ordered dinner for five o'clock – later than was usual in the country – which meant that a tea-table must be provided for those in the household who could not last until such an hour. There was, in addition, a constant stream of callers and customers who must be offered some refreshment and supper to be made if the Lamfords had guests; the baby, of course, insisted on sustenance throughout the night.

Into this generous and easy-going home Beatrice brought an agitation greater than her everyday unhappiness and more in need of being hidden. She had no appetite but, wanting to provoke as little comment as possible by acting normally, let herself be taken into the remains of breakfast where she drank a cup of chocolate and forced herself to eat a muffin. There were grass stains on her skirts but no-one saw them because it did not occur to them that they would be there to see. She explained the untidy state of her hair by saying that she had removed her bonnet to adjust a pin and found herself to be in a windy situation. As her sister and mother were taken up with disapproval of Daniel for sending no-one to guard her they did not question her explanation nor the length of time the drive had taken – which they considered was only to be expected if she had had to handle the pony alone.

If Beatrice had had a different character Thirza and Mrs Randall would have suggested that she sit quietly to rest but, knowing her spirit, as soon as her muffin was crumbled they fetched baskets and took her marketing. The Bridport streets, though of an extraordinary breadth, were so crowded with stalls, drays and the lengths of rope and twine that made the town prosperous that walking was fraught with adventure. An hour spent struggling through the clamour and bustle restored her enough to be sure no-one could guess of her morning and the early afternoon found her in Thirza's bright drawing-room to all appearances her usual self.

She was sitting at the old pianoforte and had folded back its shutter so that she could finger the familiar yellow keys of its five octaves. As children both sisters had equally loathed their music-practice but Thirza had realized the value of its result and rarely argued against it while Beatrice had frequently been dragged from the garden and tied to the stool of their spinet by her apron-strings. It was Thirza who achieved the distinction of playing with the backs of her hands so perfectly level that she could complete one of the Italian airs she favoured without dropping a guinea placed on her knuckles but it was Beatrice who was urged to give the lively ballads and country dances that gladdened a family party. She was now tapping out snatches of tune and watching Arthur and Henry, Thirza's two boys, herd a flock of wooden sheep from one edge of the carpet to the other.

Thirza and Mrs Randall were seated in the two high-backed winged chairs that stood one on each side of a small but cheerful fire. The sun was still shining with a thin, spring-like brilliance so that it was the gleam of the polished walnut and mahogany furniture and the general lightness of the room that caught the eye, not the warm winter flames. Every ray of the sun was thrown back by the white walls so that the pale rose and green colours of the furnishings were fresh and delicate against a lustrous background. There was a blue porcelain dish of lavender on the mantel and when the heat flowed through it a clean, astringent scent briefly filled the room and was lost as soon as it was noticed.

Mrs Randall was sewing. Thirza was amusing herself by dandling the infant Charlotte, to whom they all occasionally addressed imbecile remarks. In colouring no-one would have taken the dark Anne Randall for the mother of these two young women but in build and manner, in upright, slender stateliness and handsome features, Thirza and she were obviously alike. The sisters followed their father in their fairness but Thirza's hair was not the vibrant burnished gold of Beatrice's, being a softer, gentler shade and of a thick wiriness that would spring suddenly from its neat coils and would not consider a ringlet. Nor would ringlets have suited either mother or daughter. There was a dignity and composure about both that Beatrice envied and sometimes despised, for she had not yet reached a maturity which could tell her that it was not only she who sought to hide uneasy feelings beneath an untroubled exterior.

At this moment Mrs Randall, a picture of serene womanhood, her white-work dazzling against her turkey-red gown, was tormented by two longstanding anxieties. She had never been able to discuss anything personal with Beatrice. A love of openness had been thwarted in her relations with the girl, as it had been in so much else in her life. She had never understood her daughter's secretiveness nor her open sensuality and, although there were strong ties of affection between them, every remark they passed together seemed to be charged with an undercurrent of aggression. It had always been Thirza on whom she relied to keep peace within the family and in this she felt she had failed Beatrice. It had been wrong to leave so much of the persuasion not to marry Daniel to Thirza and wrong to allow the marriage for fear of having mistakenly undervalued him and of Beatrice's tantrums or elopement. She blamed herself severely for not having tried to prevent the girl taking so irrevocable a step before her majority and, although she admired and pitied Beatrice for her courage in trying to conceal her mistake, she was now constantly afraid that Beatrice's impulsive nature would not accept the narrow path but break out into actions that would make her a pariah in their community. She herself had personal reasons for knowing the strength of feelings which were not sanctioned by society and the law and despite having carried her own burden for so long she did not believe that the younger generation had the same moral stamina to resist temptation as her own.

It was strange that so intelligent a woman should not recognize the secretiveness of Beatrice as an inherited trait but what is a sign of staunchness and resolution in one's own character is often mere obstinacy and self-will in one's children. The object of Anne Randall's second obsession could now be heard talking to Henry in the hall and would shortly be seated on the sofa near her chair, taking the cake and madeira that was his habit at this time of the day.

George Lamford was now fifty-six years old and had already been married to the peevish, idle Susannah for five years when he had taken over the affairs of the newly widowed Mrs Randall. He had noticed at once that she was a fine-looking woman and had admired the way she neither reviled a husband well known to be worthless nor affected any show of grief. She was determined to do the best for her daughters with what little resources she had and he, with his shrewdness in investment and his ready, common-sense advice, saw to it that she did. For two years each had been startled by their feelings for the other and ashamed of their eagerness to discuss business matters and the anticipation and joy that came with knowing they were both to attend the same social event. Then, on an autumn spring morning when the clear cold sun filled the sash-window of Mrs Randall's small front parlour, lighting the round tea-table on which their documents lay, touching the silver ink-stand and throwing a large, grey shadow of the goose-feather pen against the white wall, they had suddenly felt comfortable together. Long, crisp, amber leaves were being blown slowly from the horse-chestnut that grew in the garden across the street, dropping so slowly through the gently-moving air that they were like something that had almost been able to float on deep water. Inside the room the two had understood each other and no longer been afraid of what their eyes showed.

They were both self-contained, uncomplaining people who expected high standards of behaviour from themselves. Neither considered George parting from his wife nor an illicit affair. They rarely spoke of what was for both an enduring love and they had never touched except when dancing or shaking hands. The secretiveness that Mrs Randall so feared in her daughter had allowed her to preserve such discretion in public that after all these years George's wife still suspected nothing of his disloyal feelings – although had Susannah been less lazy she might have noticed more.

For George his interest in the mother led to a correspondingly warm interest in the daughters and he was the nearest they knew to a father. Both naturally turned to him when they wanted an opinion of an older man – even if it was only to ignore it as Beatrice had done over Daniel – but, as yet, it was only Thirza who saw more than her mother intended her to see. At this moment as Henry, George and

Molly with a tea-board entered the room Thirza saw the habitual, almost imperceptible, lift in Mrs Randall as a small boat is lifted by the gentle wave of a passing vessel.

'Papa! Papa!'

Finding himself with two small sons wrapped about his legs Henry disentangled them from his high boots and swung them about in an alarming way. Beneath the squeals and cries for more the rest of the company greeted each other. George took his place on the sofa near to Mrs Randall's chair and was helped to saffron cake and a glass of wine.

'Beatrice, my dear,' he said, 'I was afraid we wouldn't find you today.'

She played two notes quickly and glanced at him sidelong. 'Afraid,' she asked, 'or hopeful? You always say the house is quieter without me.'

He moved to make room for Henry, who was subsiding beneath his offspring.

'I'm not so old that I long for a quiet house,' he said. He removed Arthur's small hand from its grasp on his plate and went on. 'And if you're already at the piano then let us have music.'

Beatrice began to search through the sheets that lay on the top of the instrument.

'Not those,' said Thirza. 'One of your songs. Henry, if the boys are too much—'

'No, no.' Henry arranged his sons more comfortably and recklessly took a glass of madeira into his freer hand. 'One of the lively ones, Beatrice. Something merry.'

Beatrice held her fingers above the keys and played them in the air, then suddenly pouncing them down

she gave herself a jigging accompaniment and began
to sing.

'Come all you kind husbands who have scolding
   wives,
Who through living together are tired of your
   lives,
If you cannot persuade her nor good natured make
   her
Place a rope round her neck and to market pray
   take her.

'Should anyone bid when she's offered for sale,
Let her go for a trifle lest she should get stale,
If sixpence be offered and that's all can be had,
Let her go for the same and not keep a lot bad.'

Here she let her rich contralto voice grow slightly
more lilting.

'Now come, jolly neighbours, let's dance, sing and
   play,
And away to the neighbouring wedding, away.
All the world is assembled, the young and the old,
To see the fair beauty that is to be sold.

'So sweet and engaging the lady did seem,
The market with bidders did presently teem,
A tailor sung out that his goose he would sell,
To buy the fair lady – he loved her so well.

'But a gallant young publican fifteen pounds did
   pay
And with the young lady he marched away.

Then they drank and caroused and rejoiced all
   day,
The glass passed around and the piper did play.

'Success to this couple and, to keep up the fun,
May the bumpers fly round at the birth of a son.
Long life to them both, in peace and content,
May their days and their nights forever be spent.'

With a final run of her fingers up the keys she twisted
round on the stool and received her applause. She felt
it must be apparent to everyone that she had had a
reason for singing this but no-one gave any sign of
having read her mind.

'That reminds me,' said George. 'I saw the
broadsheet recently of the wife-sale in Bristol last
year. A drover offered his wife up in the market-
place but couldn't get a bid until a young man
ventured sixpence because he thought it a pity the
woman should remain in the hands of her owner. As
soon as she was delivered to him he sold her again for
ninepence. The new purchaser not being to the wife's
liking she tried to depart with her mother but was
claimed by the buyer as his property. She refused to
go with him unless by the order of a magistrate. The
magistrate, of course, dismissed the case. It said that
Nash, the husband, was obliged to make a precipitate
retreat from the enraged populace. A good time, I
suppose, was had by all. The sheet had that ballad on
it calling itself "Verses Written on the Occasion" but
I've never yet seen it claimed as anything else. Very
lively, Beatrice.'

'So the magistrate said she wasn't the wife of the
man with ninepence?' she asked.

'Naturally not. You remain the wife of the man you marry at the altar. There isn't any changing, ninepence or no. Though, considering Nash's efforts to rid himself of her he's hardly likely to demand her return, so unless the authorities force them back together because the wife is a charge on the parish they can live free of each other.'

'Supposing,' said Beatrice, carefully closing the lid of the instrument, 'Nash wanted her back and she did not want to go?'

'Then,' George said, 'he could apply for restitution of conjugal rights and she would be obliged to go back. It's not an order I'd care to draw up myself; much of our matrimonial law is not what I would wish it. But a wife-sale is bestial.'

No, thought Beatrice, the act may be but not the meaning. I have seen and I know.

'Then,' she said, 'is there no way for an unhappy wife to be freed of her husband? What of divorce?'

A shiver and stiffening ran through the members of the party at this word. Divorce was not a subject for polite conversation and from the mouth of a young woman known to be dissatisfied it was unheard of and dangerous to her reputation. A jaunty ballad was one matter, such questions were another.

George glanced at Mrs Randall who looked first at him and then her daughter but Beatrice, with an innocent expression, did not appear to notice her mother.

Putting down his glass, George said, 'If there's good reason for a marriage to be broken – the husband, for instance, has brought a successful action for damages against the seducer of his wife – the injured party should hire a proctor and bring a suit for divorce *a mensa et toro* from the Ecclesiastical Courts. He should then introduce a bill for a divorce *a vinculo matrimonii* in both Houses of Parliament and if this is passed into an Act and assented to by the King the applicant may consider himself freed. It will have cost him, perhaps, a thousand pounds. There're few of these cases and they are rarely by women. Where is the money and influence to be found? Could the Nashes have summoned it? I say nothing of the morality involved.'

Thirza bent down and lifted one of the wooden sheep for Charlotte. Both boys slid off their father's lap and joined their sister.

Beatrice watched the children and the fire. 'How fortunate we are,' she said, 'to have a lawyer in our family. It makes everything so clear. Then, for those of us who are not wealthy men with high connections, our vows are vows indeed?'

'My dear,' George said, 'when we marry it is till death.'

It was dark as Beatrice entered the millhouse that evening. A lad had been waiting in the stables to take her pony but no-one from the house had come out to welcome her and there was no lantern outside to help her find the way. She had not expected any attention from Daniel or his mother but as she raised the heavy latch and entered the damp hall, where there was never a fire to drive away the cold of the river, she felt disappointed and empty. The excitement of the day and her pride in driving drained away and became shut in that private compartment of her mind that her husband did not suspect existed. Her body felt heavy and stagnant. Walking into that house with its chill, dusty air made her believe she was a captive. The permanence of it mocked her.

Laying her cloak and bonnet over a chair she went down the hall to where a crack of light along the flagstones showed the kitchen door to be.

'Shut the door. You let the cold in.'

Beatrice accepted this greeting from her mother-in-law without reply and came forward to sit on a stool at the long, scrubbed table. It was warm here. Outside in the scullery she could hear the cook and maid-of-all-work scouring pans. Daniel and old Mrs Fayerdon were seated in the firelight in front of the open range. Daniel had brought a Windsor chair up close to the flames and was toasting bread on a long fork. He had hung the drill overall he wore in the mill over the back of the chair and a semi-circle of fine corn-dust had drifted from it to the floor. He was dark, stocky and almost good-looking, as if he were a handsome man viewed through a distorting mirror, but now before the flour was brushed from his hair he looked older than his thirty years. He nodded at Beatrice without interest.

'Have ye supped?' Again old Mrs Fayerdon spoke in her sharp, breathless voice, the sound beginning abruptly, then fading as if its user thought the expense of air too great for the hearer.

'I have.' Beatrice did not let herself be fooled into thinking the enquiry showed concern for her welfare; a meal eaten elsewhere was one less to be paid for by this household.

'Aye,' old Mrs Fayerdon shook her head so that the curls of her false hair-piece bobbed in the firelight; with her snapped mouth and shapeless assortment of clothes that she was wearing out she looked like a turtle with an eye for a bargain. 'Always free with their favours, the rich folk.'

Once the sneer inherent in her mother-in-law's words had made Beatrice answer brusquely; now she merely sat and looked into the flames.

Daniel removed a piece of toast from the fork and put it on the board on his mother's lap. She took the lid from a tin she had been heating and a strong smell of pork dripping filled the room. Taking a round spoon she began smearing the dripping on to the bread. It had not quite melted and fell on to the toast in slithering lumps. Seeing her son watching her, Mrs Fayerdon scraped up a full spoon and held it out with a smile. Daniel leant forward and engulfed it, licking a glistening trace from his chin.

'I'm tired,' said Beatrice. 'I'll go to bed.'

Later, while Beatrice was still roaming aimlessly round their room, Daniel told her the news of the day. He had washed himself carefully and brushed his hair free of dust. His clothes were folded neatly on the black oak chest beneath the window and he was sitting on the edge of the bed in his night-shirt, paring his toenails with a small, horn-handled knife. It bewildered Beatrice that a man who was so particular in some of his ways should be so appalling in others but she was no longer interested enough to try to change them. She wanted only to find a method of enduring him.

'—and the cowslips are budding up along now, Jack Meddy was saying, so you'll be able to make the wine soon. The bottles are going down.'

'Yes, I will.' Beatrice stood in the centre of the smooth, wood floor brushing her hair. Beneath her bare feet she could feel the vibration that ran through the beams from the mill-wheel. The roar of the water falling into the race had excited her when she had first come here but now she hardly heard it. Moonlight was flooding in through the lattice making her look pale and the candle-flame strengthless.

Daniel put down his knife and climbed into bed.

'And the new millhand did come. It was today we'd settled. He's done some carpentry and wheelwrighting too so he'll be useful, maybe. He and his wife are in the Fordyces' old cottage. No children.'

'Oh? What does his wife do? Lacemaking?'

'Gloving, I think it was. Garth told me she'd been prenticed to something.'

'Garth?' Beatrice stopped brushing and turned away to blow the candle out. Her heart jumped.

'Yes, Matthew Garth. Not local. Are you coming? I have to be up early.'

Beatrice pulled back the covers and took her own half of the bed. She had not shut the curtains of the window or the bed and the room was cool and white. Daniel lay on his side and was asleep in moments but his wife sat up thinking of a hill, of lovers and a kind of marriage-night and it was many hours before she closed her eyes.

CHAPTER THREE

'Will this be the turning, master?'

The carter pointed with his whip and Boaz Holt, sitting beside him on the laden wagon, turned his head from the bulk of Tarrendon Hill rising before them into the clear May sky.

'That should be,' he said.

They had made their way westwards that morning, lumbering over the bad roads and worse lanes from Wynford Tarrent and had circled round, down from the way Beatrice took to Bridport, on to the track that led along the valley, towards the farmhouse she had seen in the trees far below as she had stood on the hill.

It was a windless day, full of sunlight but cold enough for Boaz not to have thrown off the long-waisted leather coat that hung open over his breeches. He was full of curiosity about his destination but had seen too much of life for his eagerness not to remain hidden, as something to be tasted without belief in it resulting in any beneficial outcome. I must do something to mend this road, he thought, now that it is mine; there's no profit in a cart shaken to pieces.

He intended to make a profit from this land. He was twenty-nine years old, a tenant-farmer, hard-working, honest and successful at his work. It was through no fault of his that his landlord at his small sheep-run close to Salisbury had ruined himself and been forced to sell his farms to a man whose plans did not include the old occupants. It was another incidence that might have made Boaz bitter but it did not. He was an intense man, quiet and willing for friendships that would not take too much of himself away; he was naturally tender and loving and had been made grim by circumstances but not sour. There were many might-have-beens in his life and he grieved for what was past but now, as always, he faced the future with courage and resolution.

He had not seen this farm before. The fall of his previous landlord had not been unexpected by the man himself but had been sudden to his tenants. Boaz had found himself roofless and workless at a time of year when farm leases were not changing hands. His savings were small and he did not want either to squander them on his daily needs while he waited idly for a good tenancy or to take employment as a labourer. Through the friends of his landlord, who knew him to be a deserving case, he was put in touch with William Canning of Dorchester. Among his properties Canning owned a small farm beneath Tarrendon with fields so steep and awkward to cultivate and with a house in such disrepair that it was lying empty. Canning was known not to let a tenant improve his land only to be evicted for a better offer and Boaz had good references. They closed the matter without meeting and the result was this journey and expectation in a young man's heart.

If history could be changed Boaz would not have been travelling to a stranger's house with all his possessions piled around him. His grandfather had been the last of a line of yeomen who had married gentlemen's younger daughters and had land and money of their own. Bad harvests and unwise investments had lost the Holts their property but not their pride and both Boaz and his father had been educated beyond what was usual for their sunken position and taught to be undaunted by adversity. As things were it could be seen from the contents of the wagon that here was a poor man whose ancestors had seen better days and who was not yet in such straits that he must sell the few good pieces of furniture that had been handed down to him. Amongst the plough-shares, sacks of seed-corn and farm implements the high sides of the cart held two Windsor chairs made by Chiltern bodgers fifty years ago, a chest from the days of King James packed with books and a china tea-service thrown before cups had handles, a long oak table with the marks where his grandfather had been caught in the act of working his initials with a pocket-knife and carven bedposts lashed to the spars of the tail-gate. On the hour the faint chimes of a clock emerged from the rolled bedding.

The wagon itself and the driver were hired but the cob mare, the ram and the two heifers that ambled on ropes behind belonged to Boaz, as did the dog that lay amongst the chairlegs watching the world with lively eyes. He had brought no ewes with him, preferring to sell the Southdowns he had been running and buy in Dorset Horns to cross with the ram. He had money enough for a small herd but not to take on any regular workers. He intended to farm alone, hiring day-labourers when he could not avoid it and he anticipated a hard and lonely life.

The cart turned slowly into the wood. The track here was even more damaged than the rest of the lane and the heavy wagon swayed and rocked as it was drawn over the ruts. Boaz held on to the seat as the carter clucked and chirruped at the horses to make them move on. Each side of the track was bordered by elderberry and nut-bushes that overhung the narrow way and both men had to shield themselves from the straggling branches until they drew into the clear space that was the yard.

William Canning had not lied about the dilapidated state of his property. From where Boaz sat he could see that the buildings had once been substantial. They were in an old-fashioned enclosed stockyard where cattle could winter. Round three sides of a square, where young nettles were growing in untidy clumps, there were cow-stalls roofed with matted and mouldering thatch which had rotted completely away in places to expose the roof-beams. There was a gap in one of these walls of sheds where there must once have been a gate and it was through this they had driven the wagon. On the fourth side of the square, to the left of Boaz, was a range of what had been dairy- and cheese-houses and the storerooms and behind those he could see the farmhouse. Several of the windows were broken, the door of the dairy was off its hinges and paint was an unknown word. Above the roofs the trees closed round.

Unexpectedly, Boaz felt his spirits rise. Here was something challenging to his enterprise, here was matter that would eat up his energy and leave him without time to dwell on his own mental disrepair.

He turned on the seat to his neighbour who was putting on the brake. 'I'll take a look round the house,' he said. 'Bait the horses while I'm gone.'

The carter nodded. 'Will I unload then, master?'

'Aye, lift things down. Only what you can. I'll be back to help you presently.'

He climbed down stiffly. His legs felt awkward after so much sitting but a few steps loosened them. With a scrabble amongst the oddments and a fluid leap from the side of the wagon the sheep-dog joined him, its elegant, feathered tail held high. Boaz touched its tawny head and walked back through the entrance to the yard.

He had noticed as they drove in that a path led along the outside of the cow-sheds in the direction of the house. Following it, he passed along the side of the stalls and the cheese-house and found himself at the corner of the outbuildings where they joined the back of the house. The path branched; a broad, flagstoned area led to a wide and crumbling side-door. This door was divided in two horizontally and had a ledge projecting from the top of the lower half. It must have been here that the labourers came to be paid and here, thought Boaz with a smile, that he would pay his hired men when luck looked kindly at him. The other fork of the path led into the wood and, so far as he could see, curved round to take visitors to the front entrance of the house.

It was the second fork he chose. There had once been gravel underfoot but the plants of the glades had invaded it and now it was only a uniform lack of trees that marked it as a way to walk.

Boaz went a few yards along the path and stopped. It was unusually peaceful there. He was almost at the heart of the wood and, although the copse was not large, he felt as though the rest of the world had been removed. The great trees were mainly elm and ash and the bright sun falling from the cool, blue sky was lighting their young leaves into dazzling points of green. There was a crab-apple in white bloom before him and all around were bluebells and more bluebells. Their tanging, watered scent caught at his throat. A cuckoo called twice and from beyond the dairy he could hear the carter lowering the tail of the wagon. His dog was questing amongst the undergrowth with loud, grunting sniffs.

'Nancy!' He called the dog to him and moved on, releasing fresh, sharp gusts of scent as he crushed the thick growth of the flowers.

The path curved deeper into the copse until suddenly the way cleared and the house, of which he had been conscious in glimpses, was before him across a tangle of an old knot-garden of herbs.

It had originally been a small Tudor manor built of hamstone in the Elizabethan shape of an E. The long line of the letter still remained – the porch with a tiny, many windowed chamber above forming the centre stroke – but the two wings had been so altered, pulled down and rebuilt that it was impossible to say quite what form they took now. The roof had been constructed with whatever material had been most convenient during each alteration and was here thatch, there stone-slab and, over one far room that reached out into the wood, slate. It was a house, thought Boaz, that would have charmed Esther.

He knew the keys to have been left by Canning's agent in an urn in the porch and he found them and let himself through the arched, oak door with its iron studs into the hall. The smell of cold and damp was intense but it was what he had expected and he was able to ignore the neglect and discomfort and look at the house as it could be if it were cared for.

The hall was high and square with a wide fireplace that would take a log. Doors led from its side and far walls. It would always be dark but would be lighter when the dirt had been washed from the latticed windows. The stairs were broad for so small a manor and rose from Boaz' left as he came in from the porch; they turned at a landing to double back on themselves for two steps before becoming a gallery that ran in front of the small, windowed room that was the stroke of the E. Generations of farmers had stood where Boaz stood and thought how unsafe the arrangement seemed.

He did not want to stay long in the house when he had stock to see to but curiosity took him quickly through the whole. Having seen all that was there he could not decide whether the number of rooms made the house seem larger than it was or the darkness and odd jumble of cubby-holes, passages, larders, strangely shaped chambers and walk-in cupboards made it seem smaller than was real. What was plain was that if the filth were cleared away and the cobwebs dragged down from the timbers it would be beautiful. It gave a twist of bitterness to his stomach to think how well it would be to raise a family here.

Night found him upstairs in the large room to the left of the porch. He was so tired that every movement he made was done with a kind of slow concentration. A watcher might have thought him slightly drunk. The carter had left late that afternoon after they had herded his small collection of animals into the meadow at the foot of Tarrendon and carried his possessions under cover. The hall was now crowded with boxes and upturned chairs waiting for the rooms to be in a condition to receive them. This bedchamber had had Boaz' first attention inside. During the day he expected to be always out of doors. His list of necessities in the house had been – a place to sleep, a place to cook and a place to sit in the evening. He had always been particular and marriage to a woman so efficient in household matters had spoilt his ability to live without cleanliness. It had been a temptation when faced with such a task as this neglect presented to hire a girl to clear it but he needed to husband his money and had set to the work himself.

The part of the room that was nearest the hall had been panelled off to form a corridor into the rest of the house but the other walls had been left as plaster. This plaster bulged ominously and had fallen away in parts but the oak floor and the beams that crossed the ceiling seemed sturdy. Boaz had swept and scrubbed the walls and floor and cleaned the window as far as the only opening pane would allow a man's arm to reach. As such matters do, it had taken longer than he had expected and he was now arranging his belongings on the damp wood by the light of the moon and two candles.

He had brought up his bed, whose posts were leaning against the far corner, but had not had time to fasten it together and his feather mattress lay unrolled on the floor. A linen chest that he had lugged up the stairs with a blanket beneath it stood against the panels with its lid raised and he was sitting on a stool before it, rummaging amongst its contents in the confused way of the very tired. A pile of clothes and the dishes that had been wrapped in them lay beside his feet.

Suddenly, he stopped his aimless searching and

did what he knew to be unwise. He moved a bundle
of shirts and reaching down into the centre of the
chest he lifted out a cherrywood box. He set it on his
knees and looked at it. It was a pretty thing with
delicate brass handles, to one of which its key was
tied with a piece of crimson ribbon. Sitting there in
the empty house in the fluttering pool of candlelight,
he patted his fingertips on the gleaming box but did
not open it. Then, with decision, he replaced it in the
chest and stood up.

The draught from his movement bent the flames
and sent shadows shuddering about the room. He
took up one of the candle-holders and, shielding it
with his hand, went out of the room on to the gallery.
The well of the hall was black outside the range of the
light. Setting the candle on the floorboards outside
the porch-chamber he walked into the small room.

Latticed windows surrounded him on three sides
and, despite their condition, enough moonlight
shone through to make the chamber twilit under a
hatching of shadows from the lead bars of the panes.
Boaz went to the far side and looked out. Beneath
him, in the porch, his dog slept in a pile of straw.
Nothing moved.

This chamber being more prominent than the
neighbouring rooms and unprotected by overhanging
eaves, the rain had kept the outside of the glass quite
clear and, by rubbing the dust on the inside with his
hand, Boaz had an undiminished view.

The night was very still. The half-moon made the
trees grey and bleached the sun-dial in the centre of
the old herb-garden. The house felt as it was – miles
from other human life. To Boaz it did not seem
peaceful now. From this high place he could look up

over the top of the trees to the bulk of Tarrendon rising beyond. He knew himself to be exhausted and likely to be imaginative and overwrought yet could not prevent this natural phenomenon seeming menacing and peopled with ghosts. But, he thought, it is not the dead of this house, this hill, that trouble me. Ghosts of my own heart haunt me – a living woman, a dead child. He was filled with longing and with anger at himself for having let this longing escape. If he had not given in to tiredness – not touched the box – his yearning would have stayed within the bounds he set it. Or would such a day as this with its loss of old associations – its reminders of what his life would be and what it might have been – have inevitably brought this pain? He did not need to lift that cherrywood lid to know what was beneath it.

In that box were the souvenirs of what had meant most to him in his adulthood. There was a bundle of letters lying there. Letters from him to her and, in a strong, untutored hand, from her to him. 'My dear heart,' she had written, 'my own one.' There was a posy of dried flowers he had picked for her the first time they had walked out together and that she had pressed under the flour crock in the house where she worked. A plait of her hair was coiled there with strands of lighter, softer childish hair woven into its end. There was a small kid shoe he could hold in the palm of his hand. There were the white gloves she had worn to follow the coffin of the wearer of that shoe and the white sash he had had tied about his arm. And at the bottom wrapped in a linen handkerchief were two ink sketches he had made. One of a woman with a still face and restless, piercing eyes and one of that woman holding their child. Esther. What had it been about her that had made him want her for his wife from the moment they had met? He remembered her as thin, white-skinned and dark-haired. She had not been at all pretty in the soft way village girls were liked to be but was strongly, strangely attractive. She had had no other followers, she was too quick and clever and she had too deep and passionate a nature not to make most men afraid. But he had loved her and she him and for two years when they married and worked together it had seemed that nothing could hurt them. Then Rebecca – a daughter loved and cherished by her mother with what was almost ferocity – coughed and sickened and died before she could walk without his hands on hers.

Grief to a degree neither had ever dreamt of had come on them both. Neither could touch what was in the other's mind. There was no comfort to be had. Love had been the creator of this agony and Esther could bear no more. She could not endure the sight of the man who had shared her daughter and six months from Rebecca's death she had left during the night, taking nothing with her that could remind her of those she loved. He had tracked her to a farm in a remote valley on Salisbury Plain but she would not return. Mourning was like a fever in her and Boaz the heat that made her burn. Twice more he tried to bring her back until she threatened to go where he would never find her and now he no longer hoped to have her with him again.

He had not lost his hunger for her but often he longed for another kind of solace. He wanted an uncomplicated woman; a woman to sing in his house as she went about her work, who would sit sewing in this chamber on summer afternoons and run to him when she saw him come in from the fields. He wanted a ready smile and easy laughter; a warm body to curl into his on cold nights. He wanted this so much he did not trust himself. Marriage was now closed to him but if any other love should welcome him he would not refuse it.

CHAPTER FOUR

Three days after Boaz took possession of Tarrendon Farm, Canader Garth was waiting for Matthew. It was late evening and she was boiling potatoes, bacon and a sweet suet dumpling in nets hung in a pot over the fire. The water was bubbling fiercely and as she had no chimney-crane to swing the pot away from the flames she had to be constantly on the watch against it boiling over. There was only firelight in the room and she was enjoying the warmth and glow and the pleasant anticipation of her husband's return.

She moved away from the pot to lay the table. On it there was already an earthenware jug of beer that she had fetched from the village, and a round of butter with a clover impress lay wrapped in leaves. To these she added two wooden bowls, a pewter spoon and one of battered steel, a bone-handled knife, a horn drinking-cup and one of heavy glass that Beatrice had given her. She laid a loaf of dark bread straight on to the bare table.

There was some ingenuity needed for everything she did but the contriving did not worry her. The appearance of poverty in the two-roomed cottage was greater than the reality and material things would come to add to her happiness. She and Matthew had begun their life together with almost no possessions beyond his tools and the clothes they wore. Matthew was an artisan and commanded more than a labourer's wage but all his savings and what he could gain by selling his belongings had gone to buy Canader and, though Canader had always been a hearty worker, whatever she earned had been the property of her husband Nat and he had taken it for his drink and fancy-women.

The change in her life in the few weeks since she had been free of Nat Brinsley was beyond anything she had imagined. Life for her had always been hard but she had a courageous and uncomplaining nature and had not been one to whine in the face of misfortune. It was not that she was passive – she had often questioned why the accident of birth should give one a cushioned existence and another nothing but work and poverty – but she had had a realistic view of her poor opportunities and this sudden flowering of her life was completely unexpected.

She had been born in the south of Somerset and while still a small child had been apprenticed to a gloving agent in Yeovil. Gloving-women needed soft hands so there was no field work for them but this was a compensation only in winter. Canader's childhood had been spent sitting in the downstairs room of her overlooker's house, crowded amongst the piles of leather and the other children pricking their small fingers as they learned their trade. In the dark months when night came before the end of their work they sewed with candles behind glass globes of water to magnify the light, the shadows of their stitching hands moving in rhythm on the walls. The overlooker sat with a tin of embers beneath her skirts but there was no fire for the girls and it was only their proximity that gave them any warmth. In summer they opened the door and window and the smell of the tanneries came hot and heavy into the stifling room.

Her home was too far for a child to walk to every night so she returned there only for Sundays, sleeping on other days hugger-mugger with the other children in the same situation, first in one of the two upstairs rooms and then, when her overlooker's own family filled it, downstairs amongst the leather. There was no particular unkindness for her to complain of. Her overlooker treated the girls as well as she was able and when the evenings were light they were allowed to play in the country about the town, paddling in the nine springs and following the gorge up Babylon Hill. She made friends amongst the children but even so she hated the room that was her world.

When Canader was fourteen her apprenticeship was over and she became an outworker. By this time her parents had died and her brother had gone for a soldier and not been heard from for years. She hired two rooms on the other side of the town with three other girls and in these they ate and slept and worked, taking their finished gloves to their agent on Saturday afternoons and collecting the materials for the following week. Canader had become a skilled worker, using the finest leather and most intricate stitching and though she was still paid poorly, her piece-work allowed her to take the occasional few hours holiday.

It was on one such June day when a balmy afternoon of sunlight and warm breezes had tempted her to put aside her needle and walk out towards Bradford Abbas that she had met Nat Brinsley. She had been strolling slowly about the lanes, looking at the distant, shimmering hills, for several hours and was growing tired when Nat had come driving up behind her. He was a carter making an unhurried return from delivering grain to the mill in the village and as he let his two horses amble towards Yeovil, with the leafy twigs of elder nodding on their brows, he had had time to admire the girl ahead.

Canader was now sixteen and had grown into a fine-figured girl with a firm, straight and graceful walk. She was swinging a tattered straw hat by its ribbon and her dazzling red hair hung unbound down her back. Physically, she was richly attractive and Nat, bored by the stillness and heat of the lonely meadows, looked at her as he might look at a pear flushed with ripeness on its tree and wonder if it would amuse him to pick it.

When his wagon had drawn level with her he had added up her youth, her poverty, her solitariness and the look she had cast over her shoulder at him that was neither afraid nor bold and decided on his approach. He offered to let her ride with him if she was weary and, because his manner was so pleasant and unthreatening, she had accepted. Sitting beside him, rocking on the high seat as the wagon swayed down the steep, winding descent between the sand-stone walls of Babylon Gorge, with the trees closing high above them, she was surprised at what she had done but this smiling stranger was so affable and charming that she found herself talking easily to him.

She was not the type of girl he usually liked. He enjoyed loud, cheerful, flashy women, women who wore tawdry finery in ale-houses and lay down for men willing to give them gin and laughter. He was too lazy to be a seducer and if he recognized a modest girl she was in danger of no more than an unwelcome arm about her waist. It was to be her misfortune that on that first, slow ride in the warmth and sun she revealed too much about herself. Through their conversation he found that she was a girl unprotected by any family, starved of fun and affection, and by looking at her, as she sat so close to him, he saw that her slim, upright figure and broad, unusual face were fresher and more alluring than any woman's he could remember. Neither of these discoveries would have tempted him if it had not been for a third. Canader talked of her work and he learned that she was proficient in her trade. For a female manual worker she earned well and was never likely to be out of employment. Nat had no ambition beyond always having money in his pocket but he wanted that money to come with as little effort from himself as possible. Because he had a persuading tongue and was always ready with excuses for his slip-shod work he usually had a job but was never likely to prosper. He was tired of seeing to his own washing and marketing and returning to a room with no fire lit. It had been in his mind to marry if it could be done to the increase of his own comfort and with no expense to himself. He mistook Canader's self-possession for docility and it seemed to him that here was a girl – a desirable, biddable outworker – who could only be an asset as a wife.

He courted her good-humouredly and they were married the following spring, moving into a three-roomed cottage on the outskirts of the town. Within weeks she had realized that she would never see a penny of her husband's wages and she grew to dread the sight of the rent-collector at the door. She found that her own work was expected to cover all household needs while Nat's money was devoted exclusively to his pleasures. Reasoning and appealing to his fondness for her had no effect – he laughed in her face. She fought back but without success; if she rose at night to take money from his coat he slept with his purse beneath his pillow; if she did not buy food he ate elsewhere; if she economized on firing he sat in the chimney-corner of an inn and she went cold; if she hid any spare coins she had from him he took his right and arranged with her gloving-agent for her earnings to be paid directly to him. The freedom his improved financial position gave him worsened his indulgences and character. He drank more heavily; he gambled on badger-baitings and dogs in rat-pits and made no secret of his casual infidelities. He only tried to beat her once then, as he held her she bit his hand to the bone and the blood running down his wrist convinced him that this was not a practical method of curbing her. It became his habit to complain continually of the burden of having a wife and his diatribes against marriage were a standing source of amusement amongst his cronies.

Canader would willingly have seen him leave her. She had sworn to be his wife until death parted them but it was her constant hope that he would tire of their life together and find some more profitable companion. It did not seriously occur to her to leave him – her oath was sacred and she believed that she belonged to him. This view was shared by all those she knew; the neighbours and friends who witnessed Nat's behaviour sympathized with her plight – some advised argument, some resignation – but all considered a woman to be her husband's property and her fate, correctly, to be governed by him.

It was on another such warm, gentle afternoon as the one on which they met that the second decisive event of Canader's life occurred. She had been feeling more than usually tired and, because it would not serve him to have her unwell, Nat offered to let her accompany him as he drove his round. It was late September but the trees had not yet turned and the sun was hot. She accepted; despite Nat's company it would be pleasant to sit high on the creaking wagon and make the slow journey to West Coker.

They had been married over five years and Canader was not the girl she had been when she had first ridden with him. She had grown into a pale, determined young woman who saw the realities of the world but would not let them defeat her. Nor had she let her situation fade her into an unnoticeable drudge; she wore a green gown which made her red hair more startling and brass earrings swung with the movement of the cart. To those who had a taste for rarity she was lovely to look upon. Nat was drawing barley to the mill and had timed his arrival for the midday break. As they rumbled into the yard men, already whitened by their morning's work, were seated in the sunlight eating bread and cheese. Nat had been delivering corn here and returning with the finished flour for some months and was already known for his custom of riding in at the beginning of the half-hour of rest and for his invective against his wife. No-one any longer offered to share their ale but there were those who mischievously encouraged him to talk on his hobby-horse and it was with interest that they saw him accompanied by a woman that they recognized by her colouring must be his own.

All eyes were on Canader and she knew by the low-voiced comments, the side-long glances and partly-hidden sniggers how Nat must have spoken of her. It was what she expected and so it was a surprise to her when one man rose from his place on the edge of a stone trough and came forward to speak civilly to her.

Matthew Garth was then twenty-eight years old but in many ways seemed older. He was a serious man whose abilities had made him foreman over men twice his age and those who gave of their best in their trade thought him a good master. He allowed no gaming, idling or foul stories during working hours and in return he was unfailingly fair to each man and unafraid to bargain with the miller on their behalf. Strong feelings were held both for and against him to which he was indifferent. His most abiding quality was a love of justice and it was this which brought him before Canader.

In the drowsy noontime breaks listening to the monotonous complaints and the lazy laughter of the worst of the men he had learnt to despise Nat. He was a good judge of character and of whether there was substance in a grievance and it would have heartened Canader to know how strongly he had decided in her favour before he had even seen her. As she had been drawn into the yard – her hair making her unmistakable – he had been angered by the vulgarity that met her arrival. He had seen in her face all the virtues he had known would be there and the fatigue that the severity of her married life had made natural to her. Rising from the trough where he sat he had gone to greet her as a visitor should be greeted and then it was that he began to love.

He was unencumbered by any previous connection; he had no wife and walked out with no-one. Two or three times a fondness for a girl had seemed to be growing into something more but honesty and clear thinking had told him that the desire for affection, family and a shared bed were blinding him to the reality of his feelings. He had high standards in all aspects of his way of living and if he could not have a true companion he would rather be alone. There is less loneliness in solitude than in an unhappy marriage. On this morning he had looked on Canader and known that here was his woman.

The realization did not bring with it the cooing of doves. He had no illusions over the resolving of difficulties attending the love of someone else's wife nor any romantic notions about their life when he had made her his but in one matter his sense of justice eased his path. To Matthew a marriage in which one partner was treated with the neglect and disrespect to which Canader was subjected was no marriage; it was no more than master and bondswoman and he felt no compunction in trying to dissolve that bond. The law and society might say that he was wrong but it was fundamental justice which had his allegiance and it was not just that a good woman should not be free to rid herself of a rogue.

And for Canader this was a moment that lived for ever in her memory. The sunlight whitening the stones of the yard, the heavy sounds of great horses settling into rest, the dry smell of flour and grain and above all the cool scent of the river flowing down to the millrace, a child on the far bank, half-hidden by reeds, throwing bread to a single duck.

She had learnt to show no response to the jibes of Nat's acquaintances but that morning they had faded from her hearing and her world became the dark, unsmiling man who stood beneath her, holding out his hand to help her climb down. She was all eyes and heart. Her trust went out to him and though she had never known the things his look spoke of – warmth and love and safety – she recognized them and believed them to be real. Before her feet had reached the ground and she was standing by him – all green and red and glinting in the strong sun, her tender glover's hand in his – she had basked in what could have been hers and rejected it. Her pride forced her to remember her condition and the shamelessness of showing attraction to a man other than her husband. During the hour she was waiting in the yard she made no remark and gave no look to which Nat could have objected but she was too late to hide her feelings; Matthew had understood her first astonished, yielding glance and her fate was already sealed for the better.

From that day on Matthew cultivated Nat's acquaintance. He did not join in the insulting of Canader but sympathized with the position of a man with an unwanted wife. Nat, flattered by the friendship of one he recognized as superior to himself, revelled in his company and was encouraged by Matthew's belief that a worthless marriage should be ended. On a pretext of having other friends in Yeovil, Matthew began calling on the Brinsleys on Sundays. Nat was rarely at home and Matthew was free to accept Canader's ale and learn to know her better. He never stayed long enough to excite the neighbours' gossip and at first he did not speak of his love. That Canader held the common conviction that she belonged to her husband and would be unshakeably loyal was soon apparent to him, as was her warm but secret return of his own feeling for her. When he had first come visiting she had been tense and reluctant to sit at her table with him, afraid as she was of revealing too much of herself and precipitating unwelcome events, but quickly as she learnt that Matthew would not act dishonourably towards her she relaxed and talked openly to him.

It was on one such November afternoon when the rain fell against the small window and soaked into the sacking placed beneath the door that Matthew opened his heart to her and asked her to consider a halter divorce. Unlike many of his class he was not sure of the legality of such a measure but he was certain of its rightness in this case and of the appeal of the formal handing over of a wife as property to a woman of Canader's mind. He did not lie to her over his suspicions as to how the law regarded such divorces, but to one of the poverty and origin of Canader the legal system was merely a mysterious and remote conception which touched her fellows only to punish them for trying to have more than the prosperous thought suitable. It was not a machinery that would be concerned in who was her domestic master. Her idea of her duty to her husband was derived from tradition and confused religious scruples. It was the custom for working-class wives to be transferred in this way and in it she saw her freedom.

The sudden rush of hope engendered by the thought of being united to a man who loved and respected her and who answered all her needs was soon over. She knew how useful she was to Nat and that, for all his complaints, he would not lose her earnings by releasing her. It was then that fortune favoured the lovers in three ways.

The illness that Nat had suspected when he treated her to the wagon-ride came upon Canader and made her unfit to pursue her trade. It was no more than the result of years of neglect and over-work, made worse by anxiety about her future, but to Nat it seemed a permanent end to his easy life. She was nervous, feverish and love-sick and, though he was obliged by the opinion of their neighbours not quite to let her starve, Nat was so angered by the thought of being linked to a useless invalid that he let her suffer near-destitution. It had been agreed while she was failing that Matthew should give her nothing to alleviate her condition – in order to increase her husband's worries – and Matthew was able to watch a growing desperation in Nat as he felt the hurt to his pocket.

It was at this time that Nat's employer lost patience with the smooth talk that covered his shoddy work. He was turned off and found himself with no chance of similar employment in the area. Wherever he applied he found his reputation to have preceded him. The prospect of going on the parish was made the more fearful as Nat fell into infatuation with a woman who liked money. Sarah Poole, now taproom maid at the Four Feathers, was the type of girl who suited Nat. Brassy, cheerful and callous, she had followed the drum around the garrison towns of the West until the disappearance of an infantryman's watch caused her to retire from the service. It amused her to dangle herself before Nat, giving little and promising much if he could only show her gold.

Five days after Nat's loss of work – when he had

had time enough to feel the terror of the coming weeks – Matthew sought him out and sat him snugly in the corner of the ale-house, where he had listened to so much complaint against Canader. There, over a pitcher of rum from beneath the counter, he put it to Nat that a man without money and with a wife he did not want and a man with money who had a taste for that wife could find a way of agreeing that was to the advantage of both. The divorce was suggested and laughed over; the price was bargained upon; they spat on their hands and the matter was sealed.

It had always been in Matthew's mind to take Canader away from where they were known so that there should be no talk about them, and to prepare for this he had been enquiring about work in other mills. Through a corn merchant visiting West Coker he had heard that Fayerdon of Wynford Tarrent had a growing business and was in need of an able man. In a fair hand that spoke of his abilities he wrote offering his services and Daniel, glad to get an experienced worker at beneath his previous wage, accepted his references and himself.

There was now only the formality of the divorce standing between the lovers. None of the three involved had a relish for the public spectacle they would make transacting their business in a market-place yet they knew it was traditional for wife-sales to be held in a prominent situation. Unexpectedly it was an idea of Nat's on which they settled. He knew the area around Bridport slightly from the occasional long hauls he had made and had heard of Tarrendon Hill. The promontory, so massive and unhidden yet so isolated served their purpose well and it was agreed that on the day that Matthew was due to arrive at his new mill Nat would bring Canader to the earthworks and the exchange would be made. Matthew would enter his new life as a married man.

It puzzled Canader why Nat should be prepared to travel so far to be rid of her – he could as easily have taken payment where they were – but Nat had a double reason for leaving Yeovil. He was not a man to look to the future and if he had money he spent it. To him the five sovereigns he would have for Canader was wealth enough to make holiday. Rumours of the gaieties to be had in the expanding and fashionable seaside resorts had long tempted him and his plan was to make his way from Tarrendon to Weymouth and from there to Bournemouth. After tasting the entertainments he would return for Sarah with the story of having abandoned his wife and gained an employment which had put gold in his purse and would do so again. As a prelude to his enjoyment he intended to hold Canader to the most humiliating and established aspect of the divorce. In public he let it be known that he and his wife were leaving to tramp for work and in private he prepared the rope for her halter.

And so it had come about that on a clear April day, when Beatrice first drove out alone and hid her restlessness on the heights of Tarrendon, Canader had been brought like a beast to the hill and a new existence had opened for her.

As she moved this evening between the table she was laying and the fire beneath the pot she was still in the state of bewildered contentment that had come upon her the first day they had entered this house together. All things in their life were novel to her; her evenings strange in their companionship; her nights a revelation of love and tenderness. She knew that soon Matthew would come in with open eagerness to see her; there would be friendly conversation at their table; later he would put his arms about her and show her that he was strong and gentle in all his ways. What she had expected to have to bear for the sake of being his wife had become the flowering of a passion that was growing upon her. It had been no intention of Nat to father children for whom he might have to provide and after the early weeks of their marriage he had taken little interest in her. The cold and loveless workings of his lust had not prepared her for the fierce and singing adoration she felt for this man who showed his devotion to her in all things. Beneath her quietness she lived fervent with joy, and health returned to her day by day.

The sound of footsteps interrupted her thoughts. She paused at the table, her hand on the jug. The steps would reach the point of the lane level with the end of the cottage and stop. There would be the stamp, shuffle, stamp of a dancer running through a newly-learnt jig and Matthew would come in. She smiled at the gravity there would be on his face. Outside in the dusk, hidden by the elder tree that grew by their wall, Matthew shook the corn-dust from his clothes. The long, linen coat he wore at his work was hanging in the mill and his hair was watered and rubbed clean but the fine powder of the ground meal still settled about him and for a moment the foreman, serious and responsible, beat his legs and pranced in the shadows so that his love should meet him at his best.

He opened their door and, as always when he entered, she was smiling. The room was warm and savoury from her cooking; what little they possessed was neat and tended; she had free-stoned a white pattern on the brick floor – a wide border with a circle in its centre – and she stood straight and welcoming in the firelight. Such red hair and the flames gleaming on the brass amongst it. When he was able he would buy her golden earrings.

He went to her and embraced her. They rocked together, their faces touching, then she pushed him from her, leaning back and patting his chest when he was reluctant to let go, and turned back to her nets in the pot. Matthew hung his jacket on a nail by the door and sat at the table as she lifted the potatoes and bacon on to a trencher and brought it to the table. He broke the bread and poured their beer as she divided the meat.

'I have a message for you,' he said. 'The young mistress wants you tomorrow for the cowslipping. You can walk up with me in the morning.'

'Tomorrow?' said Canader. 'I thought the day was changed to the one after.'

'Aye, but old Mrs Fayerdon will have it there'll be rain on the morrow and young Mrs says there will not and so she'll have the flowers tomorrow to cock-a-snoop at the old lady.'

Canader sliced the impress from the butter and laid it on her bread.

'There'll never be peace in that house,' she said, 'the young one so lively and reckless, the other so crabbish and sour, and the master—'

'The master in love with his pocket,' said Matthew. 'No thought for his wife or his men and not a penny paid out to put things to rights. His business prospers yet will he mend where it's needed? Grindstones worn thin, timbers rotten. I had to cross the bridge over the wheel this noon to fetch him from his house to a buyer and the planking was splitting beneath my feet. I could see the water in the race under me. When I told him repairs would make it safer he bid me bide my place. If I were Mistress Beatrice I'd spite his mother.'

Canader laid down her spoon.

'Will you often have to cross that bridge?' she asked.

Matthew looked up and met her eyes, green and wide. He reached across the table and clasped her hand in his.

'No, honey,' he said. 'I'll go by the yard way. No man with someone to love him would walk on that bridge.'

CHAPTER FIVE

In the mid-afternoon of the following day Boaz came riding easily down the long hill that led to Wynford Tarrent. The skirts of his leather coat hung open over the sturdy flanks of his mare and he wore a sprig of gorse at his chest. There had been a low mist amongst the trees in his valley the previous night, so that he could stand in his porch-room and look down on a cool, white smoke of moisture, but a dawn wind had risen enough to disperse it before dying to leave a still, sunlit day.

The world was fresh that morning and the mellowing of the light as the day drew on had not impaired it. The season at the brink of ripeness was painful to see. The rising of his spirits as he had entered his farm had not left Boaz but the optimism brought out by change and enterprise was not an unalloyed sensation. It brought with it a strengthened longing for someone warm and uncomplicated to share this new life and a deep feeling of treachery towards Esther. He wanted to forget and replace her and yet he did not want to admit finally that he had lost her. He put it to himself that it was a simple matter – he was a young man and he was lonely – but the simplicity of his problem did not help him bear it. And, he thought, as he raised his face to the bright sky with its sparse and ragged cloud, there is another straightforward aspect to consider – I have a wife living and can take no other. If I meet a woman who could suit me I must either forsake her or destroy her good name. To have her with me would be to demand a trust it would be unfair to ask.

He drew his mind from personal worries and forced them on to business. In the four days he had been in possession of Tarrendon he had not been idle. He had walked the farm and studied the field maps. A day had been spent in cleaning an outhouse and making elementary repairs to the roof and doors so that his implements and seed-corn were stored in safety. It was late to be sowing but he wanted to plough a sheltered meadow at the foot of the great hill to grow enough oats for his use in winter. The farm journal showed that this field had been arable years before and had been left fallow without reseeding with good grasses – it would serve him to take a crop before putting down clover. He had barley to fill a strip along the meadow that would be sufficient for his brewing but he needed more oats and roots. It angered him to think of the rows of seedlings he had left behind on his last farm and the money he would have to spend on winter fodder if the weather was against a rushed harvest. To provide these necessities he had ridden to Bridport the day before to search out a grain-merchant and after closing his deal over a glass of Thirza's currant wine had asked Mr Lamford to recommend a miller. Henry, who had a good opinion of Daniel's meal if not his behaviour as a husband, had spoken highly of Wynford Mill and it was there that Boaz was riding to make his introduction and bring away a stone of flour.

His sense of activity and work well begun was in

tune with the day. The dew had dampened the track enough for there to be no dust and as he rode down the long slope he could look out over a valley brilliant with the colours of new growth and early summer sky. Sand martins were darting above the white hawthorns that edged one side of the lane. Down in the village the river that fed the mill wound its shining way through meadows and gardens and beyond a copse on its banks was a field of the muted yellow that was cowslips. It was warm and quiet; a day for friendships.

A few cottages, spaced well apart, led into the village and he went by them without asking his way. He had passed the mill before on his journey to the farm and it was easy to find. He could see it clearly for some distance before he turned into its yard. It was a three-storeyed building made – unusually for the district – of brick, which had weathered to a soft, lichened red, and was built in a substantial L. The river had been running to his right since he had met houses but just before he reached the yard it crossed under a bridge and ran at a right-angle from the road up to the mill where it turned abruptly again, disappearing behind the building. As he tied his mare by a trough Boaz could see that the end of the mill that was enclosed on two sides by water was the dwelling but could see no-one there or in the workplace. A cat slept by an open door.

He could hear the roar of the wheel and the sound of the millstones grinding and was debating whether to shout or explore alone when a man came out of a storeroom. The man, white from head to foot, was grave-faced and, incongruously for a miller, was carrying a tool-bag. He seemed preoccupied by something that displeased him but when he noticed Boaz his expression cleared and he came forward pleasantly.

'Can I help you, master?' he enquired.

Boaz nodded. 'Ay,' he said, 'if you can tell me if Mr Fayerdon is within.'

Matthew shifted the bag so that it hung more balanced in his hand. 'He'll be up in the corn-hutch still,' he said. 'Will you wait or better prefer I take you to him?'

A childish curiosity prompted Boaz to be taken inside and with this he again felt a prick of remorse. A lively interest in the world around must show a reawakening from grief. He followed Matthew up steps through a door high enough for men with corn on their shoulders and pulled it to behind him.

At once he was engulfed by sound. In the great room the monotonous thunder of the wheel and the rumble of the stones as they ground and ground the fine meal swelled in a deep resonance that filled the chamber. The air was soft and white and could be felt on his face; it was thick in his mouth as he breathed. High in the walls windows laced with corn-dust filtered the sun and let it down on the lads tying sacks in a pale haze of light.

A wooden stairway rose against two walls and up this Boaz followed Matthew. As they climbed he could feel the clamour reverberating in the steps and rail but in moments he had become used to the din and from stunning him it became an agreeable and exciting sensation. As they reached the second storey Matthew turned and called into Boaz' ear.

'Keep to the wall. The wood's come away.' He pointed upwards and peering through the ghostly air

73

Boaz saw that the handrail had split from its post and was hanging out over the drop. They both went on, walking a little sideways, their shoulders brushing the plaster. At the break Matthew put down his bag and Boaz saw again the look of displeasure on his face as he saw the crumbling wood.

In the corn-hutch the air was different. Here on the highest floor vast mounds of grain lay bathed in the pure gold light that spread in from the open doors where the tackle that drew up the sacks from the drays hung down into the void. The scents of barley, rye, wheat and oats were drawn out by the warmth of the sun and lay dry and fragrant in the drifting dust.

Daniel was standing to one side of the gaping doorway, rolling a handful of grain between his fingers and staring out into space. He glanced at Matthew as he entered and Boaz, climbing quietly behind, was in time to see him ignore his foreman in a studied and petulant fashion.

'A gentleman to see you, Mr Fayerdon,' Matthew said and stood back to let Boaz pass.

Daniel turned and instantly became the merchant. He walked across the floor, thick as a bird's cage with corn, and offered his hand. Before he had reached Boaz he had assessed him and decided that here was a client to be cultivated. A farmer who was not a gentleman but who had enough of that quality in him to justify Garth's use of the term; a straight eye; health; a firm step – all meant a man likely to rise and bring trade to the mill. He took the stranger's strong, calloused hand and felt the work it had known.

They greeted each other and as Matthew went back to his tools, Boaz stated his business. It was Daniel's intention to take him down to the house but while they spoke the sound of a heavy wagon was heard beyond the roar of the mill and a cry interrupted them. Daniel excused himself and leant out into the air.

'A moment and I'll let down the chains,' he called.

He turned back to Boaz. 'A delivery and I'm short-handed today.' Thrusting his head out of the staircase door he shouted, 'Garth! Garth! Leave that and come here!' and then again addressed Boaz. 'Are you in haste to return, sir? If not my wife would be glad to entertain you until I'm free. A glass of wine after your ride?'

Boaz, accepting the invitation, found himself once more in the yard. The scene was busy now with sacks of barley being hoisted noisily by labourers calling back and forth to Daniel and Matthew in the corn-hutch. His mare still stood placidly brushing her muzzle over the mottled water in the trough but the cat – a lover of peace – had taken itself elsewhere. He approached the open front door and, reaching into the hall, rapped the brass knocker. No-one answered. Outside the turmoil of business threw its shadows on the sunlit day; inside the stillness of an empty house slept in the passage. He took off his hat and went in.

Doors lay to left and right but if their rooms had been occupied he would have been heard. The stairs were ahead but he was looking for a kitchen and a servant in it to announce him. He walked down to the door where Beatrice had seen the sliver of light the evening she had first driven alone from Bridport and as he did so, leaving the noises of the workmen behind, he noticed that here too the sound of the great wheel filled the room with thunder. He wondered how long you must live with this sound before you could not rest without it.

Tapping on the door he listened. A cheerful female voice bid him enter and, lifting the latch, he went in.

Sweetness assailed all his senses. The room, now receiving as much sunlight as its window would allow, was in a condition of picturesque upheaval. The heavy kitchen table was standing aslant before the dresser and had plainly been dragged there to allow more space to be found for the work being done. On its scrubbed surface, on the settle, the great flour crock, the floor, stood basket upon basket of cowslips, filling the chamber with their pale yellow and green and their delicate, fragile fragrance. Amongst them sat two handsome young women, their laps overflowing with the flowers, engaged in picking the peep from each cowslip and throwing the stalks and sheaths on to a mound on the flags. On the open range an immense preserving-pan released the vapour of the syrup it was brewing and enriched the scent of the room.

Canader clutched at her flowers and tried to rise but Beatrice put a hand on her arm and held her back.

'You have the advantage of us, sir,' she said, gaily. 'We're quite unable to be civil.'

Boaz smiled. He looked at Beatrice sitting so golden amongst the fading blooms and thought the tawny cat asleep in the sun had become a woman.

'My name is Holt of Tarrendon,' he said. 'I came to begin business with Mr Fayerdon, ma'am, and he offered me wine.'

'Then wine,' said Beatrice, 'you shall have. Am I

76

to be less ready than my husband to welcome callers? No!'

She untied the white apron that fell from the high waist beneath her breasts and wrapped it about the cowslips it held. Placing it beside her chair, she stood up and began dancing about the kitchen, closing the door behind Boaz, showing him where to sit, pouring a glass of sparkling, yellow wine from an open bottle and handing it to him.

Boaz, sitting opposite her own Windsor chair, was seized by an urge to take this happy creature into his arms and press her to him but it was countered by a lazy conviction that he would be content to sit in this warm, soothing kitchen all afternoon.

Beatrice was in good spirits. Her mother-in-law had gone to spend the day with friends and she had been free to have Canader's company in the most pleasant of household tasks. It was not only love that she missed in her marriage – it was liking. She liked Canader and found whatever excuse she could to bring her to the mill. They had gathered the flowers while the morning was still cool and on their walks to and from the meadow in the fresh, clear air and in the hours in the still kitchen they had talked of this and that and been more comfortable with each other than either had been with another woman for years. It was almost a holiday for Canader to be summoned by Beatrice. The work she was asked to do was not strenuous and she never left without a packet of broken meats or some small article for her home. She returned her mistress' liking and admired her for being so brave and blithe in the face of her circumstances. An unhappy marriage was a matter of pity to her and though she did not think Beatrice to be in such a plight as she had been herself yet she was able to feel and sympathize with her suffocation. It would have startled her to have known that this vivacious girl was withheld by delicacy from admitting to Canader that she had witnessed the divorce on Tarrendon Hill and she would have been astounded to learn that because of it Beatrice looked on her as an exotic and a symbol of freedom. But had she known she would not have been afraid that her secret would become common talk; she recognized the strength in Beatrice and trusted her.

The three sat together in the scented kitchen and drank each other's health in another year's wine. Boaz relaxed into the well-being of the moment and Beatrice, full of the felicity of a day unusual in its pleasures, regaled him with laughter and curiosity. In answer to her questions he told her the little of himself that he told to acquaintances and the compassion in her eyes as he said that his wife would live elsewhere almost overthrew him. He could not reconcile her, glowing and joyful as she was, with the miller and his petulance.

When the copper pan threatened to boil over Beatrice pressed him into giving his service. She measured peeps into wide earthenware bowls and they ladled the hot, sweet syrup over the flowers. With Beatrice holding a candle he carried the heavy dishes with their swaying contents down into the damp cellar and set them on slab shelves to cool. They walked back through the pantry together and the smell of her – of dew and flowers, sugar and wine – was an unbearable invitation to him. He wanted to take her on his lap, let down her hair and dandle her as he would a kitten. Sensual hungers in him were being fed by her presence. As they went back into the kitchen they found Canader holding up a large, drooping bloom.

'An oxlip, ma'am,' she said. 'Whose turn for a wish?'

Beatrice came over and took the flower. 'You've had one,' she said, 'and so have I. The next is for Mr Holt.'

Boaz stepped close to them and she put the oxlip in his hand. Her fingers were soft and warm. 'Don't tell us what you wish,' she said, 'or it won't come true.'

He looked at her. How strange that he should be taking part in this afternoon.

'Shut your eyes, sir,' said Canader, 'and think what you would have.' Boaz shut his eyes, and he did not tell Beatrice what he wished.

CHAPTER SIX

Throughout that summer as he ploughed and sowed, tended the sheep bought from Beaminster, hedged and mended house and buildings, Boaz thought of young Mrs Fayerdon. He pictured her brewing the wine he had helped her begin, stirring the bowls of cowslips at morning, at noon, at night, straining the liquor through muslin as Esther had done for their wines, pouring the brandy that would hearten its maturing. He lay alone in his bed as the owls called in the wood and remembered each move she had made. He wove his fantasies upon her and used them as solace to his loneliness. He built an elaborate dream-world in which she, so vibrant and welcoming, was singing in his tangled garden, watching from his porch-room windows, walking in the long-grassed meadows, resting beside him in the moonlit nights. It was not love – he knew that – but he made no struggle against infatuation.

Once, as he looked up from clearing a water-course, he saw her standing high above him on the ramparts of Tarrendon, a small figure that he knew by her shining hair; once he met her again at her husband's house where he had been invited to sup and play a hand of whist; twice, when he learned of her visits to her sister, he was on the road above the farm as she passed and rode beside her to his turning.

He meant her no harm. There was no intention to compromise her in his actions. She seemed to him so merry and it refreshed him to be near her. In early June he wrote to his wife in the bare valley amongst the downs that were so far away but though he sent the price of a letter's carriage beneath its seal he had no answer and he did not cherish hopes. An imaginary woman of smiles and warmth and corn-coloured braids gave less pain than the living flesh.

For Beatrice the summer was long. It was as she had feared in spring. The heat, the growth, the hope of the ripening season stirred her already frustrated nature until she was half-mad with the need to assuage her loneliness. Her yearning focused on what seemed could be the only escape from her isolation and, though she felt not a whit of desire for her husband, before the fruit had sprung on the trees she had coaxed and begged him to give her a child. Daniel, preoccupied with business and enjoying her distress, had put her aside with such contempt that she did not approach him again. He called her a trollop and, because she had cajoled him without any love on her side, she believed him and lived in disgust of herself.

She supposed that he had shut her away like unwanted linen. He would bring her out to be put to her use when self-love turned him from his pro-fessional prowess to the urge to reproduce his own image. It revolted her to think that she would be used as coldly as any breeding animal and that, if she had her wish, the young one in her arms might look back at her with Fayerdon eyes. She wanted to be looked at as Holt looked at her when he rode beside her trap above his hidden farm. There was no love that she could see in him but there was such longing that she did not know why she had no fear.

If she had not had Thirza she could not conceive how she could have borne her desperation. There was no formal Aunt Fayerdon at her sister's home; she was Aunt Bea who could be dragged by the skirts to see the yard-pups, who knew cat's-cradle, who could tell a good tale – and if she wept once as she carried Charlotte down to the arbour, Charlotte was too young to understand. Her days in Arland House, so rare and welcome, were all that sustained her and she grew to brood on them until she would not hear what was said to her at the mill. They would sit in the kitchen firelight, saving candles, and Beatrice would be among friends in a drawing-room with a nephew in her lap. Seeing her face, rapt and distant, old Mrs Fayerdon, not knowing that passion could be innocent, would exchange glances with her son and frown with an intake of breath.

Her withdrawal enraged Daniel. By word of mouth, by Henry's goodwill for Beatrice's sake, by the satisfaction of those who did not see the corners he cut in producing his meal, the reputation of his mill spread and as he prospered he felt less need of Beatrice's gentility and connections. He began to be slighting towards her in public and took a malicious amusement in watching her keep up an appearance of not noticing insults. With his balance at his bank growing he felt it unnecessary to preserve the gentlemanliness he had affected to court his wife and his boorishness became more evident in all that he did. Both he and his mother enjoyed making it plain to Beatrice that she had sunk in rank by marrying Daniel and took a pride in subjecting her to all she found offensive. To demonstrate his power and stop what he considered to be the extravagances she had introduced into his home Daniel returned control of the housekeeping allowance to his mother and if Beatrice required a sixpence she was obliged to ask for it.

A diversion from this stifling monotony came in August. A grand Harvest Home was to be held by John Treves, a substantial and hospitable farmer at Toller Porcorum. This was not to be the usual feast given to the labouring men, where they and their families were able to eat their fill for once in the year and toast their thanks to the man who had kept them hungry. It was to be a gathering of farmers and their equals at the high tables and the upper farm servants at the lower. Amongst those invited were Miller and Mrs Fayerdon and Boaz Holt.

It was to be an evening celebration in order that the guests might enjoy the Harvest Moon and as afternoon drew to an end on the day of the entertainment Beatrice was to be found in her bedchamber, gaining a little peace alone. The day had already been long. Old Mrs Fayerdon, irritated by the prospect of her daughter-in-law's pleasure, had found fault with her since early morning and Beatrice, goaded until her hands began to shake, had excused herself from joining the family at the tea-table and taken an apple and slice of fruit-cake up to her room as if she were again a school-girl.

This had given her time to make leisurely preparations and as she slowly bathed and dressed and untied her hair she grew less noticeably agitated. It had been so hot a day that even this room with its thick walls and river-chill was warm. The sunlight still entering the windows was milky with the floating corn-dust and as she moved about from sun to shadow she changed from a real and living form to something pale and ethereal. She had put on a gown that was unusual for her colouring – a chrome yellow muslin with white figures – because it took her fancy to mirror the harvest. To this she added a twisted gold chain and beneath her throat, which she had left bare, she pinned a silk and wire confection of orange blossom and ribbon. She went to the looking-glass that hung above the cabinet where her brushes and salve-pots lay. In its soft and bronzed reflection she gazed upon herself. Her hair, waiting to be arranged, still hung thickly waving about her shoulders, making her look as young as she had forgotten that she was. Except in the expression of her eyes that were both bold and sad there was nothing in her face to tell of her sorrows. It was not vanity on her part to see that she was lovely. Her clear skin, fresh lips, the hair like burnt barley, her ripe and graceful body – all were enough to make her desired even if she had not had her loving disposition. Why then was she condemned to so barren an existence? She could not believe that it was God's law that her heart should be wasted in this way. If she were bound for a lifetime to a man who despised her it would be the action of human rule-giving not natural justice.

She unscrewed the silver jar at her right hand. 'Scent of the May', an old receipt, tender and heavy with lilac and hawthorn, rose into the sultry air and she, so susceptible to her senses, could have wept for its sweetness. Would this be her life forever? She thought of Canader and the sale on the hill. If she disclosed what she knew the same authorities that tied her to Daniel would force this woman from a good man and bind her to the husband who dragged her with a rope about her neck. She would never tell Canader's secret but would there ever be such an escape for her?

Drawing off her wedding-ring she looked at it. It was said that a girl passing bridal cake through a ring would dream of her true love. She broke a piece of her own uneaten cake and held it above her ring. In the old glass her face was serious and ardent. She pushed the cake through the ring and waited. In the silence of the afternoon she found her heart to be beating harder. She stirred the crumbs on the plate with her finger and smiled at her foolishness.

There were steps outside her door. Hurriedly she pressed the smeared ring back into place. Daniel entered and found her doing nothing and looking roguish, an attitude of hers that annoyed him more than any other.

'Have you not made your hair yet?'

He walked over to the washstand and Beatrice picked up her brush. She did not speak.

Daniel poured water into his bowl. He looked her over as he threw his shirt on the bed. Runnels of sweat had trickled down his back, turning the dust on his skin to a paste.

'Preening and peacocking,' he said. 'And I haven't seen that gown before – it must have cost me a pretty penny.'

Beatrice did not turn from the glass. 'It cost you nothing. It's from the piece Thirza gave me at Ladyday.'

He grunted. 'Dressmaker's bills.' He washed

himself vigorously, scattering water over the clothes Beatrice had laid out for him.

'I sewed it myself,' she said. 'In the afternoons.'

He picked up the towel and began rubbing his arms. 'It's a pity you've nothing more useful to occupy you. Fal-lals. There's always bread to be baked.'

Beatrice did not reply. She coiled her hair and searched for combs. Together they finished their toilet without speaking and went out into the yard where the trap was waiting. They did not offer each other their hands to mount the step and Daniel drove on before Beatrice had settled, so that throughout the journey her skirts and the cloak she held on her knees were awkward and uncomfortable. Walkers that they passed looked on their youth and fine dress and envied them.

The evening was so warm that the air flowing by their faces as they rolled through the village felt dense as water. As they climbed the long hill there were swallows darting against a heat-bleached sky. All about them had lost the vigour of its colour. The verges and hedgerows were whitened by the lane; the leaves and flowers sapped by the sun. In the meadows the cattle stood head to tail, sending long shadows across the drying dew-ponds. In uncut cornfields pale oats rattled as the rabbits that had lain all day underground ran amongst them and far down in the valley distance spread the brightness of the poppies, turning whole acres to red. In the ditches the watermint wilted as the mud hardened and the first rust-brown spores were seen on the ferns. Beatrice watched a goldfinch tugging up thistledown with backward sweeps of its wings before the trap frightened it into flight. She thought how much she preferred to drive alone.

They turned to the right in Toller Porcorum, away from the Bridport route, and wound upwards to Treves's farm. The squat stacks in the rickyard told of a successful harvest for, though this was not corn country, Treves owned enough sheltered land to make him warm. They were not the first to arrive. A variety of vehicles stood amongst the ricks and saddle-horses were being led to join others in the wide shade of a chestnut tree.

The sound of a fiddle was heard from the great open door of a stone barn and when Daniel had tied a nose-bag over their pony's head he and Beatrice walked towards the music. For this he offered her his arm.

Treves was standing in the doorway talking over his shoulder to the schoolmaster and his wife who he had just greeted and who were passing down to their table. He turned and clasped Daniel's hand.

'And Mistress Fayerdon,' he said. 'Well, ma'am, you had a driver today – but never was a husband who could do a thing as well as his lady, eh? Alice!' he called across to his wife and she left the niece whose sash she was tying and came to her guests.

'Miller,' she said. 'Mrs Fayerdon.' Her narrow, high-boned face worked itself into the smile which so enlivened her. 'I see you driving through the village, ma'am. A very pretty whip.'

With her hand still pressed into the crook of his arm, Beatrice could feel Daniel stiffen. His growing confidence did not yet encompass a disregard for his neighbours' opinions of what might be thought unconventional in his behaviour. It had plainly been remarked that the miller's wife was allowed to travel alone. Was this to his credit?

'I was never used to a manservant in my youth,' Beatrice said. 'I prevailed on my . . . on Mr Fayerdon not to curb my visits to my sister from . . . from fineness. I keep no maid.'

Daniel's arm was tense now and the familiar emptiness was in Beatrice's chest. Treves watched her, regretting his words. He looked at Daniel.

'Who wouldn't be indulgent?' he asked. His wife touched him lightly on the back. 'Ah,' he said and glanced round at an old man who was standing at her side. 'Reuben, show our visitors to their seats.'

Beatrice and Daniel followed the servant down the middle of the barn. It was not yet dusk but beyond the light cast through the door they would have been in shadow. Instead, they moved in a haze of candlelight. Along the tables that lined the walls of the barn, in silver, pewter and china sticks, in basins and bottles, in lanterns hooked into the sail-cloth that screened the grain from the dancing-floor, candles burned with a smoky, flickering flame. When darkness came they would be brilliant but now in the indoor twilight they seemed to draw mist into the barn.

Even so the scene did not lack for cheerfulness. Green garlands of oak and beech leaves were ranged along the roof-beams and bound to the walls between sheaves of barley and meadowsweet. From end to end of each white-clothed table swags of convolvulus were looped, already shedding petals. A fiddler stood on a platform playing a tripping melody and with him two other fiddlers and a boy with a penny-whistle sat waiting to join in. Most seats were filled and conversation and laughter burred about the barn. As she passed a central table Beatrice became conscious of herself and, looking at who sat there, met the eyes of Boaz Holt.

She felt herself colour and bowed slightly. Boaz knew himself to be staring but followed her as she was taken down the line to a table next to the one at which the Treves would sit. He saw Daniel assessing his own importance by this placing and appearing satisfied and he met Beatrice's eyes again as she glanced down the row to his bench. Then both took their chairs and were no longer in view.

Throughout the beef and plum-pudding Boaz talked to his neighbours but thought of Beatrice. For him her fascination was no less when he saw her in person. It did not please him to see her on the arm of a man whose perfunctory manner towards her spoke of neglect. He had watched her as she arrived and witnessed her saying something to her host which hardened Daniel's face and made her anxious. It angered him that so easy natured a wife should be disparaged. He wanted to go to her table, catch up her hand and take her home with him and wondered whether he would. The evening, as did much of his life, felt unreal. He seemed to sit enclosed by unseen barriers from those around him; their movements were a little slow, their voices muffled. It was to counter this growing isolation that he had come here tonight.

He lived as a recluse and it was not through choice. Apart from the fortnight when he had hired rounds-men to break stones to mend his lane he worked alone. He recognized that the constant calculation of wind and weather that could make or mar his late crops, the hard physical labour without the respite of comfort at home, the weeks that passed without a word spoken to another soul, the deep grieving for his wife and daughter and the longing for the dreamlike Beatrice were making him inward and unnatural. He had nothing to sell and few needs to supply but he rode to Bridport market twice monthly simply to exchange a few remarks with other farmers. The price of the communal market-dinner at the Bull was too much for him to risk in this establishing year and he could not stand treat at an ale-house. This harvest dance with the hours he had spent at the mill and the day he had drunk currant wine with Mrs Fayerdon's sister and the corn-merchant were the only social occasions he had seen since he had come as a stranger.

The cloths were cleared and brushed and flagons of cider and the spirits that had come up the valleys on moonless nights were set out. It had grown dark beyond the doors and the guttering candles made a dazzle of warmth and light that did not reach to the high rafters. At a nod from Treves the first fiddler called the 'Four Hand Reel', the strings sang out the theme and as its hearty, jigging rhythm swelled into the air the sets formed. From all sides of the barn couples rose; young men bashful or sure drew out girls from among their cousins; stout fathers stood up proudly with their daughters or rallied their wives so that both went on to the floor laughing.

Beatrice glanced at Daniel but he was sitting turned half away from her talking to the maltster from Chilfrome and two brothers who farmed beyond Norden. All were in their middle-age and none watched the dancers. They had filled the churchwardens that had been passed amongst them and were handing the gin jug between them. They did not address any remark to Beatrice and she had nothing to say to them.

The dancers' feet were stamping as they wove in their reels and stepped to each other. Carefully coiled hair was falling down over white shoulders and eyes were bright. As each dance succeeded and the girls' colour deepened and they forgot any polite restriction, they relaxed into the music and swung into the figures with no thought but for their partners. Beatrice, sitting at her table, accompanied yet alone, gazed at them with hunger in her smile. She thought: how handsome, how handsome they are. Hardly younger than myself, and some no younger. They give themselves so gladly to their men, as I did. Will their unions be as mine? And the matrons dancing amongst their sons – have they come to terms with disappointment or are they truly contented? Beside her Daniel and his companions leant their heads together and listened to a tale the maltster told in a low voice with a flickering of his eyes towards Beatrice. At its conclusion they laughed and banged their glasses on the cloth. Is this all any marriage is, Beatrice wondered, boredom pierced with embarrassment and distress? And am I always to see happiness and sit separate from it?

Between dances Treves called for songs and the verses with their burdens of gaiety, melancholy and desire rang out pure and clear in the high barn.

'Love it is pleasing; love it is teasing.
Love is a treasure when first it's new.
But as it grows older it waxes colder

And fades away like the morning dew.

'Thyme it is a precious thing
And thyme brings all things to my mind.
Thyme with all its labours, along with all its joys.
Thyme brings all things to my mind.

'Come all you maidens young and fair;
Maids who are blooming in your prime.
Always remember to keep your garden fair.
Let no man steal away your thyme.'

God help me, thought Beatrice, or my heart will break. She closed her eyes, afraid that tears were in them.

'Mistress Fayerdon – do you dance?'

She looked up, startled. Boaz stood before her. His face was almost angry and his eyes were full of pain. This was not as he had looked at her before yet she felt its origin to be the same.

'Willingly,' she said, 'when I am asked.'

Daniel looked over his shoulder and made an acknowledging wave. Beatrice pushed back her chair and edged between the tables on to the floor. As she walked beside Boaz into their set she felt her body lighten. The fiddler called 'The Soldier's Joy' and each couple linked hands. As they cast down the line, following their other three pairs, she could not look at her partner. The touch of his hands on hers exalted her and filled her with a sense of intimacy that she had never felt with her husband. It was a shepherd's hand, calloused and weather-burned yet with skin smooth from the oils in the fleece, and it held hers harder than was needed for the dance. They returned and stepped towards each other. As she turned she was close enough to smell that his breath was cider-dry and for her skirts to brush his legs. They crossed hands and she leant back as they swung while he held her with a grip that pressed their palms together. Standing apart as the first pair passed between them she thought: this is guilt. The music rose and fell, flowing like rising waters in her mind, the leaders danced back swinging to change their places and all this while Boaz neither took his eyes from her nor smiled. Back and forth they danced – now their hands were clasped, now their fingers intertwined – and with every touch her elation grew. She looked at him, her face as serious as his but her eyes wild with exhilaration.

The fiddlers stopped and she stood shaken. Her lips were dry and she slid her tongue along them. Boaz still stared at her. They did not speak. She was breathing with quick, shallow gasps. This is wrong, she thought, I know that this is wrong.

'Well, sir, will you favour us?'

Treves was at Boaz' side. He held a large, earthenware jar and gestured with his head at the fiddlers' platform. Boaz turned his fierce gaze from Beatrice to Treves.

'Ay,' he said, 'I will.'

He took the jar by its handles and drank. The dancers were moving slowly back towards the tables, standing in clusters to await the next song. Beatrice followed to a place close to the musicians. Boaz gave back the jar and stepped up on to the platform, the boy jumping down to make room for him. He closed his eyes and for a moment there was silence, then he lifted his head and sang.

'Come all you maids who live at a distance
Many's the mile from your swain.
Come and assist me this very moment
For to pass away some time
Singing sweetly and completely
Songs of pleasure and of love.
For my heart is with her altogether
Though I live not where I love.

'When I sleep I dream about her;
When I awake I have no rest.
Every moment thinking of her.
Her heart trapped within my breast.
Though far distance may be assistance
From my mind her face to remove
Still my heart is with her altogether
Though I live not where I love.'

His voice was deep and alive with longing. Daniel
looked up from his glass and saw his wife as she had
not been since the early days of their marriage.

'The world shall be of one religion,
All living things shall cease to die
If ever I prove false to my jewel
Or any way her love deny.
The world shall change and be most strange
If ever I my love refuse
For my heart is with her altogether
Though I live not where I love.'

Beatrice, shivering though not with cold, thought:
dear God, protect me; I must hide myself from this.

'So, farewell lads and farewell lasses
For now I think I've got my choice.
I'll away through yonder meadow
Where I hear my true love's voice.
If she calls then I will follow
Through the world though it be wide
For this pretty maid has promised
She will be my wedded bride.'

The song ended and Boaz stood looking into the distance as if there were no walls about him. That she might not make an oddity Beatrice did as the other women were doing and attended to the ravages of the dance. She pushed hair back into her combs and spread her skirts. As she lowered her eyes from Boaz she saw that the flower had fallen from her breast and had been crushed.

The fiddler called 'Strip the Willow' and pairs began to gather. Boaz stepped down, hesitated and began to approach her. She glanced over to Daniel and saw, to her surprise, that he was no longer at the table but was crossing the floor in the company of George Lamford. Both men were grave and watched her as they walked. She turned to Boaz and saw that he had followed her gaze and was waiting for her husband to come to her.

The two men wove through the sets and reached her. As Daniel did not speak, George made his greeting.

'Mrs Fayerdon,' he said. 'Beatrice, my dear, you will not have expected to see me. Will you come outside?'

Beatrice turned and the three walked towards the

door. Before she led their way she had time to see that while Daniel's face wore the gravity of one hiding annoyance at an involvement in something which holds no interest for him, George's showed the concern of one who must give anxiety to a friend. Physical fear for Thirza's safety subdued her. As they passed out of the great doors she found it necessary to tell herself that punishment could not be so swift.

Outside the moon had risen. The air was still so warm that it did not suit the dusk. There was the sound of horses stirring amongst the ricks and the quick saw of crickets, then the fiddles sprang into 'Drops o' Brandy' and the three moved further from the door.

George took Beatrice's hand and she flinched.

'My dear,' he said again, 'I've driven post-haste to fetch you if you will come. A sad accident—'

'Thirza,' Beatrice broke in. Her hand, which had been lifeless, clutched his. He covered it with his other.

'Not Thirza,' he said. 'Arthur. He slipped from his nurse to play in the corn-loft. He tried to jump to a wagon as it passed beneath and struck its tail as he fell. His leg is broke and now a fever . . . He cried for you and Thirza believes you will be best for him.'

'I'll come,' she said. 'There's no question.'

Daniel turned abruptly, catching sight of the dancers in the lighted barn, and as abruptly turned back.

'Daniel,' said Beatrice. 'I must go.'

'Ay,' he said, 'it seems my concerns are to be little thought of.'

George pressed Beatrice's hand and let it go.

'My gig is at the gate,' he said. 'If Mr Fayerdon will release you I will wait for you there.'

Beatrice waited for him to walk from them.

'Your concerns!' she said. 'How will they prosper without the Lamfords? Good God, Daniel, Arthur is but five years old.'

Daniel grasped her wrists. 'Then go to him. You dance briskly enough without your master, now let us see you run to another.'

She tried to pull herself from him but he held her too tightly. 'You disgust me,' she said.

In the moonlight she saw his face harden. She had never spoken so freely before.

'Do I, ma'am? Do I?' He drew her closer to him so that she leant back to avoid his spittle. 'Then let me remind you that you are mine to disgust. You have your uses – few though they be – and it doesn't profit me to offend your family yet, but the time is coming when you will dance to my tune. Remember me as you sit at the bedside. Remember to whom you will come home.'

CHAPTER SEVEN

The full August light fell in narrow shafts of
brilliance from the open windows. The day was so
bright that Thirza, sitting beside her child, could not
look towards the sun without blinking. She sat in her
upright chair – a bowl of cool water and cloths to lay
on her boy's head at her feet – as she or Beatrice or
their mother had done for twelve days and as they
would do until his fever broke. It was quiet in the
room. The yard and the street had been strawed but
this being market-day there was a clamour outside
that could not be dampened yet, despite this and
Arthur's breathing, no sound seemed to penetrate
the calm. Perhaps, thought Thirza, this is the
personal silence of waiting and I do not hear because
there is no place in my mind for anything but my
hope.

She sat in luminance, a whiteness glowing pristine
and radiant about her. Her boy was fortunate in his
apothecary and the good sense of his parents. As a
young man Mr Wharton, who had attended the
Lamfords these many years, had walked the wards of
the Norfolk and Norwich Hospital – exemplary in its
cleanliness – and had been much impressed by John
Howard's reports on the condition of hospitals and
its relation to disease. The two influences resulted in
a passion for hygiene. On his orders Arthur's room
was denuded of all furniture but his bed, a chair and

small table. The hangings of the bed were removed that they might not trap air about him that favoured the propagation of putrid fever. His night soil was instantly carried away to prevent noxious vapours rising from it before the maid came in the morning to empty the pots. The floors and walls were scrubbed and white-washed. The curtains were taken down and only muslin filtered the light from windows that were always open. There was to be no possibility of a harmful miasma lingering about the invalid.

Wharton was not a rich man. He was regarded by many as a crank who rode a hobby-horse derided by more robust surgeons, yet the Lamfords put their faith in him and, in the past, had felt themselves rewarded. They had need of their faith now. Arthur, in striking the wagon as he fell from the loft, had received a compound fracture of his left leg and this injury, with its open wound inviting infection to travel deep into the system, was notorious for leading to a fatal fever. Fever, indeed, had quickly come upon the boy and Thirza and Henry, pale and tense in their bedchamber, had decided what course must be pursued to defeat it. Their decision caused many amongst their acquaintance to shake their heads. They had never observed blood-letting to strengthen a patient and would not allow him to be cupped or leeched or starved. Perfect cleanliness together with an abundant supply of lemonade and possets of the best milk and brandy were to be relied upon.

This action was hard upon the parents; not only did they bear the worry natural to the illness of their first-born, they also laboured under the uncertainty of whether they were right and the knowledge that, if he were to die, their consciences would say that they had killed him. The bones were already showing in Thirza's face and she had refused to greet visitors after being enjoined to prayer too often for her normally equitable temper. The recommendation of a neighbour, bringing neat's-foot jelly, to search her heart for the reason why the lord had seen fit to chastise her had brought Beatrice, valiant as a lioness with cubs, out of her corner to escort the pious one firmly from the house. It was said that Mrs Fayerdon did not have the courtesy of her sister.

Thirza would not have been without Beatrice. It gladdened her to see how, in his lucid moments, Arthur recognized and was cheered by his aunt. There was also comfort for herself in the presence of her childhood companion, for though Henry supported her as best he could his business necessarily claimed him. The two sisters were often together in more privacy than they had enjoyed since Thirza's wedding and from much in Beatrice's manner and from much that was unsaid Thirza understood that the Fayerdons' marriage was more empty than any of her family had yet guessed. She thought she saw despair behind her sister's smile.

A band of light had reached the bed and she rose to draw the muslin hangings closer together. As she turned from the window the door opened softly and Beatrice came in. She was wearing a round gown of Thirza's for, though Henry had sent one of his men to the mill to collect Beatrice's necessities for her stay, the few, ill-matched garments, seemingly chosen at random, that had been sent to her were not adequate to her needs. The gown was not a perfect fit and trailed on the floor as she crossed the room. It drew from Thirza an increase of tenderness for her sister. They met at the bed and looked down on the boy. Arthur, his face flushed and damp, slept a laudanum sleep, twisting his head occasionally up and to the side. A wire cage held the sheet away from his injured leg.

'How does he?' Beatrice asked, her voice almost a whisper.

'The same,' said Thirza, 'or perhaps a little cooler. I can't tell. It may be only my wanting it to be so.'

'I think he is not so red.'

They stood a moment quietly watching him, restraining their impulse to disturb him by unwanted smoothings and adjustments of his linen.

'I came to relieve you,' Beatrice said. 'Henry has ridden into the yard.'

'Thank you. Then I will go down. Call me if—'

'You know that I will.'

Thirza walked slowly down one flight of the stairs and went into her bedchamber to collect a shawl. As she stood looking down into the crowded street, where a dray was waiting while sheep surged noisily to each side, she thought tiredly how much better a view she would have if the drawing-room were on this floor. But, she told herself, gathering the folds about her shoulders, it would not be so convenient; Henry could not talk through open windows to his men as he did now in what he called his leisure. As she descended the last stairs she saw Henry go into the drawing-room, then immediately come out as if in search of her. They met in the hall and she leant against his chest briefly as he held her arms. As she stood straight again he raised his eyebrows and she knew what he meant.

'He sleeps still,' she said, 'but not so restlessly. I

101

think he is not so warm and Beatrice agrees.'

She laced her fingers into his and they went into the drawing-room. Wine and biscuits had been placed on a table as the master had ridden into the yard and he threw his riding-gloves into a chair and poured two glasses.

'I'll send for tea,' Thirza said.

'No,' he handed her a glass. 'You'll take wine. Sit and rest.'

'I've sat too long.' Again she looked out into the street. The sash was down but the clatter of market-day was much louder here than in Arthur's room. She raised the madeira – too rich for her taste in the afternoon – to her lips and the shawl slithered down her back to the floor. She glanced at it absently and let it lie. Henry stooped and lifted it. He held it as if he would put it about her.

'Are you cold?' he asked.

She looked at the sunlight flooding into the room. 'I suppose I'm not,' she said, 'but I seem to have sat so long it feels like evening.'

He draped the shawl on to a stool. 'Does Beatrice watch him now?'

'Yes, as she did this morning. It's only my fancy that makes the time so strange. Mamma has taken Nurse and the children and driven to the sea.'

'Drink your wine.'

She smiled. 'I'm quite hearty, Henry. There's no need to fear for me. If I didn't have Beatrice it would be another matter but while I do—'

'I haven't seen her today. Does she still keep strong?'

'She does but, oh, Henry . . .' She slid the tips of two fingers into his waistcoat pocket and tugged

102

sharply. 'I told her at breakfast that however much we need her she must go back to the mill if she felt Daniel wanted her. And her face! She hid what she thought soon enough but . . . How bitter to have a home you do not want to return to and yet you must. She said that it was here she was wanted and that heart and duty do not always run in harness. It's the most she has ever spoken of her life.'

'And there has been no word from Fayerdon?'

'Not a note nor a message since she came.'

They stood in silence with their wine. Outside the traffic passed amongst the stalls with the cheerful din of the time of day when serious business was past and friends were loitering together between the slowly-moving carts and the animals being driven to their homes. A man had drawn in his cob before the house and was staring at it as if uncertain whether to call. Tired as she was it took Thirza a moment to put a name to his face.

'Is that not Mr Holt?' she asked. 'Does he have business?'

Henry unfastened the window and raised the sash.

'Good day to you, Holt,' he called. 'Did you have need of me?'

Boaz slid from his mare and drew her close to the window, obstructing the passage of walkers. He took off his hat to Thirza and nodded at Henry.

'Thank you, no. I came to enquire how the lad fares but with sickness in a house a caller may not be welcome.'

Thirza moved nearer to the sill and Henry took her empty glass from her.

'You're most considerate,' he said, 'in your intention and action. My wife hasn't drawn breath these twelve days. We think the boy to be improving. Nothing is certain yet but we think his fever to be dropping.'

Boaz looked at Thirza and saw in her eyes the hope he had seen burn in Esther's as she had sat by another bedside.

'It's a troubling time for you, mistress,' he said gently.

'Yes, sir,' she put both hands on the sill, playing her fingers along the wood, 'but I trust it will end well. And I'm not alone in my nursing – my sister, Mrs Fayerdon, is with me. Family is a comfort.'

It was in him to reply 'I had a daughter' but he prevented himself, nor did he say that on the night of the Harvest Home he had followed Beatrice as she went out into the moonlight with her husband and seen her treated as no wife should be treated. She was in this house and there was no method he could employ to see her and nothing he could say if they met. He put his hand into his coat and drew out a toy.

'If you would allow me,' he said. 'I made this for your son. It may amuse him as he grows stronger.'

Thirza reached out and took the gift. It was a wooden horse, plump and unpainted, that could be pulled on stout wheels by a halter of blue cord. It was for a boy who was beginning to be active and at this gesture, so positive and optimistic, she found her eyes to be filling uncontrollably.

'You're so kind,' she said. 'I . . .' A tear ran down her face. 'I will . . . Excuse me.'

She turned away and carried the horse from the room. Climbing the stairs, she bit the inside of her cheek and was mistress of herself again by the time she entered Arthur's chamber. He still slept and she gave the toy to Beatrice to await his wakening. In a few words she told her sister how it had come before she went to bathe her face and rest. Arthur was long in waking and all that afternoon Beatrice sat and did not put the horse out of her lap.

CHAPTER EIGHT

'Do you have everything?'

'I brought little enough. Yes, all's there.'

Beatrice ran her eye over the collection of her belongings that lay in the trap. She was standing in the cornyard with Thirza as Henry made a final check of the harness. Behind them Mrs Randall and George Lamford were talking together. George held Beatrice's cloak over his arm and was winding its ties around his finger as he spoke.

It was an ordinary day in the yard. A wagon, very like the one involved in Arthur's fall, was being unloaded and men, bowed beneath sacks of barley, were passing into one of the barns. In a corner four heavy horses were being groomed before their journey to outlying farms and everywhere there was a constant to-ing and fro-ing. Each time two men met they asked if the weather were warm enough for them.

To Beatrice, standing in the enveloping heat, it was no ordinary day. Arthur was now recovered sufficiently for her to have no justification of her stay. It had been decided three evenings before that as Henry was to pass the mill that Thursday he was to call in and bring the trap back with him. Daniel, unusually truculent in his speech with Henry, would neither fetch his wife himself nor brook any delay in the vehicle's return and so on this Friday in early

September Beatrice was preparing to drive back to what was called her home.

The action did not please her. Although she knew herself to be unhappy in her marriage and reluctant to enter the mill after even a few hours' absence it was only with these weeks of complete freedom from her husband that she realized how much she abhorred him. The release their separation had given dismayed her and she dreaded the resumption of their life together. She had a physical shrinking from this journey and each step that took her from the house was an act of will.

Mrs Randall came forward to stand at her younger daughter's side.

'Does your head still ache?' she asked. As she spoke and Beatrice turned to her she noticed that the girl smelt of the lavender water they had used to bathe her brow; a cool, clear scent on this hot afternoon.

'It's a good deal better, Mamma. I'm glad I waited. I couldn't have driven this morning.'

'Won't you reconsider and let Henry send a man with you? You know he would.'

'No, I'd rather not . . . and,' she smiled slightly without humour, 'you know Daniel has no fears for my safety.'

Mrs Randall touched her daughter's cheek. 'But we have, my dear.'

Beatrice looked from her mother. 'What could befall me between here and the mill?' she said.

The trap was judged ready and Henry came to take Beatrice's hand.

'We've given our thanks,' he began but she interrupted.

'Then don't give them again,' she said, and this time her smile had warmth. 'Don't weary me.'

'Dear Beatrice.' Thirza took her sister in her arms and clasped her. Beatrice dropped Henry's hand and returned the embrace. 'Dear Bea, how we shall miss you.'

'Mercy!' said Beatrice. 'Shall we all set to crying?' She transferred herself to her mother's arms and shook hands with George before climbing briskly into the trap. George passed up her cloak and she laid it on the seat.

'Will you lead me into the street, Henry?' she said. 'The turn is so sharp and, at this moment, I can't see so well.'

The pony, more content with its routine than was its mistress, wound its way on the accustomed journey without feeling the touch of the reins. At first, through habit, it kept to its usual pace – walking the rise and fall of the hills, bouncing at its wide jog-trot where the lanes were level – but as they progressed and it felt no encouragement from its driver it slowed to an amble, tearing mouthfuls from the hedgerows as it went.

In the trap Beatrice sat unseeing. With every mile her resistance to what she must do increased upon her. She felt her mind to be like a frantic beast digging its feet into the ground as it was dragged to slaughter, yet even as her thoughts fought against her return she allowed her body to be conveyed inexorably to where its presence was demanded and despised. For over three weeks now she had lived bathed in an atmosphere of love. The anxiety over Arthur, the pain of witnessing his suffering and the relief at his triumph over his malady had not strained the affection in the household. It had rather drawn the family together in an intensity of emotion that now as she left its source seemed without direction. She carried with her a desire and capacity for love which would be scorned where she must spend her lifetime and, as she travelled further from Thirza's home, she felt unneeded and superfluous to all.

The heat oppressed her. The luxuriance of the lanes, with their heavy, overhanging borders of bushes whose leaves had hardly begun to turn, trapped the thick warmth of this day of full sun. Her skin was moist and her mouth dry. There was a ripeness in the air. At valley farms orchards of apples, plums and pears were being harvested and the richness of the scent of fallen fruit hung in the coombes.

As she reached the long ridge of the downs that led to Tarrendon her thoughts – of love, of need, of harvest – fused into her remembrance of the night that had begun this separation. Somewhere below her in the meadows of sun-bleached grass and uncut oats Boaz Holt was working. She craved for more than the brotherly fondness she had had from Henry or the odium of her husband and her memory gave her a man's hand in hers as they danced. Guilt had been in her mind on that evening and as she had sat in the stillness of the sickroom she had examined the details of their meetings and known she was right to be conscious of sin. She recognized passion in Holt – repressed, restrained yet barely so. Their actions had been innocent but their wants could not face the light of day.

She was being drawn towards the green lane that

led to Tarrendon. Soon she would have left this place and be back amongst her duties without one moment of fulfilment to sustain her. Once before she had grasped her pleasure by walking on this hill and seen a new world open in which there was release from lovelessness. She would do so again. For the first time she gathered the reins and stirred the pony to her directions. Concealing the trap in the hollow, she uncovered her head and followed the path to the fort. She intended only to be near the one who showed that she was desired; she would not seek him out nor approach him but she could not return without this instance of gratification, of secret satisfaction unseen by those who could make her walk paths of their choosing.

The heat was great here. Far below, the valley shimmered and the woods blurred in softened greens. No birds sang. The shade from the hedgerow gave no relief. She walked with purpose and desperation. The further she left the road behind the greater was her fear that she hoped for more than a distant sight of Boaz yet her hunger was too fierce to allow her to turn back. Part of her prayed that he was far away – on the other side of his land, elsewhere for this single day – but still she walked, reaching the earthworks before she had realized she was there, climbing the ramparts as if they had no rise.

She was silhouetted against the sky as she crossed the ridge, a lonely figure with hair glinting in the brilliant afternoon. Passing the hollow where she had witnessed the halter divorce, she strode on almost to the curve of the hill where the dips were deepest and most like a maze. Her mind was besieged by memories of her marriage, of Canader's release, of the want in Boaz and tormented by the strained and violent emotions of the past weeks. She gazed into the valley for Boaz and he was not there. Standing quite still in her anguish, she covered her face with her hands.

At the furthest end of the fort, where the land fell away almost vertically into the coombe below, a spur of the hill left the earthworks and continued the promontory into the vale. It was from this vantage, as he stood in the shade of a stunted copse, that Boaz watched Beatrice as she approached. The few small thorns and elders, with the brambles between their knotted trunks, cast a contorted shadow from their wind-bent forms that hid all within it from the eyes of one dazzled by the brightness of the day. As he stood amongst the leaves, dappled with their broken grey, he knew himself to be unseen.

Tomorrow he was to reap his late harvest. Today, since noon, he had been walking the hill considering whether to move his flock. He had found the first ripe blackberries, plump and glistening where they caught the light, amongst these trees and had stopped to gather them. It was hardly cooler here but it rested him to stand without the glare of the sun on his face and pick this fruit. He had lined his hat with dock-leaves and when he had filled it to the brim with berries he turned from the brambles to gaze out over the hill.

It was then that he had seen Beatrice. She was close to the turn of the ramparts and the recognition of her sent a shock through his body. His impulse was to go to her but he did not move. He did not trust himself if he were near her. His obsession with her had not diminished; fed by his knowledge of her husband's contempt and by his compassion for her care of the sick child it had grown until his mind was never far from thoughts of her. He felt pity and tenderness for her and it was his nature to be aroused by these emotions. On sultry nights, when he could not sleep, it was not Esther but Beatrice who lay beside him and there were days when he could not say whether these nights were dreams or truth.

He watched her as she came towards him. There was enough of reality left in him to keep him hidden. It was a pleasure for him to have her before his eyes yet he wished her away. He did not want to harm her but had no faith that he would not. Alone on the hill before him she stopped and covered her face with her hands. There was hopelessness and desperation in her action that tore at his heart. He could not neglect one who was so forlorn; he left the shadow of the trees and went to her.

When he reached the ramparts she had gone. He walked the bank to where she had been standing. Between the ridges the hollows were deep and narrow. He looked below and saw her sitting on the turf with her head on her drawn-up knees. There was no more hesitation; he climbed down. She raised her face to him and her eyes were so full of pain and longing that they might have been mirrors for his own. He sat beside her.

They did not talk. They sat in silence feeling the heat trapped within the steep earth walls. Each felt a heart-beat that must surely have been heard. At last Beatrice said, 'The horse – it was generous of you.' Her voice was low; she could not control a breathless-ness in it.

'It was less than I wanted to give,' he said. 'My thoughts were of you.'

Again they fell silent. Dry stalks of the pale grass rose around them, still and untroubled by any breeze. Beatrice could not look at him. She bent her head. Boaz exerted himself to resist his desires yet the exertion was not such that would restrain him. He, who had never been a seducer, held himself ready to seduce. He could not believe his own actions but here was sweetness where all else was bitter.

He touched her neck; his hand ran from her hair to the shadow of her gown. His fingers curved and stroked the soft skin on her throat. She was as still as a hawk. He ran his hand over her shoulder to her arm and felt her firm and warm and real against him. Her mouth was dry. She leant and took from the berries he had brought. As she raised the fruit to her mouth the juice ran down her hand and stained her. Boaz reached for her hand and put the juice to his own lips. He kissed her palm and each finger. They lay together in the long grass.

CHAPTER NINE

In the machine-room Daniel wiped the grease from his hands and tossed the cloth into the corner. He and his mother stood in the dim, roaring room and watched the great axle driving the gears that carried the power of the water up to the millstones. The newly-lubricated cogs gleamed in the green light that fell from the small, high window. The floor was beneath the level of the river and damp saturated the walls. A thin black mud oozed up from between the loose flags. The cold was penetrating.

Outside the wheel moved sluggishly. The river had fallen through the summer months and the mill's trade was dropping. Old Mrs Fayerdon hugged the shawl she had knitted out of two of her husband's old waistcoats and folded her arms in front of her. She jerked her head towards the churning water.

'The noise don't get any lower,' she said.

Daniel put his hands in his overall pockets.

'It's less than it was,' he said. 'You don't come here so often.'

His mother chewed at her lips.

'Still,' she said, 'it's a mighty sound. It's not every man can lay his claim to this.'

'I'll not be laying claim to it if the river keeps to falling. A little child could tumble in the race and come out safe; it's that smooth.'

'You'll do, lad, you'll do. The water will come again. It do always return.'

Old Mrs Fayerdon patted her son's arm. She took a pride in Daniel's sullenness as a sign of his ambition. It delighted her that he was a thrusting man in business. She gazed about her gleefully as if she could see through the walls and up through the storeys at all the workings of the mill.

'A mighty sound,' she said again. 'It was your father's before you and will be your son's hereafter, if Mistress High-horse ever does her duty as a wife. It's time there was a new boy for us, Daniel, time there was a full cradle. You did ought to speak to her on it.'

Daniel stared impassively at the revolving axle. ''Twouldn't be speaking to her that'd do it,' he said.

His mother cackled and then looked grim. 'Well, if she's barren,' she said, 'we've got us a bad bargain. You could've got the trade without her.'

Daniel did not reply.

'Gentry,' continued Mrs Fayerdon, 'fancy folk. They count for nothing if you've no son to follow you.' She wrapped her shawl more tightly, not seeming to notice his silence. 'She ran after her sister's boy fast enough. Couldn't get free of us too quick. Thinks we bain't good enough for her. And come home with her head full of notions to look at her. Always in a dream and never a word spoke to us.'

'You don't like to talk to her anyhow.'

His mother made an angry movement that brushed her long, outdated skirts over the glistening floor. 'I should have talk or no talk with who I please in my own house. A hoity-toity chit! You didn't ought to give her leave to see that family if she do return like this.'

'She'll stir or not stir,' said Daniel, impatiently, 'as I say and no-one else. I'm her master. Lamford is still useful to me with the river like this.'

They stood together without speaking; a look of testy satisfaction on the face of each. The cogwheels turned and turned.

Matthew Garth appeared in the open doorway. The noise in the room was too great for them to have heard him descending the steps and the suddenness of his appearance startled them. He was completely white with corn-dust and the damp air began to seep into it, making his clothing slimy. The yard-cat, that had followed him down, crossed the wet flags in two fastidious bounds and leapt into Daniel's arms.

'Tibby, Tibby, Tibby,' he crooned and brushed his face against its fur.

'We'll be finished for Lower Mead in about the half-hour, sir,' said Matthew. 'Then the stones'll need adjusting. Jackson wants his rye very fine.'

'I'll come in good time,' said Daniel, his cheek still laid against the cat.

Matthew made no move to go. Daniel's periodic and uncharacteristic displays of sentiment towards the animal offended him, less for themselves than for their frequent abrupt descents into the contempt his master showed for the rest of creation. Some spark of affection in Daniel was kindled only by the cat but having enjoyed it Daniel could extinguish it at will. 'Could I have a word about the staircases, master?' he said. 'There was a mishap this morning while you were away. Jacob's lad, that'd come to run the errands, leant on the rail in the milling-room and fell through. Not hurt, he came down on sacks but the post's come away. We need a carpenter.'

'Am I never to have a day without the stairs shaken in my face?' asked Daniel.

'I'd say naught about them, sir,' said Matthew, 'if there was not so much danger. They're rotten through in places. If they collapse a man may be badly injured and how would we trade without proper access above? I patch them as you tell me but it's not enough. We must have a carpenter.'

'Must, is it?' Daniel threw the cat from him and it twisted in the air, landing lightly and running from the room. 'Let me tell you, Garth, if Jacob's lad damaged my property then Jacob's lad must pay for its mending. A carpenter should soak up his wages for a week or two, eh? Unless you'd like to repair it yourself when the day's over. And a new flight altogether is out of the question. I'll be laying men off at this rate, never mind taking carpenters on. Nail it yourself if you've such an interest and let me hear no more.'

'There was a time,' said old Mrs Fayerdon, 'when a workman was glad of his job.'

Matthew did not look at her. He kept all expression from his face. The meanness hidden within this mill disgusted him more than he admired the expertise of the miller. He was a craftsman and it went against his grain to be continually hampered in his actions by poor equipment and the parsimony of his employer. Such niggardliness and disregard of safety annoyed him more here than it would have done at a mill where the master had no talent for his profession. It infuriated him to see Daniel miss excellence for the sake of his love of cheese-paring. He had begun to consider leaving his place but was worried what impression so swift a change would

117

have on potential employers and whether Daniel would give him a character. Whenever he was with Daniel he was tempted to give notice but, at this moment, his own pride and love of work well done prompted him to pass on his news.

'The carrier brought me a letter, sir,' he said. 'From the foreman at my old workplace. He says there's an engineer, a Mr Belton, coming down from the north to look at the Somerset mills. He has a knowledge of steam-engines and is hiring himself out to install them. If a message was sent maybe he would come here.'

Old Mrs Fayerdon snorted. 'Expense!' she said. 'What for do we want an engine? Don't we have the river?'

'The river's low, ma'am,' said Matthew, 'as it will be most summers and trade's low with it. If we had steam to drive the stones at these times 'twould be a different story.'

Daniel put his hands in his pockets and looked first out of the high window and then at Matthew.

'This Belton,' he said. 'He's viewing properties and making tenders for the work? Nothing need be agreed beforehand?'

'There's no cost involved,' said Matthew. 'Or only a night's lodging.'

Old Mrs Fayerdon drew in her breath to speak but Daniel raised his hand to silence her.

'It'll do no harm for him to look us over,' he said. 'I'll send word to your mill to ask him here. Now, you've left the stones long enough. I'll come presently.'

As Matthew left, Daniel and his mother looked at each other. Daniel rocked back and forth on his feet as if he were considering.

'Garth,' he said, 'his manner offends me. I can't single anything out. He never stints his work but . . .'

Mrs Fayerdon nodded, her eyes sharp. 'And Beatrice is thick as thieves with his wife.'

Daniel shrugged.

'Don't never trust a woman with red hair,' she said. She thought for a moment. 'Didn't you find,' she asked, 'that he were given more wages at his last place? Didn't you say that?'

'I did.'

'Then why was that, eh?' She folded her arms tightly within her shawl. 'Folk don't leave good money for no reason. You'd best find out what it be, boy. Then you'll get no more sauce from he.'

In the milling-room Matthew went to the open door for a breath of clear air before returning to his work. He had not expected thanks for his news but still Daniel's attitude rankled. There was no question in his mind that Daniel would stop the boy's wages if the stairs were not righted and so his own day was made longer. He was a man who did not grudge extra hours to a master who appreciated willingness and ability but he felt it to be a nonsense and an imposition for his time to be eaten away in haphazard repairs to a structure that was rotting about their ears. It was said that the previous Mr Fayerdon had bought the mill cheaply because the old miller had not been able to afford the rebuilding necessary to preserve his business. There was talk of the refurbishment that had taken place when the mill had changed hands, of the new wheel that was brought from a distance, of the painting and mending and the

119

stones shipped from France of the finest burr. It was not mentioned that Matthew was the first experienced millwright hired by the Fayerdons and so the first to be able to judge the true condition of the mill. In his opinion, apart from the importing of the stones – now long in need of replacement – there had been no changes which were not merely cosmetic. Even the great wheel, so bruited as a marvel of outlay, had not been new but had been brought in sections after years of use elsewhere. Daniel was too familiar with his home and workshop and too much in love with miserliness to notice the dangers that were all about him but Matthew did. A mill was no place to play fast and loose with safety; there was too much power in cranking machinery, too many heights from which to fall from crumbling platforms. Matthew looked out across the yard that was bathed in the warm September light and considered the future for Canader and himself.

He was distracted from his thoughts by Beatrice emerging from the house and beginning to cross the yard in front of him. She was dressed for walking and was wearing a wide, straw hat, bound under her chin with a broad, white ribbon and she was swinging a linen bag from her hand. Her appearance was as fresh and charming as a young girl; she made him think of sunlight. It occurred to him that she might be paying one of her visits to Canader and he stepped forward out of the doorway.

'Mistress!' he called.

Beatrice stopped and turned on him an expression of brightly startled humour.

'Mr Garth,' she said, laughing.

Matthew crossed the yard to join her. She puzzled

him. He had noticed that she had always tried to maintain a cheerfulness that was not in keeping with the atmosphere of the mill but since she had returned from her sister a joy seemed to radiate from her.

'I wondered, ma'am,' he said, 'seeing you pass, if you were going down to my wife?'

'Yes, how clever. I've been home three days and this is my first chance.' Beatrice marvelled at her words. Was it rather three hours or years? Time was unaccountable now.

'May I trouble you to take a message for me, ma'am?'

'It's no trouble to me.' Beatrice smiled. 'What shall I say?'

'That I'll be late home tonight. I don't know how much.'

'Oh? Is the river rising? Is Mr Fayerdon milling while he can?'

Matthew's face betrayed a little of his feelings. 'No,' he said, 'the stones are still sluggish. The sluices are wide open but the wheel hardly turns. No, the stairs are broke again and I must mend them. But I'll say this to you, ma'am, for you might have influence with the master, there's not an inch of woodwork in this mill that I'd trust without it be completely replaced and if that's not done one day the whole of it will be about our heads.'

'Then,' said Beatrice, her own expression bitter, 'be about us it must. I give you confidence for confidence, Garth – your concern's leading you astray. You're a man who looks about you and you know what my standing is here. It's not with my husband that I have influence.'

*

The walk across the meadow and down the lane to the Garths' cottage was not long but it served to banish the venom against her situation that had erupted in Beatrice at Matthew's warning. It shamed her to be connected with the meanness implied in his words and her shame fuelled her loathing of Daniel yet her other emotions were too intense to be overwhelmed or soured.

She was in an exalted state. She knew herself to be loved and for the first time had freely expressed the passion of her spirit in the medium that was natural to her. Physical love was no longer meaningless but was the completion of her life.

She walked through the lea, where the aftermath was rich enough to bear the scythe, with her face lifted to the sun. Foul names that Daniel had often called her could now be cast at her with justice. She was aware that she should feel guilt but was not a hypocrite to pretend to feelings that she did not have. A stranger, riding towards the town, looked over the tangled hedge and saw a woman, straight-backed and lovely, walking as if in rapture and did not forget a beauty beyond the sum of her features.

She did not know what would come of this love. It was in her heart to adore Boaz. She did not look to the future except in her desire to keep silent to preserve him from harm. Every part of her reason strained to keep their secret secure yet her senses were so bathed in him that she could not help being changed to all who had eyes to see. How could she have known a man could touch her so? It was not in her power to be as she had been before.

Leaving the meadow, she followed the lane to the Garths' cottage. Before she had reached it she could see over the low wall that Canader was collecting water. A stream that ran into the river which fed the mill passed through the small garden and Canader was kneeling on the plank that crossed it, carefully lifting a jug on to the grass. The water was shallow, hardly covering the stones that littered its bed, and plainly had not filled the jug which had been lying in a scooped hollow with its mouth to the current. Canader took the cup that was beside her on the plank and began using it to bail water from the stream to the jug. Every time she bent forward her heavy braid fell over her shoulder and brushed the water. She sat upright and wound the plait over her head, tying it loosely in place with the ends of its leather thong.

'Do you need one of my pins?' asked Beatrice, over the wall.

Canader turned on the plank and looked across at her. She was startled out of a day-dreaming concentration but her still face did not show surprise. As she moved the thong undid and the braid slithered down her back. Realizing who had come, she pulled her skirts from beneath her knees and stood up.

Beatrice let herself in through the gate and made her way round the rows of potato plants. She was more full than ever of curiosity to know Canader's story but still she knew she would not ask.

They greeted each other as friends but with the reserve that their different circumstances and secrecies always made present.

'Matthew told me you were home, ma'am,' said Canader. 'Is the boy well?'

'Bravely. I left him plaguing his papa for a pony.' She smiled and Canader saw that it was as Matthew had reported – the young Mrs Fayerdon had returned changed.

'Will you come inside, ma'am?' she asked.

Beatrice looked at the stream. 'Do you fill the pail first?'

'I'll leave it to fill itself.'

Canader squatted on the plank, forcing the bucket into the hollow on the bed of the stream. A trickle of water began to flow over its rim.

'Every day,' she said, standing up with the jug in her hand, 'I d'wish for rain. If the bourne dries I'll be walking to the river. And the summer's no good for the mill.'

They began moving towards the cottage, Beatrice leading the way along the path. The doors of the house had been propped open and they went straight in. Inside the room was as neat and clean as always and it was warm from the fire that was boiling a cauldron. A pile of docks lay on a sack beside the hearth and a curious smell came from the steam drifting from the pot.

'If you're cooking for your husband,' said Beatrice, laying her bag on the table, 'I have to tell you that he'll be late home.'

Canader set the jug on the floor for the grit to settle to the bottom of the water. 'No,' she said, 'I'm boiling down the juice from these leaves. They do make a fine, dark dye to decorate the floor. I like my house to be smart.'

'It's before I would work,' Beatrice sang, seating herself at the table, 'I would rather sport and play.'

Canader pressed more docks into the pulp within the cauldron. 'This is play to me. This is the first year I haven't been at the gloving every hour of the day.' She stopped, remembering how little she thought was known of her.

And this is the first year you've been Garth's wife, thought Beatrice. How did you make your husband free you? How could you broach such a subject? Tell me for I need to be released.

'Then don't let me interrupt you,' she said. 'You work and I'll sit. I like to look at you.'

Canader brought the two cups and a stone flagon to the table. 'Do you? Why?'

'Because a man loves you. Because you delight in him.'

Canader took the cork from the flagon. It was her own ginger beer and the strong smell of the spice overcame the dye. She poured it and caught the white froth at the rim with a steady hand but her thoughts were rapid. She is in love. While she was away she met someone. Shouldn't I recognize this? Oh, do nothing, do nothing; it's safer for you. Fayerdon won't let you go. Don't let him see.

She set down the flagon and tested her suspicion. 'You're the one to be looked at,' she said. 'You've come back . . . you look like a bride.'

Beatrice flushed, first gently, then fully over her face and neck. What have you done? thought Canader. Don't you know that anything you do in the country is known by someone?

Beatrice opened her bag and pulled out three packages. Her blush was fading and her voice was under control.

'I haven't come empty handed,' she said. 'See – I've brought you tea and sugar and this,' she took a cloth from the largest object, revealing a jar, 'is my sister's damson cheese. It will be something to give your husband when mine has done with him tonight.'

They sat together and talked. Beatrice asked for local news and to make their converse seem easy Canader told her of every small happening while she had been away. Beatrice listened but her mind was on another place and presently she took her leave. As she walked away down the lane, Canader called out to her but when Beatrice stopped and turned all Canader said was, 'Take care.'

CHAPTER TEN

As it was not yet winter a fire had not been lit in the mill parlour and the damp that was an ineradicable part of the walls was making its presence known. It was Sunday afternoon and the Fayerdons were at tea. The strict Sabbath piety of Daniel and his mother demanded cold meals on their day of rest and a complete absence of any form of entertainment for Beatrice and their kitchen staff. They had attended the church, at which Daniel was warden, that morning and would do so again in the evening. At intervals during the rest of the day old Mrs Fayerdon appeared suddenly in the back regions of the house to ensure that the cook and maid were at their duties or their bible and became discontented if they were. She had already had to speak sharply to Beatrice for singing as she bathed and this had cheered her.

At this moment Beatrice did not feel inclined to sing. She found Sundays long. When she had first come to the mill it had puzzled her to understand what determined what was suitable for the Sabbath and what was not. Why was it acceptable for the cook to mull Daniel's ale but not to heat broth? Why might the maid prepare, serve and clear at these dreary meals but not talk to her family in the yard? Beatrice's own experience was of Sundays as pleasant times of relaxation and excursions and she could not get used to activities being curtailed in this joyless fashion, nor could she grow used to the word 'Sabbath' though it was often flung at her head. After a few months, however, she had seen the principle which governed their day – if Daniel said that something was proper then this, and this alone, they did.

She was now pouring tea. This was sometimes performed by her and sometimes by her mother-in-law and she had never yet been able to guess when old Mrs Fayerdon would be insulted by her assumption of superiority in taking charge of the teapot and when by her idleness in leaving chores to the elderly. She no longer cared whether she gave offence.

They had just sat at the round table and the bread, the ham, cheese, preserves and a caraway cake lay untouched on the white cloth. The steam rising from the cups as she filled them gave an illusion of warmth but the sunlight falling on the river outside the window seemed to emphasize the chill in the room. The cat was sitting uprightly beside Daniel's chair and, as she poured, Beatrice fought an annoyance at what she knew would be next.

She set down the teapot and, as she put out her hand for the cream jug, Daniel, apparently oblivious of her action, reached for it first. He carefully filled an extra saucer and set it down before the cat which stood, lashed its tail, and lapped. He put back the jug and returned to his paper. Beatrice took up the jug. It was almost empty. They had cream only on Sundays and she knew there would be no more. She added what was left to the tea and passed the cups.

Daniel folded his newspaper noisily and dropped it on the opposite side of his chair to the cat. He helped himself to bread and the women followed him.

'I thought Mr Hibbard spoke very well this morning,' he said. 'We've to thank him for many a good sermon and this was another.'

He had expressed this opinion several times on the walk home from the church but it struck his mother as an agreeable novelty.

'Ay,' she said, sighing and shaking her head. 'A word in season. You're right there, Daniel.'

He spooned gooseberry preserve on to his buttered bread, spread it, considered the result, then skimmed it with his knife, returning half of the jam to the dish and scraping the knife clean on the edge, so that a lump of crumbs and butter formed on the rim and slid down into the fruit.

Old Mrs Fayerdon looked at Beatrice.

'You taking ham and cheese to your bread?' she asked tartly.

'I am,' said Beatrice.

She continued to stare at Beatrice but finding it had no effect transferred her attention to her son.

'I see that Mrs Norris was there in a new shawl and gloves,' she said. 'Trigging herself out fine as a turkey-cock and her no better than she should be.'

'And not the only one that can be said of,' Daniel reached across for the ham. 'That Mrs Tozer – Elizabeth Lee as she was – was sitting there in her father's pew as if there was never such a thing as a husband in the world.'

'Elizabeth!' said old Mrs Fayerdon. 'Bessie were good enough for her mother. Nothing's too grand for she.'

'She's above being a wife, that's for sure. Runs away from her lawful husband and sits in church as if she'd a right to be there.'

She ran away, thought Beatrice, cutting the rind from her cheese, as we all know, because her husband is a drunkard.

'I'd right her with the flat of my hand if she were my girl,' said old Mrs Fayerdon.

'She needs whipping at the cart's tail.' Daniel, noticing that the cat had finished its cream, lifted the jug and, finding it empty, glared at Beatrice. 'She married for better or worse and she's got no call to think she can go free. When a woman's wed she's wed. She promised to obey and obey she must. St Paul says, "Wives, submit yourselves unto your own husbands, as it is fit in the Lord."'

His mother shook her head sorrowfully and took a slice of ham. She dearly loved to hear Daniel quote a text.

'He also says,' said Beatrice, '"Husbands love your wives, and be not bitter against them." Her husband is not safe to be with.'

Old Mrs Fayerdon brandished her butter-knife. 'The Lord's name in vain!' she said. 'Daniel, Daniel, what d'ye say?'

Daniel searched his memory. '"A continual dropping in a very rainy day and a contentious woman are alike."' He smiled maliciously, showing scrapings of cheese on his teeth.

'Good, good. Good on ye, boy!' His mother laughed gleefully.

And you long for rain, you fool of a miller, thought Beatrice. She looked out of the window at the river. I will be quiet, she thought, but I too have texts. 'Stolen waters are sweet, and bread eaten in secret is pleasant.' 'Come, let us take our fill of love, until the morning; let us solace ourselves with loves. For the

goodman is not at home, he is gone a long journey.'
Oh, Boaz, Boaz.

She wrapped herself in thoughts of her lover. They closed about her mind with warmth and comfort. Since she had visited Canader she had been more circumspect. There had been that in Canader's eyes that had given her a warning. Looking back on her behaviour during those first days of her return had made her fearful. It seemed that she had been proclaiming her love from the hilltops. It astounded her that she had not been accused. This and the appearance of her monthly show had made her cautious. It was only with the proof that she had not conceived that the possibility of being with child by Boaz occurred to her and she was amazed by her own obtuseness. The present joy had been so great that she had not considered the future. Even now, when the awareness of danger had broken through her preoccupation, she dared not imagine the consequences of discovery. There was still a spring about her that had not been there when she had left the mill but her happiness was soiled by outbreaks of anger and frustration with the way she must live.

Daniel had enjoyed his success and assumed an expression that was between solemnity and spite.

'There's too many women these days,' he said, 'who think lightly of their vows. Man is set at woman's head to be looked up to in obedience as Christ is set at the head of man. There's no gainsaying it. If a wife won't follow the holy rule she must be broken to it. It's for her own good.'

My heart may break, thought Beatrice, but I will not.

'A wife should be grateful to her man,' said old

Mrs Fayerdon. 'He do give her a home and the proper duties of a woman. She did ought to thank him every day of her life.'

Daniel took the last piece of ham. 'Duties,' he said, putting the meat on his bread and holding it in place with his thumb. 'There's one here that would do well to mind them. You,' he turned to Beatrice. Can't you say my name? thought Beatrice. Is it so hard? 'You,' Daniel pointed his finger at her. 'You've been giving away good food again. Don't deny it for you know mother keeps her eye on the levels in stock. Better than a quarter of tea gone and sugar. All so you can play the fine lady with your charity. You'll not be doing it no more.'

Friendship, thought Beatrice, friendship not charity. She clenched her fists under the table.

'Extravagance,' old Mrs Fayerdon chimed in. 'Never nothing but extravagance. No care for your husband's money, no child at your breast. Never nothing but airs and graces.'

'You'll have to change, my lady,' said Daniel. 'You'll have to pay heed to your duty. Look . . . look now, there's Ma ready for her cut of cake and what're you doing? Sitting like a lord. Neglecting her and she your husband's mother.'

Beatrice stood up. Deliberately she pulled the cake-stand nearer and reached for the knife. Holding the knife downwards in her still clenched fist, she looked from Daniel to her mother-in-law and, at her look, they fell silent. She raised her arm and slowly, savagely, she stabbed the cake.

During the night it rained heavily and the river began to rise. The sound of the rain against the window was a relief to Beatrice as she lay awake for she knew that it would distract Daniel from her behaviour the day before. The shock at her introduction of so strange a violence into what they considered to be a normal family party had initially curbed the tongues of Daniel and his mother but after church that evening they had closeted themselves in the parlour and she had known that they were talking of her.

She rose late that morning, regardless of what comment it would cause. It was still raining, though more lightly, and, as she brushed her hair, she looked out on a yard that was fresher and cleaner than it had been for weeks. The brickwork shone wetly in the sun that was brightening the showers and a blue sky showed between the dark clouds.

She had missed breakfast and, when she had dressed, went straight down to the kitchen to find herself something to eat. The room was empty. The maid was turning out old Mrs Fayerdon's bedroom and it was the cook's routine to go to buy yeast on a Monday morning. Beatrice took a cup, saucer and plate from the dresser and set them on the table. The fire was alight and she put the full kettle over the heat. Returning to the dresser, she reached out to take off the lid of the bread-crock and it was only as she was making this automatic movement that she realized that the crock was not there. There was a mark on the flags where it always stood but its place was empty.

She looked round the kitchen. The crock was not to be seen, nor was there any evidence in the room of any food or drink. She went to the pantry and tried the door. It would not open. Knowledge of what these changes meant began to come into her mind.

The Fayerdons kept their servants in too much fear for there to be any risk of theft by them. There was only one person who would need to be locked from anything they did not wish her to have – the mistress of the house.

She leant her head against the closed door. How much more humiliation would there be in store for her over the years? How could she bear it? Mamma, Thirza, Henry – why didn't I listen to you all? There was a sound behind her and she turned abruptly.

Old Mrs Fayerdon was standing at the entrance to the kitchen, gloating at her daughter-in-law.

'Well, missy,' she said, 'that's righted you. This'll teach 'ee to lie-a-bed all the morn. If you don't come for meals you'll be hungry. And there'll be no more charity. Y'll mind your husband's property like a good wife. Daniel's been too—'

Beatrice stayed to hear no more. She strode across the kitchen and pushed the old woman aside. The stairs were before her and she climbed them two at a time. She could feel the blood throbbing in her temples. Tools, she was thinking, tools in the mill. I'll smash the lock. They'd bar me from bread. I must have tools.

She threw open the door to the right of the stairs. This was their drawing-room. It was rarely used as such except when they had company but Beatrice would sometimes sit here for the view of the river and Daniel did his accounts at the massive walnut desk. The noise of the waterwheel was always great for it turned almost beneath the windows and there was a door which led out to the bridge that connected the house with the working part of the mill. There was a bell outside the door so that a hand could summon

Daniel if he were needed quickly while at home but it had not been rung since Matthew had discovered the condition of the bridge.

The key was in the lock and she turned it and ran out over the wheel. The planks were green and slippery and her thin shoes slid on the wet wood, throwing her off balance. She caught at the rail to prevent herself from falling, throwing her weight against it to keep her feet. The post held but a nail that had rusted through in the rotten wood was shaken loose and fell down into the millrace, more turbulent now with the rising river. She stood upright, her heart beating with her anger and shock. Beneath her feet, where the planks were eaten away, she could see the wheel turning, turning, the water sparkling in the sunlight as it dropped from the rungs.

She had a sudden, terrible desire to press through the thin, mouldering planking and cast herself into this incessant power. The wheel would beat her down deep into the race and who could say it had not been an accident? The temptation made her shudder and she tore her eyes from below to the far bank. The rain still fell lightly, dimpling the surface of the river. It cooled her face and she struggled to be calm. She would not give Daniel the satisfaction of knowing that he hurt her. Had not someone come into her life to give her reason to live it? She would armour her mind against the Fayerdons and she would live through him.

It was a constant worry to Beatrice during the next week that Daniel would exert his authority over her by forbidding her to visit her sister. If she could not use the trap she had no means of reaching Boaz and though they had made no arrangements to meet again she believed that he longed for her as she longed for him.

By a severe mental effort she returned her behaviour to what it had been before she had left the mill. She felt that a too great and sudden meekness would arouse suspicion and she had decided not to let the Fayerdons see that she was wounded. Her rage was forced back within her and her joy at being loved, which now manifested itself as a desperation that one afternoon should not be the sum of her experience of being worthy, was stifled and disguised. Daniel and his mother watched her and felt that she had been successfully chastised.

She need not have been anxious over her rides to Thirza. Daniel had been frightened by the slump in his trade and was no longer as confident that he could prosper without the goodwill of the largest cornmerchant in the area. Though he did so grudgingly, as a favour, he gave Beatrice permission to drive out as usual.

Nor was this the only move he made in his business interest. His frustration over the reduced power from the low river encouraged him to write to the engineer Matthew had spoken of as visiting mills with a view to installing steam. He wrote to Mr Belton at Matthew's old mill and, because he had not forgotten either his dislike of Matthew or his mother's warning that a man who takes less wages must have something to hide, he wrapped it in a covering letter to the miller. He had no clue to what Matthew could have done that he wished to conceal and nothing had happened while Matthew was in his own employ for justifying him in suggesting that the good character his hand had brought with him was false. It was impossible to ask outright if Matthew had a bad reputation without seeming to accuse his fellow miller of supplying references which were a lie. The most he felt able to do was to say that Garth and his wife were finding it difficult to settle in their new situation and ask whether this had been the same at their old mill or if the miller could put forward any reason for it.

The letters were sent out on the Tuesday following the locking of the pantry and it was not until a week later that Beatrice was once more seated in the trap and guiding her pony up the long hill out of Wynford Tarrent. It was her plan to leave Bridport early to enable her to go to Boaz on her way home, without returning late to the mill. Her family was not surprised to hear that Daniel had instructed her to leave before her usual time. They had expected a display of his ability to order her as the result of her absence from his house. Beatrice's hasty departure was not questioned and, only a little after noon, she was again upon the road.

Throughout her drive her one thought was of Boaz. Her hands shook as they held the reins and her heart beat quickly but not through fear. She was perfectly confident that he would welcome her and her eyes were bright with the joyful anticipation of their meeting. There was no room in her mind for concealing her actions and when she reached the turning to his farm she did not take her route over the ridge to Tarrendon but recklessly guided her pony on to the track that would take her directly to Boaz.

She had never been in this valley before. As she drew near the copse that hid the farmhouse the great rise of the fort encouraged her to be oblivious to danger. She felt too small for anything she did to be seen or condemned. Her want of Boaz was all that she was conscious of as she drove down his lane in the view of all those who travelled the road above.

Where the track forked to go into the wood the ruts were too much for her trap. She drew up the pony in the shade of the hazels, whose pale green nuts hung out over the path, and went towards the house on foot. When she reached the yard she stopped. She could hear sawing and the sound seemed to come not from any workshed but from within the dwelling.

Taking the path that led along the outbuildings attached to the back of the house she found herself where it branched. She crossed the flagstones and tried the side-door but it was locked and the noise of the saw was still muffled as if it came from far into the house. Looking about her, she went back to the branch and followed the path into the wood. There was a light wind in the coombe and the trees were all in motion. The stirring and sighing of the fading leaves excited her and the sight of the old house across the herb-garden gave her an impatience for Boaz that she could hardly contain. The sensation of being with her love in a place that was his own pierced her and sent her without hesitation across the tangled garden to his door.

She did not knock. With both hands she lifted the heavy latch and went in. The hall was not as it had been when Boaz first came. It was swept and scrubbed and a chair and table with a pewter dish

138

stood against the wall. A hat had been thrown on to the chair and a pair of high boots stood within the door. She bent and righted the boot that had fallen against the wall and the sense of intimacy – of being here amongst her lover's most personal things – overwhelmed her with an almost intolerable desire to belong wherever they and he might be.

Following the sound of his work, she made her way through an empty room and a passage until, at its far end, she saw him. He was in the kitchen, surrounded by sawdust and woodshavings, cutting a plank that lay over a trestle. His back was towards her. As she stood watching him, he laid down the saw and taking up a plane began to smooth the edge he had cut.

She walked forward, advancing eagerly into the room.

'Boaz,' she said.

He was startled by her voice. His back straightened and he was still for an instant before he turned. When he did she saw at once that their meeting would not be as she had imagined it. Shock at the change apparent on his face made her apprehensive of her welcome and Boaz, seeing the happiness in her eyes replaced by alarm, laid down the plane. He said her name gently and, partly reassured, she crossed the room to him, standing before him amidst the tools and shavings that had had no place in her fancies.

Boaz looked down on her with relief that he now need wait no longer for this inevitable moment. He was anguished by her obvious desire to be with him but it did not shake his conviction that what they had begun so rashly should have no continuing. He was eaten by guilt over his seduction of her. His dreamlike vision of her had vanished and he was in dread of what damage he might have done. In the two weeks since he had lain with her, as he reaped and gathered his harvest alone in his silent fields, he had brooded over his double betrayal: of Beatrice who had trusted him; of Esther to whom he was sworn.

He took the shame on himself. He did not blame Beatrice or dislike her or think worse of her in any way yet he had wished that she had never been born. Now that she was close to him – her face near to his that was thinner and tauter since their parting – he knew that all this while he had wanted her here, the smell and touch of her, her softness and pleasure in him. He must tell her that there was no future for them but his thoughts told him that it was his desire to enjoy her again and he feared that he could not resist a temptation that was so willingly displayed.

Whatever he did he must hurt her. He searched his mind for words that would have the least cruelty in them but Beatrice was too quick for him. The blood fled from her face; she felt a faintness rise in her.

'Oh, God,' she said, 'you think me a whore.'

Her voice sank as she spoke. As she had done on the hill she covered her white face with her hands and again Boaz was torn by her pain.

'Never that,' he said, 'my heart, never that.'

She turned away from him. She wanted to hide herself from him, to leave this house and take her disgrace where no-one would know of it. The illusion she had fed on seemed now like a plaything for a child. Her memory told her that in all their hour of tenderness and passion he had said nothing of love.

She could not challenge him with deception – her own need had put meaning into their action and reality was too harsh for her to bear.

Her legs were weak. She felt him guide her to the settle and she sat with her face still covered. He pushed aside the shelves he had been making and fetched a cup of water that he held to her lips. She drank, lifting her eyes to his as she did so and she did not see a man who thought her base. She felt herself stripped of all that had made her glorious; she was an adulteress, sordid, degraded – yet she looked into his eyes and this was not what she saw.

She said loudly, 'I love you,' as if her firmness could summon truth to her words.

He put the cup on the flags amongst the shavings and took her hands.

'No,' he said, 'you love my want of you.'

Her fingers gripped his. 'Do you want me?' she asked.

'God forgive me – I do.'

They sat together, holding each other's hands. There was much love between them but it was not for each other.

'Did you come here,' he said, 'because you're in trouble?'

She shook her head. 'No, I'm certain. No risk of that. You know why I came.'

Outside they could hear the rustle of the leaves as the wind increased. Shadows of the elder at the window played about the room.

'I want you to stay,' he said. 'I want everywhere I look in my house to be filled with you. I want to wake each morning knowing I shall touch you. You gave me comfort. But I have a wife and you a husband and we're bound to them. If they're not to our liking still we've done them a wrong. We can't meet again – you understand that? We have no escape and I won't injure you this way.'

She said nothing; she clung to his hands.

'The fault was mine,' he said. 'It was wrong.'

'It was sweet,' she said.

'It was very sweet.'

Again they were silent and again they did not let each other go. At last Beatrice gave a sigh that was like a shudder.

'I will never come here again,' she said, 'but I'm here now and . . . we have the afternoon.'

CHAPTER ELEVEN

It was a failure of Daniel's business acumen to misjudge Isaac Belton's manner of arrival and the quality of the man with whom he had to deal. Perhaps this failure was to be expected for Isaac was of a kind who had never crossed Daniel's path before. Isaac was a man of the revolution in industry which had barely touched the West and was as exotic in the Dorset valleys as a bird of Paradise, though rather less flamboyantly clad.

Daniel imagined that a man who tinkered with new-fangled machinery would be a lowly artisan, glad of any interest shown in him by potential buyers. He therefore expected that the best transport Isaac would be able to afford was the carrier and, knowing the cart to reach Wynford Tarrent in the early evening, did not reckon to meet the engineer before nightfall on the day he had designated for his arrival. The result of this expectation was that there was no-one to greet Isaac as he rode into the mill-yard in the late morning on his own sturdy and well-kept cob.

There had been a delivery of wheat an hour before and all hands were indoors either milling or arranging the corn in store. Beatrice and her mother-in-law had gone marketing. The servants were at the back of the house. To the eye the place seemed deserted but the ear was presented with the true state of activity.

As Isaac sat his mare, taking in the lie of the mill, the sounds of the wheel, the stones and the shouts of instruction filled the still October air. If his hearing had been extraordinary he would have caught the maid singing, as she was wont to do when the master and old mistress were not at home.

He continued to sit for some minutes; his mind already quick with possibilities. Even before venturing on his profession he had been no stranger to mills. His father was a miller and if he had been the owner and not the tenant of his workplace it was probable that Isaac would have followed in his footsteps. What would have been considered a misfortune by most was looked on as a lucky chance by Isaac for, not being bound as strongly by family tradition as if the mill had been their property, he was freer to trace his own inclination and was encouraged to do so by his parents.

They lived in the north of Warwickshire and early in his life Isaac became aware of the movement in the textile factories that were so prominent in the midland counties. The new machines excited him. As a youth he worked a year in a foundry but, finding his interest to be in the use of machinery more than in its making, he moved on to the cotton and worsted mills, learning his trade in their engine-houses where heat, steam and metal were driving the world forward into a place it had not supposed existed.

He had intelligence, enthusiasm and manual dexterity and was sought after as an employee but his love of independence was too great for him to be content as he was. He wanted to be his own master. Looking about him for means to achieve this end, he remembered the anxiety in his childhood home when the river fell too low to turn the wheel effectively and considered the usefulness of an engine to supplement the flow of water. He knew the mills of the manufacturing districts, where engines were common, to be already introducing steam to their workplaces and he wanted an area where he would have no competition. He needed a region where mining, good rivers or the sea could ensure a supply of coal. There was also the question of providing the engine once a sale and installation had been agreed. He intended to buy from the Round Foundry in Leeds which had established a reputation for their self-contained steam-engines but was interested in Trevithick's whim engine in use in some Cornish mines. He had never seen one of these devices but knew them to be both smaller and cheaper than either the Newcomens or Watts that he was used to. However warm the millers might be, Isaac did not expect them to be able to rival the prices paid by the Manchester men for their machinery or have properties to which an engine-house could conveniently be added. A foundry in a region ripe for development and producing a more attractive engine would be of benefit to him. For these reasons he began travelling west, trading as he went.

He prospered at once. 'I sell, Sire,' Matthew Boulton said to King George, 'what all the world desires – power,' and Isaac, scouting slowly through the countryside, planting his new ideas, ordering engines, returning to install and demonstrate them, found power to be as coveted as he and Boulton had imagined.

Now, he sat his cob on this bright morning, watching the breeze drive ripples into the reeds at the river's edge, thinking of the potential of this mill and of his own affairs. He worked hard and seriously and derived great satisfaction from his success but he was not a solemn man. For several weeks he had had no rest from concentrated labour and he felt the need for relaxation and amusement. He had a lively nature and liked to enjoy himself. An inn where there was music in the evening was his notion of a good lodging. He read, fished, sang and could not have enough of dancing. If these activities took place in the company of clever, spirited, pretty women so much the better. He had never been in love and would not trifle with a girl however strong the temptation but would be glad to marry if he happened on a woman of his own mind. He felt today that after he had dealt with Fayerdon he would make a holiday in this place.

No-one looking at him would have guessed his thoughts. His face was naturally severe and his light brown hair, though short, gave an impression of being tied back. This and his plain, dark clothes of worsted gave his appearance a gravity which stood him in good stead as a character reference and was useful to one who had only this April seen his thirtieth year.

His contemplation over and preliminary calculations made, he dismounted and, leaving his mare at the trough, he crossed the yard to the working portion of the mill. For civility he rapped on the main door but, not expecting to be heard above the stones, did not wait for an invitation and walked in purposefully. Daniel, coming down the stairs, did not recognize this confident stranger as the man to whom he had written and was puzzled by the appearance of one who was neither local nor a farmer. A hope that here was a land agent from beyond his present reach of trade come to bring an estate's business to the mill crossed his mind and brought him promptly to Isaac's side.

Their meeting entertained Isaac. He was used to the suspicion and disbelief evident in the manner of each master as he discovered the identity of his caller. There were occasions when the ignorance and prejudice behind this reaction irritated him too much to divert him – especially when expressed in a patronizing belligerence towards foreigners and invention – but, in general, the rapid submerging of surprise beneath everyday politeness appealed to his sense of the ridiculous. He enjoyed judging the effort involved in the transformation and in Daniel he felt it to be both extreme and smoothly achieved.

It being evident that his arrival was unexpected and inconvenient Isaac did not press for a full examination of the mill. He asked leave to walk about it quickly while Daniel returned to his work and Daniel, still startled by the boldness and self-possession of his visitor, granted his request. It was agreed that the morrow should see the detailed investigation of the mill's possibilities and that later that day – so that Daniel could more readily take the measure of this singular man – Isaac should return to dine.

Isaac stayed an hour at the mill and before he left he had already drawn conclusions.

'Are you just standing there?' Old Mrs Fayerdon darted from side to side of the parlour, adjusting what did not need to be moved. With her turned black silk and her sudden, jerking halts she was like a

147

moorhen agitating its chicks. 'Where there's work to be done it's sure you'll be found idle.'

Beatrice did not turn her gaze from the window. 'If I were mistress of my house,' she said, 'I'd see to its running but as I'm not I shall stand as I please. And,' she added, 'there is no work to be done. You're meddling with what is ready.'

Outside the river was higher than it had been since June. A night of heavy rain two days before had brought so much water down from the hills that the sluices had had to be half-raised for the first time that autumn. It was almost five o'clock and, though the light was fading, there was still sunlight glancing on the flowing river and filtering through the yellow and orange leaves of the copse on the far bank. Beatrice was able to stand and admire the scene with no feeling that she should help her mother-in-law with the preparations for dinner.

She was sadder and more subdued since she had taken leave of Boaz. In the long nights she felt that heart-break would have been a more suitable emotion but, now that he had spoken plainly, she was too honest to pretend that he was her love. She had a liking and tenderness and need for him but this was not the same as loving. She told herself that it could only be love that could raise adultery from degradation but that, too, she knew was not the truth. Since her first burst of shame in the farmhouse she had not felt herself to be sordid and did not try to make herself out a sinner.

Her loneliness remained and her home life had not improved but in the fortnight between that day and this she had been numbed and her despair at the trap in which she lived was in abeyance. She could not rouse herself to any active defiance of Daniel and his mother but she mustered a passive refusal to take up a wife's duties where she was not given a wife's respect. It was this attitude with which she was annoying old Mrs Fayerdon as they waited for the engineer to arrive to dine.

They had a roast fowl and a plum tart and the smells of the cooking were drifting into the room. A dish of pears, too beautiful to eat, lay on the white cloth. The yellow fruits, flecked brown, flushed pink, were plump and lovely in the blue china. A tiny fire burnt on the hearth and this surprised Beatrice. She had not realized that their visitor was a man Daniel wished to impress – but she noted that the engineer's status was not such as to take the chill off the room.

A rap at the knocker warned them their guest had arrived. Despite herself, Beatrice felt a slight lift in her spirits. A life-long love of company and curiosity about her neighbours rose in her. Where there is a stranger there is hope of change.

She did not follow old Mrs Fayerdon to the door, knowing from past experience that she would not be immediately introduced. Standing with her hands on the back of a chair, she heard Daniel greet Mr Belton and make his mother known. As Isaac replied, the flicker of interest that had risen in Beatrice became stronger. His accent was entirely new to her. It gave a harder tone to the words than the West's round vowels, yet the voice that spoke was pleasant and unthreatening in its strength.

They came into the parlour. Neither man was in evening dress but Isaac, whose heavy baggage had been delivered by coach to the inn, wore a dark frock-coat that fitted his waist and trousers strapped beneath his boots that gave him an air of severe elegance that Beatrice had not expected.

Like Daniel, she had made mistaken assumptions about Isaac's profession but her reappraisal was more thorough and complete. She felt immediately that here was a man who could have the better of her husband and it made her smile.

'My wife,' said Daniel, dismissively.

Isaac, catching the tone of his host's presentation and putting it with Beatrice's hanging back and the mischief in her eyes as she smiled, thought there might be more entertainment in the evening than he had anticipated. He went to Beatrice and bowed over her hand; she, feeling it odd that it should be a man of iron and steam who made her think herself back in civilization, gave a return bow that rustled her silks. Isaac, calculating upon her expression and attraction in herself and sea-green gown, found her captivating, incongruous in this cold, damp parlour and totally unsuitable as wife to a dour egotist whose mill was crumbling with neglect. He took his seat and prepared to be amused.

At first he was disappointed. Beatrice, so used to being ignored or made the subject of criticism, was silent during the early part of the meal and Isaac was left to tackle his tough and aged fowl without the salt of lively conversation. It was a bird which may have seen better days but which had certainly reached the end of its useful life and it did not escape Isaac's notice that Daniel readily agreed with his mother that there was meat enough on the bones to be saved for the morrow nor that he carved the parson's nose for his wife who returned it to the dish.

Daniel's talk was ponderous. He wished to convey to Isaac that he was a man of substance and position without giving him the idea that he could charge what he pleased for any work undertaken. The difficulty involved for his host in portraying himself simultaneously as enviably wealthy and yet in need of conserving every penny was such that Isaac was able to await Beatrice's entry into speech with a mounting sense of enjoyment. It was plain that Daniel was undecided in the matter of buying an engine and likely to be persuaded by the cost to continue to rely on the river and Isaac began to see the evening purely as a social call. He would examine the mill more fully the next day and make his recommendations but he thought it probable that nothing would come of it. He had refused before now to act for millers who seemed likely to be troublesome when asked to pay and his policy had kept him in credit. He had not, however, completely ruled Daniel out as a customer and was prepared to discuss the merits of various engines.

'Of course,' he said, leaning back to let the maid take his plate, 'the Newcomen engine is cheaper to buy than the Watt but it's more expensive to run because of its free use of coal. It's popular in the Midlands where the price of fuel is low. Here,' he glanced behind Daniel at the dying fire, 'you have the Somersetshire coalfields and it might reward you to have the Newcomen.'

'Explosions!' said old Mrs Fayerdon, suddenly. 'Steam and boiling water! Ye said nothing of safety, young man. Newfangled doings. Like as not we'll be scalded in our beds.'

They had now embarked on the plum tart. The cook had made this to old Mrs Fayerdon's own economical recipe which called for half the usual amount of butter in the pastry and gave the illusion of the fruit being encased in a fragile plaster of Paris. It was a moment before Isaac found himself able to answer.

'I assure you,' he said, 'the new boilers are well able to withstand high pressure. Wrought iron with a central—'

'It means naught to me.' Old Mrs Fayerdon was unable to control her grievance. 'You bain't telling me it's safe. And expense! Engines and workmen and coals? There's one in this house ready enough to spend money and now looks like there's another. And what for, eh? The river's been good all these years. Why bain't it now? I say have no change and we'll all be better off.'

Finding Beatrice to be looking at him Isaac addressed her directly. 'And you, ma'am,' he said, 'would you keep the mill as it is?'

Beatrice fixed her eyes on his. 'There are many changes I would make, Mr Belton,' she said, 'but none of them is within my power.'

'I've found with machines that all parts influence the whole – if only by their absence.'

'Absence?' She took up her glass. 'There are those who like their possessions firmly kept in place. Don't ask me my opinion of the mill; I've no more say in it than I have in the kitchen.'

'You have your duties,' said Daniel, grimly, 'but you don't attend to them.'

Beatrice struck the shell of her pie with her spoon and the pastry shattered.

'Flour and water are the substance of a mill,' said Isaac.

'But,' Beatrice pushed the fragments to one side, 'to be palatable there should be something more.'

''Tis good tart,' old Mrs Fayerdon looked at Beatrice with an air of suspicion. 'Will I give 'ee another slice, Mr Belton, or will I keep it for the morning?'

'My thanks,' said Isaac, 'one piece was quite sufficient.'

'The fruit,' said Daniel, 'was from our own trees. We husband our resources.'

'Will you have a pear?' asked Beatrice. 'My sister sent them over. They're very fine.'

She lifted the bowl and held it out to Isaac. Taking one, he cupped it in his hand and admired it before reaching for his knife.

'Would this be from a brother-in-law's orchard?' he asked.

'It is,' said Daniel.

'I suppose it is,' said Beatrice. 'By law, yes. But I always think of the fruit as Thirza's. She and Henry talk of their household as family property.'

'I meant to ask whether she was married.'

'Why, yes, and with three children.'

Isaac cut a segment from the pear. The flesh was ripe and dripping. 'And do you have any more sisters, Mrs Fayerdon?'

The next morning Isaac returned to make a fuller examination of the mill in Daniel's company. He was not impressed by what he saw but thought it possible to install a self-contained engine in the cellar adjoining the present machine-room if his advice on repairs was taken. His first thought had been to knock out part of the wall between the two rooms but on closer inspection had decided that not only must the bricks be left but considerable shoring-up would be essential for the mill to withstand the added vibration. This suggestion did not have a happy effect on Daniel who took offence at what he thought to be an insult to his property and Isaac found himself all but accused of exaggerating to increase his charges.

He was still uncertain whether to take Daniel's business if it were offered but was inclined not to become involved with one who reacted so badly to suggested improvements, despite their obvious necessity. For his part, Daniel, while tempted by the thought of no longer being reliant on the river, was afraid of the cost and inclined to withdraw from the idea. Nevertheless, out of curiosity and a wavering mind, he rode out that afternoon to visit a farm leaving Isaac to take measurements and form an estimate of the price.

When his master had been gone an hour Matthew went in search of Isaac to see whether he needed help and to discover what prospect there was of gaining an engine. He found him in the cellar, folding up his rule with his pocket-book under his arm and a pencil thrust behind his ear.

Isaac was interested in Matthew. He had learnt from Daniel the previous evening that the venture of asking him to Wynford Tarrent had been the foreman's notion and he wondered why Matthew should be more eager to improve the mill than the miller was himself. Having now seen the conditions here and compared them with the position of chief-hand at Matthew's old workplace he was intrigued by what reason could have brought him to exchange his previous employment for this. There had been no bad feeling between master and man that could have driven him away. While at West Coker, Isaac had heard the miller regret Garth's leaving and congratulate Fayerdon on acquiring a sound servant, yet it was plain that it was not within Daniel's character to value a man of integrity.

He put the poor state of the building to Matthew and Matthew's impatience with Daniel's methods and attitude was soon clear. It became evident that Matthew's suggestion of consulting an engineer had been from a professional pride that was continually insulted by his master's acceptance of the second-rate and that if a character were obtainable Daniel would shortly be losing his most competent workman. He found himself liking Matthew as he had liked Beatrice the night before; it was ludicrous that Daniel should have authority over two such people.

Reaching an understanding on the neglect of the mill, the men felt easy with one another. Isaac lifted his coat-tails to sit on a box the better to discuss matters but seeing the damp in the wood, changed his mind. Raising his voice against the roar of the wheel, Matthew asked him to intervene on behalf of the restoration, not just of these rooms, but of the whole structure.

'I'll do what I can,' said Isaac, returning his pocket-book to his coat. 'I'd be a fool to do otherwise – any accident and it'd be blamed on the engine – but it's not likely I'll be employed here. I don't trust Fayerdon to pay for the best. Nor,' he gestured to the doorway, 'to want it. The cogs on that machine are near worn away. How's he thought of in the district?'

'Better than he deserves.' Matthew set his hands in his pockets. 'But he has talents as a miller; he knows to a nicety how the stones should be set for what meal; he never lets the seed sprout in his keeping; he gives weight for weight. 'Tis that which makes it worse that he fails in other ways. He'll love his gold till his workplace falls about him.'

Isaac opened and shut his rule. 'I supped with the family yesterday,' he said. 'He's thick enough with his mother but the young mistress is slighted at every turn.'

'She is. As open-hearted a lady as you could wish to find but the master don't care that much for her.' He snapped his fingers. 'What brought her to marry him is more than I can say but there's many a marriage that's a puzzle once the wedding's over.'

'And comely to look upon,' said Isaac.

'Kind and always generous to my wife.'

The mention of Canader reminded Isaac of something said at West Coker.

'I should give you my good wishes,' he said. 'Your old master sends you his. It seems Fayerdon mentioned you'd taken a wife when he wrote.'

Matthew felt alarm but did not show it.

'We didn't tell,' he said gravely. 'Neither of us likes our private matters published abroad.' He considered, judging whether Isaac would be offended by his invitation. 'Would you make your supper with us this evening? Canader'd like to have company. Or are you promised to Mr Fayerdon?'

The rule was folded and put away. 'I've no such pleasure. Give me directions and I'll come gladly.'

Despite having no offer of the renewal of Daniel's personal hospitality, Isaac had not been abandoned completely to his own devices. Before leaving the mill Daniel had instructed him to call at the house for refreshment when the measuring was over and this Isaac duly did. He expected no gastronomic pleasure from the enterprise but he wanted to see Beatrice again. He had been immediately drawn to her as Boaz had been before him but there was less of longing in this attraction and he did not think himself likely to fall a victim to sentiment.

It happened that the maid, assisted by the cook whose work was not limited by her title, was upstairs turning the beds and it was Beatrice who opened the door. She was expecting him and the interest he had aroused in her had enlivened her morning. In the past week she had been feeling exceptionally tired and, attributing this to the depression of her spirits, she had hopes that the spark of a new acquaintance might warm her out of lethargy. Isaac's enjoyment of her peculiar household had not been lost on her and she found it cheering to be reminded that even the tragic is ridiculous.

She asked him to come in, saying that she would fetch wine, and Isaac, not knowing the whereabouts of the drawing-room, did not wait in the hall but followed her down the passage to the kitchen. Beatrice, whose exhaustion was accompanied by a somewhat absent mind, did not notice that he was behind her until they were in the room and then a look of embarrassment fled swiftly over her face and was gone.

Isaac was no less quick-witted than he had been the previous evening. He did not think her to be the kind of conscious miss who would flush because she was alone with a man. There must be another cause. He glanced about the kitchen. It was as devoid of food as it had been the day Beatrice had discovered herself locked out of the pantry except that a tray was in readiness on the table. On it sat a bottle, two glasses and a single, uninviting slice of sponge-cake. Matthew had asserted that the young mistress was generous; she herself had claimed that she had no say in the kitchen. He went to the pantry door and tried it. It held fast. He turned round on her.

'Where are your keys?'

The question, spoken in his foreign voice, seemed blunter and less affronting than if it had been asked by a local man. Her skin darkened again but she did not look away from him or hang her head. His boldness attacted her. The simplicity of his presumptuous action made them allies. He knew she would not complain of him to Daniel.

'I have none,' she said. 'My husband's mother has full charge of the house. Surely, it doesn't surprise you?'

As answer he returned to the table and pulled out a chair for her. She took it and he sat opposite.

'I dare say,' he said, 'you weren't trained to a trade?'

'Oh, I was,' she took the cork from the bottle. 'I was trained as a gentlewoman. It fits you to be a wife.' She spoke calmly with an edge of bitterness but his words had startled her. His meaning was clear – if you left your home could you support yourself? This prospect had never before presented itself as more than fantasy and it suggested that there was another world where independence could be real. It also comforted her that a stranger should have assessed Daniel and found him wanting. She poured two glasses of last year's cowslip wine and pushed one towards him.

'That,' she said, 'I made myself. I could be a still-room maid. Would you like this cake?'

'Did you bake it?'

She shook her head. 'The cook, with ingredients weighed out for her by her mistress.'

'Then I will drink and go hungry.'

They each tasted their wine.

'I would suppose,' said Beatrice, 'that it's unlikely you'll have business here?'

'I think it very probable.'

'But there are other mills. There's one in Bridport not far from my sister's house. My brother-in-law is a corn-merchant and knows of more. He would be useful to meet.'

'He would indeed.'

'I could give you an introduction if you wish it.' She passed the bottle to him and this time he poured for them both. It was disappointing to her that his stay would be short and she was eager that he should judge her by Thirza's liberality not her own.

'I'd be grateful,' he said. 'Does your sister make wines as delicate as yours?'

Beatrice smiled. 'Thirza, Mrs Lamford, is superior to me in every way. She's never taken a false step.'

'Then,' said Isaac, 'I'm the more desirous to make her acquaintance, for I think she will prove unique.'

The evening was fresh and bright with a westerly wind that brought a soft dampness to the air. As Isaac rode out to keep his appointment with Matthew the sun was setting before him in a radiance sharpened by the glinting reflection of its light on the river and the glistening hedgerows. He had closeted himself all afternoon at the inn, drawing up estimates

159

and studying a map of the district, and was in need of air to clear his mind enough for company.

There was no other traffic in the lane except a woman travelling on foot some way ahead of him. As he rode he watched her, giving her no more nor less attention than he gave his surroundings, but gazing merely because she was there. Being on horseback, he had the advantage of her and gained ground as they left the village until, just before the track to the Garths' home, he was abreast of her.

'Sir.'

For an instant he thought she would beg of him but a glance at her face as she raised it drove out the idea. He reined in.

'Ma'am?'

She was a young, lean woman in half-mourning and the grey shawl that had slid from her head threw her black hair into relief and emphasized the whiteness of her skin. Her face was disquieting. Her features were still and tranquil but her dark eyes were full of a piercing restlessness that leapt out unnoticed by their owner as if their thirst were permanent. Yet there was nothing importuning about her. She carried a lidded basket which she laid in the grass.

'Do I take this road to Tarrendon? Is it this turning to Toller?'

Her voice was low and quiet but firm. He wondered what her purpose was and knew he would not ask. His cob stirred a little but she did not take her eyes from his.

'It is the road,' he said, 'but don't turn here. Take the second branch after this. To the left.'

She nodded her thanks and taking up the basket,

turned to go, but after she had walked a few yards Isaac, who was still sitting where he had halted, called out to her. She stopped and looked back.

'It's a long road,' he said, 'and lonely on the hills. Were you warned how solitary it is? There is nothing at Tarrendon.'

'There may be something for me.' Her face remained without expression. She turned again and walked on and after a moment Isaac guided his mare down the track towards the Garths. He twisted once in the saddle to look over the corner of the field but the hedges were tall and she was gone.

Autumn was on the hills. In the valleys, remnants of summer still lingered but on the uplands the trees were bare and stark against a reddening sky. Esther walked with a steady, measured pace that told of one used to walking and her feet stirred the leaves that had softened the lane. As she climbed the incline to the high country, she faced into the wind and it strengthened until her skirts were flattened against her and the debris of the season was blown in rushing gusts along the ground. At intervals she changed the basket from arm to arm.

She had been travelling for five days in search of Boaz. The letter he had written to her in June lay at her breast but she had his direction by heart and did not refer to it. Occasionally, she touched her gown and the feel of the paper folded within emboldened her. 'My dear wife,' it said, 'dear heart, think once more of that which you cast off and could have again.' She had not answered him. It was not in her power to find the words to explain herself. It was love of Boaz that had driven her to part from him and how could she say that to convince one whose needs in his grief were quite contrary to her own? If she had not loved him so deeply and completely she would not have loved their daughter with a savagery that had all but killed her reason when death had taken its object. Their love had created the child and she had wanted no more of a passion that could cause such bitter pain, nor could she bear to watch her husband's suffering and know that she could do nothing to help him.

Jealousy had also been in her. In the first months of her despair, when her mind had grown obsessed with her loss, she had wanted no-one else to mourn and it angered her that Boaz shared her sorrow. Their life together was a torment to her. Enough of her old thoughts remained to tell her how much she had changed but, from the knowledge, she drew the wrong conclusion – that Boaz would be relieved by her absence. She craved for strangers and seclusion and she fled. She did not consider that a secret leaving must show that beneath her distress she understood that he would not want her to go and when he traced her to the remote farm where she found work she would not return with him.

There was a way in which her action had been right. Far from all reminders of her past, her senses were not rubbed raw by old associations. The monotony of her days numbed and exhausted her, drawing her down into a thoughtless depression that was so foreign to her nature that her spirit began to stir and awaken. Though she was sick at heart, she found her yearning to be for Boaz and in her dreams the unobtainable that she sought turned and was not a child but a man. Had Boaz known it, his letter was seed sown in fertile ground and now, as healed as she would ever be, she followed him, ripe to accept his love at his own valuation of it.

When she turned into the lane to Toller she was more sheltered but the sun had set behind the hills and the way was not easy. The moon was rising and the sky, where the first stars were showing, was clear of cloud. Before she had walked another mile the night would be brighter. She had ridden from Dorchester on a woodman's cart and as yet the road had not tired her. There were lights in the valley as she went down into Toller but, beyond them, the steep lane that rose to the hills seemed darker by contrast. She did not linger in the village for fear of being taken for a vagrant but when she had climbed halfway to the high downs she stopped to drink from the wooden flask of milk she carried. She did not want the bread she had brought with her. Walking on, she began to feel her solitude. The shadows cast by the risen moon moved as the trees answered the wind and there was a melancholy in the damp air. Thickets that she passed were black on their moonless side and the sound of the branches stirring was a lonely accompaniment to her footfalls.

The uncertainty of her position was lending itself to her setting. She had not told Boaz of her coming. Afraid that her long rebuttal would make him refuse her, she had not trusted a letter as petition. She was not confident that he would welcome her and she recognized that her fears made her invest the atmosphere with more menace than it held.

Once upon the heights of the ridge she felt stronger. Here the open country fell away in coombes that were grey with moonlight and offered no hiding

163

place for nameless threats. It was colder where there was no barrier to the wind but she was warmed by her walking. Knowing that she was nearing Tarrendon, her heartbreat quickened. She had been told by the woodman what landmarks to look for and as she saw the bulk of the hill-fort, her breath, that had been steady throughout her climb, shook in her throat.

Her driver had told her of the track to the farmhouse but she had begun to grow tired and apprehension was making her impatient. She could not yet see the farm but because she had reached the earthworks she knew she was above it. There were hawthorns to her right that prevented her leaving the lane but some distance ahead the hedging was replaced by a fence of hurdles and this she used to enter the meadow.

The field was almost level for twenty yards or more but when she had crossed these she set down her basket and stood considering whether to go on. Before her the ground dropped away to a copse far below where she knew the house to be. She kneaded her arm where the handle of the basket had been. The wind swirling out of the coombe lifted her skirts and blew the hair back from a face that was more deathly white than it had been at Wynford. The hillside fell so steeply that it offered her an excuse to take the longer route. She hesitated to go forward but because it was dread that tempted her, she gathered herself and went on. The turf was too short to give a good handhold but the slope was ridged from side to side with the paths that sheep had made and stepping askance from one to the next, carefully, laboriously, she began to climb down.

★

In the copse, in the house that was full of the moaning of the swaying trees, Boaz walked through his dark hall. His face was no less taut than Beatrice had found it but there was a change about him. Disgust with himself had become a stimulant. He had searched his memories of his time at this place and traced out a growing slovenliness of thought and deed. A condemnation of the laxness of mind that had brought him to such a decline was tightening every aspect of his life. That he should be an adulterer shocked him far more than it did Beatrice. Though he had gone about his work with no lessening of skill, he felt his standards to have fallen in all other ways and, while he knew he could not repair the moral damage he had done himself by outward alterations, a new discipline was entering his life. Small adjustments were returning him to what he had been.

He now no longer came in from his day to sit brooding and field-stained over a loaf and cheese until the hour of the final round of his stock. To be clean and cook and wear linen especially kept for the evening refreshed him. He could not vanquish the loneliness of his situation by such actions but a barrier could be built against it by minute gains of self-respect. It was now his habit after eating to take a cup of ale up to the porch-room and sit quietly until the last inspection. When his work was done he read in the kitchen firelight but in the porch-room he simply took his rest.

Tonight, the tumult in the topmost branches disturbed the peace he tried to find in this room. Leaves torn from the half-bare trees were whipped against the lattice and held there, pressed like moths in a case, until the gust died and they fluttered down on to the path. Because there was moonlight, he sat without a candle. He looked out into the unrest in the wood and, though often at this time he did not see what was about him, the motion of the trees unsettled him.

He left his ale untried and, pushing back his stool, stood against the window with his chin resting on his arms. The glass was cold on his hands and the chill and the wildness of the night spoke of winter. He raised his eyes from the copse and gazed at the hill. The fort was grey and desolate and was made the more massive by its stillness. He watched it for some moments, his eyes attuning to the dusk, and then a movement at the edge of his vision arrested him.

He looked more narrowly. Far on the distant hillside, where the coombe met the earthworks, a darker shape was slowly descending the slope. He had no stock in that field and the form did not move like a deer. There was nothing it could be but a man.

At once he was alert. There had been sheepstealing in the district and he did not intend to lose his flock. He considered what this single figure meant. It seemed to have no companions and was not keeping to cover. If it was part of a poaching gang he would not have seen it. There were always vagrants tramping the roads and it was likely that this was such a traveller, foraging where he did not know the lie of the land.

'Nancy!' Boaz called, as he went down the stairs, and the dog left the hearth in the kitchen and came to him. Taking up the leather coat that would be a protection against any blows if the malefactor did not run at the sight of the master, Boaz thought that a gun would serve a good purpose as a threat but his tenancy had no shooting rights and the expense of such an implement was not worth its use. He opened a cupboard in the passage and brought out his drove, the heavy, pointed iron rod he used to make the holes for his hurdles, and thus equipped went out into the night.

He circled the copse and came round in the meadow between the woods and hill. His flock was huddled in the angle of the hedgerow but, though disturbed by the wind, was showing no other alarm. The sound of the bells was muffled by the crowding of the ewes and their bleating was the plaint of an unmolested herd. He did not try to hide himself as he walked towards the trees that divided the hillside from the level field. It was his intention not to lay hold of the intruder but to frighten him away before harm was done. The gaols were full enough of these wretches.

He could not see the figure as he crossed the meadow but when he reached the edge he saw that it had only been concealed by the trees. It was still slowly descending the steep side, its shoulder turned to him, and from this distance the moonlight revealed it as a woman.

He thought of Beatrice. Had trouble come to her that had driven her to leave her home for him? But before his mind could form the words recognition was growing. The dog at his heels was staring ahead and, as it stiffened and leapt forward, the woman straightened and turned to see how far she had left to descend.

Esther. She was perfectly still as she saw Boaz.

When the dog reached her and stood up against her waist she took its head in her hands but she did not turn her face from him.

At first he could do nothing, then tensely, as if it had been he who had walked the hills, he climbed the slope and stopped before her. He was startled by his feelings. A conflict of love, desire, unbelief and suspicion was strong within him. He raged against the hurt she had caused him yet there was that in him that simply leapt towards her as the dog had done. He made a sign at the animal and it subsided. She waited with her white face raised to his and part of him assessed her as if she was a stranger. He had not thought her to be so pale.

'Why have you come?' he said.

'For love, for love of you.' Her voice was rich and low; he remembered it better than his own. He stared at her, his own eyes cold. He was less generous to her than he had been to Beatrice; he blamed her for his adultery. He wanted to throw his grievance at her and see her in pain but more than that he wanted her secured and it would be dangerous to accuse her. He needed to cry out with anger but he did not.

'Come home,' he said.

CHAPTER TWELVE

The moon that had shone on Esther's coming waxed and began to wane and ten days after Isaac had tasted her wine Beatrice was in the yard beyond the mill, folding sheets with the maid. Hens were scratching in what grass they had left and now and then entangled themselves in the feet of the two women, before flapping and squawking away. It was colder, with a blanker sky, than at the beginning of the month and the river, flowing from behind the house along the edge of the yard, looked less lively.

Beatrice did not find the maid good company. Lizzie was a dull-witted girl, without the sense to find a better master, but she did have an interest in gossip and, as they walked back and forth from one another folding the linen into neat squares, she was keeping the young mistress abreast of the news. It had been her free afternoon the day before and the hours spent with her mother and aunts had left her acquainted with particulars of the entire neighbourhood.

'Mother said Mrs Graham, that she do wash for, did want to know why you weren't in church a-Sunday and when mother said the bad cider you'd had to your supper had given you the headache Mrs says if 'twas from the same batch they'd had from Cooper she weren't at all surprised. When they'd opened their last barrel the bones of a mouse had been at the bottom and never found till they drunk it dry and took off the top. Cooper, he did say, 'twere only a bit of bone from the beef, crumbled-like in the ageing, but Mr Graham says not to talk foolish – a cow and a mouse got no article in common and he don't want vermin in his drink no more.'

She laid the finished sheet in the basket and Beatrice caught the corners of the last one as the girl removed the pegs. They brought the sides together twice and advanced on each other to begin the square.

'So he'll be going to another farm, will he?' Beatrice asked. 'When he buys again?'

'So his wife d'say.' Lizzie caught the sheet under her chin. 'And farms, that's another thing. That Mr Holt, the one over to Tarrendon—'

'What of him?'

'Well, last Wednesday week he was seen riding along the high road with a woman sitting pillion behind him. Everyone did say he'd got himself a fancy-piece – living so lonely in that place – but old Jos Whitticker went out there to see was there any timber to be had and there she was. Farmer Holt d'say she's his wife.' She paused, waiting for some comment on this news but Beatrice was absorbed in the final folds so she continued. 'She d'wear a ring as if she be a lawful wife but where's she been to all this time? She d'say she's been living with relatives but what for with her man needing help on that farm and no-one to do a hand's turn for him? Folk d'say she looked consumptive so maybe she've been ill but Holt's never said nothing about her, though he's not one to talk of his doings. There, now, missus, you've let go the edge.'

Beatrice gathered up the loose linen and they completed the sheet. There were only three shirts left on the rope and she stood back while the maid took them down.

'This Mrs Holt,' she said. 'Is anything more known of her?'

'Nothing,' said Lizzie. 'She don't seem to have stirred from the farm except that one time she was riding behind he and there's never no company kept at that house. Dark, she is, and thin. What manner of woman would be parted from her husband like that?'

'I can't imagine,' said Beatrice.

The girl pressed the shirts down into the basket. 'Do you think she be his wife?' she asked. 'Or be she a-putting us on to look respectable?'

'If Mr Holt says that she is,' said Beatrice, 'then we may believe him. I've found him to be an honest man.'

She joined the girl and they each took one handle of the basket. Beatrice sighed.

'Lord,' she said. 'I'm tired. When we've carried this I'll see if the air will help me.'

Tying her cloak about her and walking out of the mill-yard, Beatrice felt as she had done as a child when George Lamford had taken her by the hands and swung her round and around until she was deposited upright with the world reeling about her. Except, she thought, then the fear of that first moment of leaving the ground and the heightened sensation were all pleasure and this . . . this was something other.

She carried a straw bag as if she were looking for

late blackberries but passed the brambles without glancing at them. It had seemed natural to take the road towards Tarrendon but as she had left the village she remembered who she might meet and, crossing Tollerford, she turned away to the left and began climbing the lane to Chammen's Hill. It was lonely here and the track that led over the downs to the old Roman road was unlikely to bring her near any traveller.

So his wife had returned to him. The wife he had mentioned so briefly the day they had brewed the cowslips and who had been the reason he had not wanted her to come to his farm. 'I have a wife and you a husband.' Yes, but there were ways in which she did not have a husband, ways which were now much to her disadvantage.

She paused and looked across the hills. The sky was a uniform grey and there seemed a great stillness in the air. Laughable, she thought, that I who have so longed for a child should greet its imminence with such apprehension. Never wish, the proverb said, for your heart's desire, for fear it may be granted you.

Walking on, her mind went back to the Harvest Home and dancing with Boaz. He had sung 'Though I Live not where I Love' and she had thought it was for her, had told herself it was for her. He had never talked of loving her; he was, as she had said, an honest man. She bore him no grudge. She was as generous in her thoughts to him as he was to her but this news of his wife frightened her. It had been her decision not to go to him for help but she realized now that she must have been holding him in reserve as her saviour. Yet what could he have done? Even if he had accepted her he would have been at Daniel's mercy and it was unlikely that Daniel would not have sued his wife's seducer until Boaz was ruined by the damages he must pay. Nor could they have fled. You cannot leave a tenancy at a moment's notice or take another without some sign by which you may be traced. And if she had gone to some secret place alone and he had followed her at the end of his tenure then the rumour that jumps out of nowhere would surely have connected them and Daniel would seek out Boaz and discover her.

She did not know what she should do. Since she had realized that she was with child it had been as if she walked blindfold across a marsh, treading now on firm ground, now sinking into depths of darkness and danger. There were hours when the joy of her conception was all that she could feel. She was glad that her child was begun in passion and indiscretion; triumphant that this precious thing was no part of Daniel. Then there were times when she was in terror of the future. There was no difficulty in concealing these early weeks of her pregnancy. She was always tired and often absentminded but neither of these symptoms were things that her household would notice and she felt only the mildest nausea which was easily hidden.

But this safety could not last. What shall I do? What shall I do? beat back and forth in her mind. It was the refrain that began and ended all other thoughts. She would not tell Boaz that this child was his. Better that no-one should know. There was too much pride in her to run to him for useless sympathy and she would not disrupt his new life. She knew enough of her own weaknesses not to blame him and she wanted him to be happy. He had, after all, given

her two of the things she most wanted. It would be a
cruelty on her part to give him word of a fatherhood
he could not acknowledge – and he with one dead
daughter in his heart.

The air was colder as she left the valley and she
pulled her cloak closer about her. She was planning if
it was possible to pass off this child as her husband's.
That was, of course, what all would assume. All
except one person and he the most important. It was
– what? – ten months since Daniel had performed his
marital duties upon her. She could not hope to
convince him that he had caused this pregnancy. Nor
was there a chance that he would keep silent from
dislike of scandal. He would not relish wearing horns
but he would never accept another man's child as his.
A stranger's son to inherit his mill? And she knew
with a sick foreboding that he would enjoy bringing
her to disgrace. She could picture him and his
mother now in their righteous anger.

So what should she do? I will ask Mr Belton for
help. He'll know what's best to be done. That she
should think of Isaac startled her and she instantly
rejected the notion. Hardly had she decided to tell
no-one when she wanted to say to a man she had met
only twice, 'I am an adulteress. Give me succour.'
She could not. And why had she thought of him? He
had hinted that she should leave Daniel but her
plight was something more than he had seen it to be
and he would be as revolted by her as all other
virtuous people would be.

Smiling briefly and bitterly, she watched her feet
as she climbed the hill. She must learn not to be so
particular; she must grow used to being known for a
scarlet woman. Shortly, she would be homeless,

destitute and infamous. Why did she wonder what she should do? All that was open to her was to throw herself on Thirza's charity until her child was born. Perhaps later she could portray herself as a widow and find a servant's situation where she was allowed to have her baby with her but before then she could only hope that the Lamfords would have the bounty to support her in some distant place.

And if her family turned its back on her, what then? She could not blame them if they did. It was wormwood to her that she should bring such a tarnish to them. But if they did? How could she support herself? There were serving-girls and labouring women in plenty, stronger and more capable than herself. She was aware of the distressed gentlewomen who slowly starved as they tried to earn their bread with their needle. A workhouse would take her child from her. Lizzie had said it had been thought the lonely farmer Holt had got himself a fancy-piece. Would that be her only means of gaining shelter?

There was a gate beside her and she leant on it, exhausted. Staring out over the meadow beyond she saw nothing. She was desperate but she was not in despair. There was that within her which she had longed for and she cherished it. It was welcome and she would not stint her love whatever she might have to do to protect it. A lie that claimed legitimacy would be the simplest expedient but how to make Daniel believe it? Could she persuade him that he had coupled with her half-asleep? That while half-conscious the natural appetites of a man, which were held to be so strong, had overcome his dislike of her? No, it would not serve. Her attempts to coax him into fathering a son had already persuaded him that she was without morals and he would not be hoodwinked. There would be no name and no security for her innocent one.

Her hands gripped the cold wood and she shook with the intensity of her emotion. Anger ran through her with the shock of entering freezing water. The world would condemn her and her child but it was Daniel, not they, who should be despised. He had entrapped her into marriage with a false portrayal of himself. He had bound her to him for a lifetime to further his business interests. Knowing her nature, he had deliberately subjected her to a spiritual cruelty and physical neglect that had left her an easy prey to temptation. If he had paid the least heed to the vows he felt to be so binding to women there need have been no deception. God knows she had tried to be a good wife and how had her openness been met?

She had already been out longer than Daniel would think suitable and if she was not to draw attention to herself she must go back. Leaving the gate, she began striding down the hill. She walked quickly and firmly, her memory presenting the succession of humiliations of which her marriage had been made. It gave her a rich satisfaction that Daniel would be a public cuckold. However much he would enjoy seeing her brought low he would still be aware that he would be a laughing-stock for many. His men would look at him sidelong and whisper about him behind his back. Her very condition meant that it was not he who had first rejected her but she who had found him wanting.

It was in this turbulent frame of mind, compounded of fear, rage and triumph, that Beatrice returned to what was called her home just as old Mrs

Fayerdon was removing her own gloves and taking charge of the house in the masterful way she had when excited by an outing. Old Mrs Fayerdon was part of a coterie of ladies of similar age who, for lack of guillotine under which to sit with their knitting, gathered in each other's parlours to drink tea and talk over the reprehensible ways of the world. They were a group continually jostling for precedence amongst themselves and quick to take offence at each other's remarks. What A had said to B concerning C after the previous tea-drinking would immediately be relayed to D who ensured that it reached the ears of C. The next meeting would invariably begin with one participant sitting straight-backed and drawn-in upon herself until compelled to break her silence with the announcement that for her part she disliked gossip but felt it her duty to . . .

On this afternoon a certain Mrs Naughton had gained unequivocal status by bringing her first grandson, who had accompanied his mother on a fortnight's visit. He was a stout child, not yet out of skirts, with a vacant face which appeared to have witnessed nothing interesting in its three years but his presence and ability to consume bread and butter gave his grand-dame a cachet that she exploited to the full. Several of her companions were out of temper by the time they reached home and old Mrs Fayerdon was one of them.

As Beatrice entered the hall she could hear her mother-in-law in the kitchen taking Lizzie to task for having banked the fire too high while heating the smoothing irons. The agreeable smell of newly-ironed linen was pervading the house but its comfort was dissipated by the sharp sounds of the old woman's criticisms. It had been an act of will for Beatrice to cross the threshold and, although she knew that it would be expedient to hurry quietly upstairs before her mother-in-law realized she was there, a debilitating loathing for the mill and its inhabitants kept her fumbling over the ties of her cloak long enough for old Mrs Fayerdon to come out into the hall and see her.

She advanced on her daughter-in-law with determination. Her hair-piece had come slightly adrift beneath her lace cap and the false ringlets were lower over one ear than the other. She did not greet Beatrice but leapt at once to accusation.

'So,' she said, 'you've seen fit to come home. Thought to take your ease because I was out calling, did 'ee? With ironing of your man's shirts left to do itself.'

'When I'm paid a maid's wage,' said Beatrice, 'I will do a maid's work.' She removed the cloak and laid it over a chair while she shook out her skirts. The bag she had taken with her was lying on the floor and old Mrs Fayerdon prodded it with her toe.

'Carried a bag, eh?' she said. 'So we'd think you'd gone a-berrying? And come back with it empty. Did 'ee think 'twould be in our minds you were working? We'd be some foolish if 'twere. Never naught but dreaming and idleness from 'ee.'

Beatrice, who had heard this so often before, lifted her cloak and hat and took a step towards the stairs but her mother-in-law grasped her arm and turned her back. The afternoon had played upon the principal grievance she had against Beatrice and she was unable to rest until she had aired it.

'Do 'ee know how I did spend these last hours?'

Her face was close to her daughter-in-law and Beatrice was able to think dispassionately that both mother and son spat when they were angry. 'Shall I tell 'ee? I bin watching that Mistress Naughton's fudgey-faced grandson a-stuffing hisself with bread and Mrs queening it for having him.' She gave Beatrice's arm a twist. 'And where's my grandchild, eh? When's my son's cradle to be filled? You selfish, good-for-nothing creature. There's never a sign of your belly growing.'

'And how can there be,' said Beatrice, 'when I'm married to a gelding?' She spoke so calmly that old Mrs Fayerdon had opened her mouth to reply before the sense of the words reached her. Dismay silenced her and in that moment Beatrice shook off her hold and moved closer so that she was driven back towards the wall.

'Harridan!' said Beatrice, viciously. 'Virago! You think your son's such a man, don't you? Let me tell you he's no better than a eunuch! You want a grandchild? Then pray for an immaculate conception, for that's the only one there'll be in this house!'

Beatrice did not come down from her room that day. She had bread and meat brought to her but she ate only because she must take care of herself for her child's sake. This chamber was as full of Daniel's belongings as of hers but he had ridden to Dorchester and would be taking supper with his cronies on the way back and so for one evening it was a private place.

She was ashamed of herself. She had let the vulgar old woman drive her into a corresponding vulgarity. There was an ugliness in what she had said and in her intention to hurt that offended her more because she had lowered herself to say it than if she had heard another speak the words. She was lonely tonight. Thirza's house, with its warmth and lights and friendship, was only behind the hills but she longed for it as if she had been transported to another hemisphere. As indeed, she thought, I have. Very shortly I will not be welcome in that home for fear I contaminate the children. My name will not be mentioned. Their world is not mine any more.

The hours passed slowly. She saw the men leave their work and Garth lock the mill door and bring the key to the house. The light faded and the room was filled briefly with a livid salmon glow as the long, rain-heavy clouds caught the last of the sunset before they covered the sliver of moon. She had grown used to the roar of the millrace and the unending vibration in the beams but tonight she noticed them and could not free her mind of their burden. The darkness deepened and settled in the room. She found herself shaking and understood that she was afraid. What would come of her accusation? Her mother-in-law would not fail to repeat it to her son and she would say it must have been heard plainly by the maid. Many times she had dreaded the long misery of life with Daniel but this was the first occasion she had sat in the dark in fear of his return.

It would show him she was anxious if he found her as she was. Undressing, she lay in the cold bed watching the hangings stir in the draught from the uncovered window. She did not even think of sleep. Once she thought of Boaz and the feel of his body against hers as she had lain so differently on another bed. Always she was listening for the one sound she did not want to hear. Her mouth was dry.

At last the sound came. A horse's hooves were heard in the yard and, to show that Beatrice was not the only listener, the front door opened from within and old Mrs Fayerdon called out into the darkness.

'Daniel? Daniel? Is that you?'

'Who else would it be?' His voice was loud and surly and Beatrice, catching the tone but not the words, knew what condition he was in. He was not one to drink to excess. He did not like to seem ridiculous or be incapable of any action he might be called upon to perform but this did not make him a sober man. A preference for spirits was common to him and his friends and he would take liquor enough to draw out the malice in his nature. It was then that the spite he felt for mankind was closest to the surface; then, that even his mother was wary of how she spoke. This brutishness was what Beatrice had feared and expected and she had been aware that on this one night her mother-in-law could fuel his savagery with no anxiety that it would be turned upon herself. It was in her mind that it must have rankled with the old woman that Daniel had never yet raised a hand to his wife and that both mother and son would gain a sweet satisfaction if he did. Sweat began to spring beneath her arms and on her breast-bone. Her hands were damp and she smoothed them on the sheet. The defiance of the plans she had made whilst walking now seemed futile. After all, what could she do? She had no-one to run to even tonight. There is no protection from a husband who has not yet attacked.

There was a silence while Daniel must be un-saddling his horse, then the slamming of the stable door and footsteps across the yard. Voices began as he entered the house. His mother must have been waiting in the hall. As they stood at the foot of the stairs, Beatrice could hear her, pious and indignant, venting her opinion of the wife's misconduct, of the outrageous suggestion. She tensed, expecting an immediate invasion of the room but the pair moved into the parlour and closed the heavy door.

There was a time when she could hear nothing and the moments stretched in her suspense. The unvarying rumble of the millwheel, that was no obstacle to ordinary life but had irritated her nerves in these dark hours, took on a malevolent intent to mask what threatened her.

A sound and her eyes widened. Steps on the stairs. The door opened and a candle-flame shuddered in the movement of air, throwing its wavering light on the hand that held its stick, on an arm and body and a face made wan and hollow by the shifting shadows.

Daniel stood on the threshold, staring at her. She pulled herself up and turned towards him, leaning on her elbow and the pillows. Beyond him, she heard a slight stirring as if his mother lurked in the dusk. He came inside, closing the door with an arm held behind him. Beatrice thought: how thwarted she will be. If I am to be hurt she would want to see it. He crossed to the bed and looked down at her. His hat and gloves had been thrown aside but otherwise he was dressed for the road and the night coldness wafted from the skirts of his coat as he moved.

He said nothing and Beatrice, meeting his eyes, saw that, within a face tight with passion, they were strangely blank. There was no recognition that she was human in his gaze. He could not comprehend her. In other matters he had intelligence but 'She is my wife' intruded on all his thoughts of Beatrice, blocking the path to understanding before he had started down it, satisfying his reason. It was not for her to have needs or preferences. She had insulted him in this most private subject and he could not even try to follow the years of hurt that could have led to her outburst. His will should have been accepted by her without question or judgement.

With his free hand, he reached out and grasped her hair. She slithered from the bed and, for an instant as her feet slid on the wood, her weight was suspended from his arm. He jerked her upright and the brandy on his breath, with the heat of pain in her scalp, sickened her. Raising the candle, he blew it out and the pungent, waxy smoke was suddenly between them, hanging unexpectedly white in the darkness. Tossing the stick on to the bed, he dropped her hair and took her by both wrists. A wraith of smoke still rose from the cooling wick.

For a moment they did not move and beyond the door she heard again the sound of a listener stirring. He slowly tightened his grip and twisted her skin so that the flesh burned beneath his fingers. Her back was rigid and her body shook but it was no longer fear that mastered her. Her hatred of him was absolute. It was not natural to her to be passive. Her mind scouted for means to injure him, to reach that steel stick with its sharp corners. She shifted slightly to have better ground to kick out but, as she began to lift her foot, she forced herself to stop. His breathing had changed. She could not see his face clearly but, in revulsion, she realized that this violence was exciting him. More than before she wanted to pull away from him but she had promised that there was nothing she would not do to protect her child. Still holding her wrists, he pushed her down towards the bed and she, unresisting, leant back.

CHAPTER THIRTEEN

It was soon noticed that there had been a change in Daniel Fayerdon. Not everyone could describe where the alteration lay for at first it was subtle but as Thirza said to her husband, after Daniel had called at the cornyard, it was the difference between a bull-frog that was considering whether to croak and one that had actually drawn breath to do so. Henry, who had had occasion to call at the mill, replied that it was as if Daniel had become a caricature of himself. He mentioned that Beatrice had also seemed curiously transformed, wearing an expression that was both hunted and smug – a combination for which it was impossible to account.

The violence Daniel had used against Beatrice had not simply excited him enough to lie with her. It had released the gall that flowed in his spirit and brought the malice inherent in his nature into the open. He had enjoyed Beatrice's pain and submission and the love of power and cruelty that had always been in him was fed by his pleasure and flourished freely. Having always considered his virility unquestionable, he had been bitterly offended by his wife's accusation and during the nights that followed grimly set to proving his manhood to her. It puzzled him that although it was plain that she loathed him, there was a disconcerting complacency about her. Far from looking like a woman who has been put in her rightful place of subjection she was, as his mother said, like the cat that got the cream. There was even a gleam of victory in her eye.

Within a fortnight, he felt this triumph to be both explained and commendable. Beatrice, who had now been struck by morning sickness, drew her malady to his attention and told him that she was sure she was with child. It was beyond Daniel's imagination to think that any woman could fail to feel favoured by carrying his son and he considered Beatrice's attitude more than understandable. For the first time he felt a faint approval of her and even, to her indignation, went so far as to chuck her under the chin.

Beatrice had risked giving him the news so early in the hope that now she had achieved her purpose, she could rid herself of his attentions and for this she found an unexpected ally in her mother-in-law. Old Mrs Fayerdon was inclined to be sceptical about Beatrice's claim, thinking it to be merely a tale told to excuse her from a duty she had found to be onerous. When Daniel's insistence and Beatrice's abandonment to retching persuaded her of the child's reality she was, initially, nettled by the loss of so substantial a ground for complaint but was soon consumed by a fever of expectation. She was indifferent to Beatrice's welfare as a daughter-in-law but was obsessed that she should thrive as the receptacle for the next Fayerdon. An opinion embedded firmly in her mind was that all sexual connection during pregnancy was harmful to the progress of the baby and this she passed on to her son. Daniel was not eager to renounce so newly-acquired an amusement but, while not recognizing his cruelty, admitted to himself that he was rough and was ready to accept that in female affairs his mother knew best.

The object of their concern was relieved beyond measure. She would need to ensure that no questions were asked about her offspring's precipitant arrival in the world but Thirza's second son had been both early and healthy and she had the symptoms pointing to such a delivery at her fingertips. Nor was there any need to fear suspicions – what could be more natural and looked-for than her present condition? With her anxiety over her future gone and her nights restored to sleep she was able to relax and enjoy the sensation of awaiting the child of a man for whom she cared. It was of infinite reward to her that Daniel would be rearing a cuckoo in his nest and she had no scruple in planning to steer its mind on another course from that of its nominal father. She hoped for a son, not because she felt one sex to be better than the other but because she believed that a boy's life would offer more opportunity and independence.

That the baby would be male was not doubted by the rest of the household. Even old Mrs Fayerdon, who thought it would be like Beatrice to want a girl out of sheer perversity, believed that her daughter-in-law would be unable to thwart Providence in so important a matter. Her son was so perfect in all his ways that it was unthinkable that he could sire the inferior gender.

Pride in the coming son fuelled the savage arrogance that was now undeniably within Daniel. With the ending of the physical humiliation of Beatrice as a channel for his newly-released malignity he needed another object on which to vent it. Energies stimulated by these surfacing passions surged within him and were expended on those who, next to his wife, were most in his power – his workmen. He knew they already feared him but the urge, for his son's sake, to have his business in the small of his hand drove him to induce an atmosphere of continual tension in the mill. He watched for the smallest departure from the many written and unwritten rules and punished offenders with public upbraiding and the rigorous enforcement of fines.

The men, afraid to lose their jobs without a character to show a new master, afraid of the dwindling of small savings and the selling of possessions that unemployment would bring, afraid of hunger and the overseers, afraid of the workhouse and roadgangs, did not criticize Daniel's methods to his face but worked with one eye to his coming and whispered of what his wife was heard to have said.

Only Matthew Garth remained uncowed. For him, the increased strictness of the regime with its pettiness and Daniel's obvious enjoyment of his men's unease was the final straw. His disgust for Daniel as a man overcame other considerations and he determined to seek for other employ. If he could not take a character from Wynford Mill he would apply to his previous master and trust to his skills and achievements to recommend him. The approaching winter delayed his leaving, there was many a slip in attaining a new post and it was wiser to stay with the devil you knew in the cold months but in the spring he would go.

A matter which had played its part in deciding Matthew was the rejection of Isaac's scheme for modernizing the mill. Isaac had submitted his plan for the instalment of an engine and suggestions for general renovation without serious hope that they would be accepted and Daniel had not proved his expectations to be wrong. Faced with the prospect of an absolute commitment to reach into his pocket, Daniel found himself unable to agree. The promise of having command of year-round power was still attractive and he tried to bargain, but Isaac was not the man to haggle for work he did not especially wish to have. The interview had ended with rancour on both sides and a severe warning given by Isaac of the consequence of ignoring the crumbling timbers and brickwork of the mill.

Despite the minor accidents that had occurred, the frequent patching of the stairs and the cautions given to him by Isaac and Matthew, it had not yet been borne in upon Daniel that there was real danger in his workplace. He had grown up amongst these buildings and their decay had been too gradual for him to notice it. Accustomed as he was to the well-worn appearance of the mill, he did not seriously consider that there was risk in treading where his father had trod. To his eyes, there had been no change. Where injury to the structure could not be overlooked, the thought of what he must pay for renewal clogged his reason as the corn-dust settled on and hampered the workings of the wheels. Rottenness riddled the bones of the mill but Daniel thought his meanness a virtue and blamed whoever had touched the damaged piece last.

Towards noon on a cold morning almost a week after Beatrice had told him of his impending fatherhood Daniel was prowling the mill, ensuring that all of his hands were up to the mark. The sky was obscured by unbroken cloud that moved in a mass before an easterly wind that penetrated every corner of the building. The fine meal pouring from the stones filled the pale air with new flour that eddied in the gusts entering the doorway and sank in drifts to soften the floor.

The men, never given to banter while the master was near, were working in a silence that seemed emphasized rather than drowned by the unceasing din of the mill. There had already been an incident that morning. The lad recently hired as odd-job boy had been affected by the increasing cold and, fearing to ask permission to make water during working hours, had suffered until nervousness caused by Daniel's sudden presence had made him wet his breeches. Daniel had held him up to derision, castigating him for filth and childishness, and the boy, shivering in the midst of the men Daniel had called to witness the correction, was too shamed to see that it was not he that his fellows were despising. The sight of the lad, known for his shy ways, going about his tasks with tears on the face he tried to hide filled the men with a helpless rage. Hands were placed on the young shoulder as they passed him but none dared speak up while the master was in the temper to turn them off.

Towards noon they became so busy that they were less conscious of their hate. A cart had come from Frome Vanchurch to take away three dozen sacks of meal and was being loaded by means of a shute when the wagon expected later in the day arrived delivering wheat. Daniel, quickened by what he felt to be the just humbling of the boy, was aware of the animosity against him and took it ill. He was not in a humour to have his authority challenged in the slightest degree and it stirred up his bile to see criticism in the set of faces and lowering of eyes. He wanted complete servility and determined to make his men bend their backs exactly as he pleased. Summoning Matthew, he gave the order that both loading and unloading were to be achieved before the clock struck twelve.

''Twould be better for the wagoner to wait, master,' said Matthew. 'There's no man to spare for the pulley.'

His tone was mild but Daniel knew what his thoughts had been.

'Are you defying me, Garth?'

'No, sir. Shall I halt the stones?'

'Have I said so? Keep them running.'

'I'll take Harris from the loading to see to the hutch.'

'Then the cart will not be filled by the strike of noon and I will have it filled. Who feeds the stones?'

'Blackstone and Samways, master, but it needs two men. The stones are running so hot we could have fire if the corn doesn't flow.'

Daniel smiled. He had been gazing over the yard as Matthew spoke but now he turned and looked into his eyes.

'Yes,' he said. 'It needs two men. Send Samways to the hutch and help Blackstone yourself.'

A twist of dislike showed itself in Matthew's expression and Daniel laughed.

'Reluctant, Garth?' he asked. 'Are you tender for your fellow men? If Samways has a fear of heights – what is it to me? Let him choose another profession if he wants his feet on the ground. The law, perhaps, or church.' He raised his hand and, extending a finger, lowered it slowly to point into the mill. Matthew did not move.

'One man in the hutch is not enough,' he said. 'He won't be done by noon. Let me help him.'

'And risk fire? Take yourself to the stones, Garth, and don't let me find I've been disobeyed or it will be the worse for your friend.'

Waiting at the open door, where he could survey the loading of the cart, the movement within the mill and the manoeuvring of the wagon beneath the corn-hutch, Daniel felt a faint self-doubt that spoilt his satisfaction. It made him irritable. Spite had prompted him to send Samways above and, however gratifying it might be to force both Samways and Garth to do his will, it was not business-like to use the least efficient man for any job. Samways was not lax in his work but a severe tendency to vertigo made his life a constant effort to be busied on the lower levels. His disability was recognized by his companions and it was accepted among them that there should be a continual balancing of tasks amongst themselves to prevent him having to climb. It would have surprised Daniel, who could not appreciate this quality, to know how much blunt good-will existed between his workmen and, although he had been trying to prove his authority over them, he did not realize what enmity his order had aroused and so the full enjoyment of his action was lost to him.

Overhead, Samways mounted the stairs with the sweating weakness that afflicts those who have a terror of heights. He could not look at the wall for the steps, worn smooth and thin with the use of years, were here loose and there sloping so that attention was needed not to stumble. Glimpses of their height sickened him so that when he reached the corn-hutch his body was no longer under his control. He passed between the mounds of grain and put his wet hands on the bolts that held the doors. The thought of Daniel timing his appearance made him want to be prompt but for a few seconds he stood, drawing breath, unable to still his shaking enough to slide the metal back. When he did and the doors were open, his giddiness as he leant out to lower the tackle was such that the men below saw him sway into the air and paused in their work for fear that he would fall.

The chains rattled and the hook holding the wooden tray descended through the void. The carter heaved a sack into it and, hearing him cry ''bove!', Samways winched it aloft. Seven times he raised the grain and swung the sack into the hutch. Seven times his concentration kept his eyes on the load. He did not look up to see the tackle parting from the wood where it was screwed; he did not have experience enough of the task to know that the feel of the chains was wrong. It was without warning to him that the block, taking the strain of the eighth sack, was pulled from the age-softened beam and dropped, straight and sudden, down three storeys to break the ground below. For an instant the chain from the winch was loosened then, as the block fell, it crashed to the floor of the hutch and the weight of the block drew it rushing over the edge. It tautened and the winch, fastened to planking as old as the beam, was wrenched forward. There was a splintering of wood, the handle of the winch was snatched from Samways's hands and, as it whipped round, struck his arm before the winch was ripped from the floor and, dragged to the doors, plummeted to the yard.

Daniel, still standing below, saw the tray tip and the grain plunge and spill beneath the wheels of the wagon. The carter cried out and turned to jump but the winch, flung beyond the path of the block, flew outwards as it fell and struck his side as it plunged on to the sacks. The horses reared in the shafts and, as his men ran to calm them, Daniel watched the carter open his eyes with a look of grave amazement and stare before him as the blood from shattered ribs seeped through his smock.

The noise of the accident brought Beatrice running from the house. Her mother-in-law and the servants followed but Beatrice was across the yard before them. As she ran she took in the gathering of men about the broken boards of the wagon and Daniel standing motionless on the steps. The men parted for her as she reached them and she saw the wounded carter, his clothing raised and the bones showing white through the torn flesh. She glanced at Daniel and realized that the emotion that held him speechless was anger. The thought – this child is none of his – flashed through her as Matthew, who had immediately climbed to the corn-hutch, came out of the mill. Matthew looked first at the carter and then at Daniel.

'Sir,' he said, 'we must have the surgeon. Will the lad run for him? Samways's arm is broke by the winch and . . .' He nodded to the wagon.

'Must!' said Daniel. 'Always free with your musts! Incompetence! Fetch Samways to me!'

'Daniel,' Beatrice spoke across the wagon. 'This man is bleeding. We need the surgeon now.'

Daniel opened his mouth to tell her to mind her place but remembered her condition. His mother, arriving at Beatrice's side, supplied his words. 'Disgraceful!' she snapped. 'To talk to 'ee like that! The damage! Never saw the—'

'Are we just to stand here?' she interrupted. Beatrice untied her long apron and, folding it into a pad, laid it against the carter's rib to staunch the blood. Matthew, with a contemptuous glance at his master, took off his neckerchief and helped her to bind the apron in place. It was to their advantage that the carter had fainted.

'The surgeon, sir,' he said.

Daniel's eyes sought out the boy he had upbraided that morning and, in answer to a gesture, the lad ran out of the yard towards the centre of the village. It was against Daniel's inclination to summon help but the carter was not his man and he did not want his business damaged by gossip. He felt that the episode had shown him in a bad light and he was stung by the attitude of his wife and Garth. His authority had slipped and he would regain it. He looked at the fallen tackle and then at his men. 'Do you see the damage to my property?' he asked.

A stolid silence met his question. Beatrice, knotting the makeshift dressing, was ashamed for him.

'How long will it take Samways to pay to replace it, I wonder?' He linked his hands beneath the skirts of his overall. His audience watched him as a walker watches an adder that has appeared in his path and it renewed his confidence. This is a nonsense, thought Beatrice, I can't let him – but Matthew was before her.

'That wood was rotten,' he said. 'We all knew it was so. Mr Belton said particular that it should be renewed.'

Daniel's face took on a dark, congested look. 'Was there aught he didn't say should "particular" be renewed?'

Matthew stared at him over the carter who had come round but did not seem to know where he was. 'He asked for many repairs,' he said, 'that would save accidents like this.'

'Competent workmen would save such accidents!' Daniel's neck was engorged and Beatrice, already astonished by her capacity for adultery and deception, found that she would not dislike it if her husband dropped dead before them all. He glared round and went on: 'Let no-one follow Samways's example. Slip-shod and a danger to us all. And you,' he pointed at Matthew, 'if you value your employ, speak to me with respect. Now,' he slid his hand back under his overall and smiled, 'go to the hutch where this Samways takes his ease and tell him my pleasure. I will not have him taken in charge for the breaking of my tackle – for which he may thank me lest I change my mind – but I turn him off without a character and let him find other occupation if he can.' The feeling amongst the men was palpable and Daniel did not drop his smile. 'Go now,' he said, 'or I will do this to them all.' He waited until Matthew had passed him and reached the door. 'Garth,' Matthew turned, 'one thing more. Tell him I retain his wages against repairs and that, naturally, the surgeon's fee must be found by him.'

The activity made necessary by the accident disguised the resentment that Daniel's unreasonable and callous behaviour had engendered. The coming of the surgeon, the removal of the carter to a work-bench in a storeroom, the setting of Samways's arm and the sending of news to Mrs Samways and the carter's master all served to occupy the millhands and subdue what desire for rebellion Daniel's threats had aroused. It was over two hours later when Farmer Comer rode into the yard to collect his injured man. The work of the mill had been resumed and the surgeon, having done what little should not be left to nature, had been taken into the house by Daniel to refresh himself.

Comer had brought with him three other of his labourers and a cart for the conveyance of the invalid, and the sight of the wagon that he had sent out undamaged that morning did not improve his temper. Hearing the sound of wheels, Matthew came out of the store where the carter lay and greeted the farmer.

'How does he do?' Comer asked.

'Badly, sir,' said Matthew. 'Half the time he's with us and half he's wandering. The surgeon's bound up the broken ribs but there's a fever rising.'

Comer made inarticulate noises of annoyance. He was not a man to put accidents down to Providence and was looking about him for someone to blame. He was harsh to his own men if their carelessness caused any hurt and saw no reason to be more mild towards Daniel's. The winch and chain had been moved back against the wall but the position of the smashed wagon beneath the hutch told its own tale.

'You'll tell me the name of the hand that let that chain fall,' he said, 'and I'll have the law on him. My man's got a wife and three children who won't get their bread.'

There was no question in Matthew's mind as to what he should answer but he was conscious as he spoke that he might be abandoning his own livelihood by being honest. The paying of compensation that could have been avoided by a lie was not

197

something Daniel would overlook and repercussions would be inevitable.

'The hand was guilty of no fault,' he said. 'The wood that held the pulley was rotten. There's no case for law.'

'Is there not?' Comer eased himself in the saddle. 'Well, now, thank 'ee. If it wasn't done by the man it was done by the master. There's a wagon to be mended and corn lost and I know whose pocket it'll come from if he wants to keep his good name.'

Towards evening, Canader was following a footpath across the meadows behind the houses that led from the centre of the village to the lane where their cottage stood. She was wearing the russet gown and crimson shawl that Beatrice had first seen her in but her figure was fuller and her appearance more healthy than on that April morning. The walk to fetch the piece of bacon and two pig's trotters had put a high colour in her cheeks where the sharp wind had caught her but it enlivened her face as she moved with her mind elsewhere.

Her thoughts were of Beatrice and they were the first that she had not shared with Matthew. The news of Beatrice's pregnancy had been quick to spread and had re-awakened the suspicion she had felt when Beatrice had returned from her stay in Bridport. It had seemed to Canader then that Beatrice was in love, a condition not previously associated with her relations with Daniel. The story of Beatrice's accusations had been repeated to the mill-hands by the maid, who had listened eagerly from the kitchen, and had been carried to Canader by Matthew. That the announcement of a pregnancy should follow so closely such a bitter claim that her husband was a gelding fitted oddly in Canader's reasoning. Nor was it like Beatrice to forget herself and retaliate when irritated by her mother-in-law in so violent and, in effect, public a manner. Some intense emotion other than habitual annoyance from the old woman must have sparked the outburst. It could be simply that the moodiness of her condition had shortened Beatrice's temper but if this was so it was strange that she should have called Daniel a eunuch. Was it possible that the child was not his? The opportunity was there, for Beatrice drove alone, and yet no rumour of a sweetness for another man had been heard in Wynford and Daniel showed pride in his coming fatherhood.

She shifted the basket on to her other arm and, bunching her skirts in her free hand, climbed the stile into the lane. Her home was nearby and she could see from the smoke rising and being snatched by the wind that the fire had not gone out. Walking again, she tried to shake off the uneasiness she felt. She did not have Beatrice running through her mind from any wish to unearth scandal. It was fondness and pity that prompted her foreboding. She knew what it was to suffer an unhappy marriage and to see an escape in the guise of a better man but though there had been release for her there would be none without disgrace for Beatrice and her heart pleaded for her conjectures to be wrong.

Her door was before her. She put her fingers to the latch and, as she did so, she noticed that the board she leant against it, lest it should rain and the water run beneath and soak the earth floor, was not in its place. It did not much concern her. The preoccupation which had led her to stoke the fire higher than she had remembered must also have prevented her attending to this small duty, although she had imagined it to be something she did as routine. She crossed the threshold and set down her basket, still looking back at the board which lay by the path.

'Good day to 'ee, Canader.'

The voice startled her. There was an instant while her consciousness fought against recognizing it, then she turned into the room. Nat Brinsley sat in the chair by the hearth. His legs were stretched upon the fender and a jar of her ale was by his side. She had not seen him since the day he had sold her. A coldness went through her now.

'No greeting for me, my dear?' Nat's voice was lazy and she wondered how long he had been sitting there, calculating upon the blow that his appearance would be. The expression in his small eyes showed how much he wished to have the advantage of her and, exerting her self-control, she determined that he would be disappointed. Taking off her shawl, she laid it on the table. Externally calm, she began to adjust her wind-blown hair.

'What do you want?' she asked.

Her lack of emotion was not what Nat had expected. He refilled his glass from the jar to demonstrate his confidence and, watching her over its rim, saw her examine him with unspoken derision. It was not a conclusion he welcomed. His fortunes had reached a low ebb and in coming to Canader he had hoped not only to refill his pockets but to bolster his self-esteem with her fear of him. Since they had parted he had forgotten with what spirit she had survived his tyranny and remembered only that she had been in his power. Now he saw her take him in – a jockey-like man in a cheap town suit – and remain unimpressed. He had decked himself to cut a sophisticated figure – his trousers and waistcoat were of large green checks, his frock-coat was a rusty brown, a tarnished brass-topped cane lay on the floor by his side, a paste ring adorned his hand – but in her presence he felt suddenly uncertain and tawdry.

'That's not friendly,' he said. 'Can't I come calling? Come to see how you do?'

She lifted the basket to the table and took out her packages.

'I suppose you're here for money,' she said.

He uncrossed his feet and stared into the fire. Her attitude was disconcerting but there was a certain satisfaction to be had from it. He was feeling exceptionally sorry for himself and angry with the world and her treatment of him was all of a piece with the general undervaluing of his character that met his efforts. It was through his generosity that she was living with Garth and she ought to be grateful. If life had not gone well with him since April she should be eager to help. He put the sole of his boot against an unburnt stick and forced it further into the flames.

Waiting for him to reply, Canader took a dish of suet and crock of flour from a shelf. It would not be long until Matthew returned and she had intended to fry the bacon with potatoes and onions so that he could eat at once but as she did not mean to ask Nat to join them she decided to make savoury dumplings instead. Their preparation would occupy her while she listened for Matthew and surely Nat would have left before they were ready to eat.

Despite her apparent self-possession, she was as shaken by Nat's arrival as if he had been an apparition. Her anxiety over her unorthodox situation had grown with the increase of her happiness. Morally, she considered herself to be Matthew's wife but she had not forgotten his doubt as to their legal status. What had seemed immaterial at the outset of their marriage – for what had lawyers to do with them? – now took the guise of a threat. Her days were not disturbed by worries but there were nights when the spectre of her old life seemed summoned by her joy in her new and a dread that Nat could reclaim her kept her fast awake in the darkness. How should she act towards him now that he was here?

She unwrapped her bacon and began to slice it without speaking again. Nat could have only one reason for coming but she could not guess what method he would use to filch from her. It was unlikely to be force, his hand still bore the scar where she had bitten him when he tried to beat her. He might use persuasion and play upon any sentimental feeling for him he supposed her to have or there was blackmail – if he spread the story of the wife-sale she would receive an interest he could be sure she would not relish. One thing she knew; at the time of their transaction he had been as convinced of the legality of such a sale as she had been before. Matthew had warned her otherwise and she did not intend to let any nervousness in her demeanour hint that she was not completely safe from him.

Nat, meanwhile, was contemplating his grievances. In an attempt to appear nonchalant he, too, was silent but his mind was loud with self-pity. When he had taken the five sovereigns for Canader and left her with her new master on Tarrendon Hill, he had felt himself to have had the best of the

bargain. With money to spare and rid of a burden-
some wife, the world seemed a gayer and more
approachable place than ever it had done before. His
plan to sample the delights of the seaside before
returning to the barmaid he coveted, with gold to
tempt her and a tale of an abandoned wife to make
her laugh, was put into effect at once. He entered
Weymouth as a man of leisure and was, at first, well
satisfied with the diversions to be enjoyed at a resort
but, finding the price of lodgings high and money to
slip away strangely amongst his new friends, he
thought he might prefer Bournemouth and took
himself there in the comfort of a coach. His luck was
no better in these fresh surroundings. The summer
costs were dear and though it was cheerful to go to
the races in a hired carriage filled with cronies he
could not bet on a winner and standing treat to his
companions sank his funds to a level that frightened
him. Sarah Poole had not been driven from what
passed as his heart and, with his resources much
diminished, he had returned to Yeovil, to the
taproom of the Four Feathers to tempt her with what
money he had left. She, who had not given a thought
to him since he had gone, noted his town-clothes, his
swagger and the shillings he scattered on her tray and
welcomed him to her bed. This was not a cheap place
to lie for although she did not charge by the night,
unless occasion demanded it, her favours could only
be had by constant gifts of trinkets and finery and
loans both parties understood would not be repaid.
Nat, laying his finger along his nose, would not tell
her how he had come by his wealth but promised that
there was more and she, being well-acquainted with
the underworld, accepted that he had found a more

profitable and less law-abiding trade than driving a cart.

It was not a position which could be held for long without the truth of his vanishing riches being revealed but Nat was an opportunist and, living for the day, hoped that somehow his purse would not empty before he had tired of his Sarah. This was not to be. A search of his belongings while he was elsewhere and the putting of two and two together soon convinced Sarah that he was not the warm man he claimed to be and that whatever activity had provided his gold it was not something that looked to produce a regular supply. Having milked him of all that he had, she discarded him and held him to public ridicule, leaving him forlorn, homeless and feeling ill-used.

He had not known what to do next. There was no work for him where he was recognized and he had no character. In thinking himself hard done by, he reviewed his past and included Canader amongst those who had taken advantage of him and the memory of her had decided him to apply to her for aid. If he only had a little money he could be set to rights again, he was sure, and she owed him this at least. Now, as he sat by her fire watching her prepare another man's food in the light of the flames, he was resentful. He looked at the whitewashed walls, the pattern of the freestoned floor, the two chairs at the hearth and thought: I gave her a home. Why did she never make it as comfortable as this? And she herself, with her graceful movements and shining red hair, had attractions. Why had she not had affection for him? He thought sentimentally of her talents in her craft and the income he could have had from her if she had still belonged to him.

'Do you ever do your gloving?' he asked, suddenly.

She smiled, moulding the dough on the wood.

'I'm a housewife,' she said, 'and when I d'have no work I sit and take my rest like a queen.'

He resumed his observation of the fire. Her composure suggested that he should use persuasion to profit from her but with every movement she irritated him more. He must search for employment while she lived in idleness. The injustice moved him to rise from his seat with a threat in his eye but as he did so, she said, 'That will be Matthew.'

She rubbed her hands on a cloth and went to the door. Nat lowered himself back into the chair and tried to look at ease.

'My dear,' Matthew came into the room and Canader saw at once that something was wrong.

'Matt,' she said, 'has there been an accident at the mill? Are you hurt? Has Mr Fayerdon . . . ?'

She hardly knew what she feared but, though she had often seen him return from work angry at the master, she had never seen the expression that was on his face now. He was looking over his shoulder at Nat.

'What are you doing here?' he asked.

Nat waved his hands. 'A friendly visit.'

Canader turned back towards Nat. 'I'm sure he's here for money,' she said.

Nat nodded. 'I've had some bad luck. Anything you wanted to offer.'

Matthew ignored him and spoke to Canader. 'Did you invite him?'

'No, he was here when I got back from marketing.'

'Has he harmed you?'

She shook her head but he, more observant than Nat had ever been, could see the distress she was hiding.

'Do you want for him to stay?'

Again she shook her head.

Matthew took a few steps into the room and addressed himself to the figure lounging in his chair. 'Leave my house,' he said.

Nat, unable to believe that violent emotions could be expressed in a quiet voice, did not feel himself to be in danger and complacently admired the glint of his cheap ring in the firelight. Now that he knew Canader to be disturbed by his presence he was convinced that he would be successful and his weasel face was smug.

'Canader,' said Matthew, 'take his bag out for him. He won't need it here.'

She picked up the leather valise that stood by the wall and he held the door open for her as she went out.

'Now,' he said to Nat, as she passed. 'Will you go?'

'I did think to sup with 'ee,' Nat said. 'Talk of old times. There don't need to be any unpleasantness for Canader. Just you give me what you can spare and there won't be no gossip for—'

Matthew stooped and picked up the cane that lay on the floor. The shocks and frustrations of the day had brought him to an uncharacteristic urge to destroy. He wanted to hurt Nat but instead he held up the stick.

'This yours?' he said and without waiting for an answer he placed his fists at either end and snapped it

206

before Nat's face. He threw the splintered pieces on the fire.

'I asked you to leave,' he said, 'and leave you will.'

He grasped Nat suddenly by the collar and, pulling him out of the chair, took him by the seat of his trousers. Nat, surprised and painfully aware of Matthew's greater strength and of Canader watching from the doorway, struggled pathetically like an upturned beetle but Matthew, shaking him twice as he would chastise a puppy, ran him from the room. Canader, standing back to let them go by, saw Nat – his legs flailing and touching the ground only every second or third step – transported down the path with a look of outrage widening his eyes. It was the first time since their wedding that he had made her smile.

Matthew reached the lane. He lifted Nat so that the cloth of his coat tore and dropped him impassively into the ditch. Nat, finding himself amongst the old nettles in the rivulet that trickled through the weeds, felt Matthew's boot prod him. He turned a humiliated and mud-stained face to his attacker.

Matthew looked down on him with an expression that kept him motionless. 'I'm a patient man,' he said, 'but I can't never stomach vermin in my house. I don't want you round my wife. I don't want sight nor sound of you. And if you come here again . . .' he raised his hands and made a gesture that wrung the neck of a chicken. 'Understand me,' he said, 'and take my warning.'

CHAPTER FOURTEEN

As autumn froze into winter and cold, crisp weather, with straggling mists and ice on the water-jugs, replaced the gusty days of November there was a good measure of private tension concealed by those who had to do with Wynford Mill.

It was Beatrice, having the most to hide, who suffered most acutely and yet was the more successful in appearing to be calm. She was in good health. The morning sickness, which she had so exaggerated to prove her pregnancy, now rarely troubled her and the rounding of her figure only lent a greater ripeness which held a strong attraction for those who saw her. There was often a languor about her but it was only Thirza, always quick to see beyond her family's defences, who realized that this was the soft disguise of a rigid self-control. Her emotions were more than usually turbulent and she was sensitive to the slightest offence. The initial joy she had felt in her conception was no longer enough and, though her reason told her that she did not love Boaz, her days were full of a fervid longing for him that had constantly to be restrained.

Her relations with Daniel were outwardly improved. He could not bring himself to like her but his approval of her pleasure in her condition and a concern that his son should be born lusty led him to cosset her in physical things. The larder door was no longer locked and she was urged to eat plenty of butter, eggs and red meat. He instructed his mother not to cross her and, despite a noticeable increase of spleen in dealings with the servants, old Mrs Fayerdon managed to bridle her tongue for the sake of the coming child. This hitherto unknown lack of insult from her mother-in-law could not satisfy Beatrice. The very sight of Daniel or the old woman filled her with guilt that she was inflicting them on an innocent baby, who had done nothing to deserve such a fate. As it was her mother-in-law's habit to sit either in the kitchen or in the parlour, she took to closeting herself in the drawing-room where she stitched small gowns and brooded, now warmly on her short season of content, now painfully upon the future. At times she opened the door on to the bridge to the mill and stood looking down on yellowed reeds at the river's edge and thought of the day she had almost fallen into the race.

Daniel himself had much on his mind. He had settled comfortably into a rut of despising Beatrice and to be shaken out of it produced a confusion of spirits. It blocked one route of release for the sadistic tendencies that had flowered since his attack on her and he had not found an adequate alternative source of gratification. There was also the problem of the rumour raised by the accident of the falling tackle. The farmer who employed the injured carter had not been well pleased by the damage done to his man or his wagon and, despite the compensation he had extracted which Daniel had hoped would quiet his tongue, for the first time it was being hinted that Fayerdon did not invest enough in the upkeep of his mill.

He felt it necessary to make some gesture that would bolster his reputation as a shrewd man. The raising tackle was replaced with new, but from sheer obstinacy and an inability to admit that he was wrong, he would not make an outlay to repair the rest of the structure. His thoughts were turning in another direction. His father had left him a business which had been improved since its first purchase and he wanted his own son to inherit a concern which would be more flourishing still. With his access to good grain it seemed to him that it would be a profitable venture to add malting to his activities. There were storerooms in the mill which could easily be converted into a malthouse if their contents were transferred to the half-used buildings at the rear of the backyard. He could afford, initially, to undercut the established maltsters and was sure that the farmers who utilized his mill would be glad enough to buy their malt from the same convenient and trusted source.

It appealed to his new energy to have this project to absorb his ambition and he was so taken by the scheme that he abandoned habit and confided his plans to Beatrice. She found it curious that a man who would not put his hand in his pocket for the renovation of his existing business or for the installation of a steam engine could be so enthusiastic over something which would require an investment before it would bring a return but Daniel became so inflamed at the mention of Isaac's name that she did not question the matter. On reflection she realized that in making repairs or installing an engine Daniel would have been accepting the lead of others whereas the malthouse was a notion of his own and in this was by far the more enticing.

However, the subject of repair did not die from the mill. Matthew was not content to keep silent and wait for the next man to be hurt by Daniel's negligence. Already two men lay ill and on parish relief and, although the carter had the word of his former employer that he would be hired once more if he recovered enough to work, Samways, with a weakened arm and no character, faced a barren future and the hunger of his wife and children. Matthew's own days were now harried by anxiety over what trouble his violence towards Nat might cause but he schooled himself to act as if the event had not occurred in order to strengthen Canader. Nat had left the district without annoying them further and Matthew could do nothing but hope that he would not reappear.

In the case of the mill there was a less passive part he could play. The turning-off of Samways had put terror into the men but as the weeks passed the memory became less intense through familiarity and the increased strictness of Daniel's governance grew to be accepted as normal. It was then that Matthew began to rouse them to approach their master again on the question of safety. He knew that the whispers after the accident had worried Daniel, who prized his reputation highly, and wanted to insert a blade in this chink in his employer's armour while the wound beneath it was still raw.

A round robin asking for repairs would be the most useful method of attack. If all the men signed it and declared themselves willing to stand by each other it was unlikely that Daniel would turn every one of them off or risk a selective sacking, which might result in a withdrawal of labour that would leave his mill without a skilled man to work it. It seemed to Matthew that if Daniel did not agree to the requests he, being aware of the name of its instigator, would confine himself to getting rid of the ringleader in the hope that this would deprive the others of courage or force himself to treat the matter as a piece of inconsequent nonsense.

With impressive persuasion, Matthew slowly heartened the men. He did not promise them that their petition would be effective but each agreed the necessity for change and one by one they made their mark on the paper Matthew had prepared. The letter was sealed and so Daniel need not feel obliged to outface a messenger, was pushed beneath his door on an evening in late December.

It was this document that Daniel was fulminating against as he drove Beatrice to Bridport on the afternoon before Christmas Eve. Thirza, sensitive to her sister's unhappy home life and fearful of the result of melancholy reflections upon the merry festivals of their childhood, had particularly wanted to have Beatrice to stay with her at this time. After making the suggestion to Beatrice during one of her Tuesday calls, she had written to Daniel recommending her idea and urging him to consider the harmful effects of the river mists upon his wife's health. Henry had given his brother-in-law the note when passing through Wynford Tarrent and added his own wishes to see Beatrice enjoying the drier air to be had in town. Daniel was a little inclined to resent the invitation as an intrusion into his affairs but old Mrs Fayerdon, who had always disapproved of the expense the season brought and was jealous of Daniel's new attitude towards his wife, had seen the opportunity to reduce household costs and luxuriate in her son's company without putting her grandchild at risk. The end was that Daniel was seated beside Beatrice in the trap, driving her over the roads she had travelled so often alone, to pay a Christmas call upon the Lamfords and leave her with them until New Year's Eve. There was a white sun hanging low in a colourless sky as they mounted the rise of the hills but no warmth was imparted by it to the day. Beatrice sat with her veil down and her hood drawn up over her bonnet – more to insulate herself against her husband than the cold – watching the gulls that rode the air above brown trees and dropped with sharp cries into the fields.

Daniel was saying: 'Of course, I know who was behind it and if he'd been man enough to give it to me face to face I'd have told him so and flung it back at him. Round robin, indeed! "Beg leave to ask!" Beg leave I'm a Dutchman! If I'd realized what his manner would be – manner! Impertinence more like – I'd never have hired him. 'Twouldn't surprise me if that was the reason his last master got rid of him. I never got an answer when I wrote asking if Garth and his wife were restless at Coker – not a proper one. Round robin! I blame him for what I had to pay out for Comer's wagon. I blame him entirely. If he'd kept his mouth shut I needn't have given a penny. He'll regret he ever crossed me.'

Beatrice pulled her cloak more tightly around her.

'It's natural,' she said, 'that the accident should have made them fearful. I walked out on the bridge myself last summer and near dropped into the wheel.'

He snorted. 'The more fool you. I go where I choose in the mill and naught's befallen me.'

213

Beatrice made no reply. Daniel's reaction to the injuries of the two men had so disgusted her that she had never mentioned the subject to him before. She did not trust herself to speak now. Withdrawing her attention, she fixed her mind on her stay in a well-run home, in a well-run yard where the family was glad to see each other and no man needed to petition for his safety to be considered.

Daniel did not require a responsive companion to encourage him to give his views. He gave the pony an unnecessary slap with the reins and continued. 'I'd turn off the lot of them if I had men to take their places straight away but I haven't. There's common labourers a-plenty that could do the fetching and carrying but you can't find experienced millhands so easily. Not in numbers. There's the stones to be dressed shortly and who's to do that if not Garth? Harris can judge the grain almost as well as I can. I can't train up all the help I need, not all at once. No, I'd best say nothing of the matter – let them worry over what I'll do – and replace them when it suits me. If I get rid of Garth the others will come to heel soon enough.'

He fell silent and the rumble of the wheels on the uneven ground, the creak and rattle of the harness and the regular beat of the hooves were all the sound they carried with them until they passed Tarrendon and Beatrice heard the rhythm of her own heart. Smoke rose from the farmhouse and drifted slowly in the quiet air and far below in the valley a figure moved amongst his sheep. Beneath her cloak, Beatrice put her hand on her belly and endured the ache that was above it.

The town was crowded when they drew into it and

Daniel could not rein the pony directly in front of Arland House. He let Beatrice down as close to the door as he could and drove on alone into the yard to attend to the trap. She made her way around a stall that was selling gingerbread and comfits, enjoying the atmosphere of vitality that enlivened the scene. It refreshed her and gave her a new optimism just to be here.

The door was opened for her as soon as she had knocked and she stepped into a hall that was encumbered by baskets of holly and yew waiting to be hung about the house. There was the noise of running and shrieking from the drawing-room and, as Beatrice took off her gloves, Henry cried, 'Catch-me-who-can!' and shot into the hall pursued by his sons. Seeing her, all three changed course and gathered to greet her. There was a kissing and hugging and an asking how they did and while the maid removed Beatrice's outdoor clothes and the boys pulled her hands and skirts, she and Henry agreed in their pleasure that she had come – and that one should go to Daniel in the yard and the other to Thirza at her cooking. He took her as far as the kitchen and, opening its door, stood back for her to enter. The two boys – Arthur with the limp he would now never lose; small Henry who was taller with every visit – each had one of her hands and dragged her forward with much information to their mamma upon the subject.

The room was busy with the last preparations for the season and the scents of rosewater, mace and nutmeg filled the warm air. Beside the range, where the fire burnt red beneath half a dozen pots, the oven door was open and a girl with a long wooden spade was drawing out the breads and pies that had been baked that morning. Two more maids were carrying them to the pantry, whose shelves Beatrice could see were already heavy with dishes. A man was bringing the furze that would be burnt inside the empty oven to heat it again and in the scullery a young girl with an unquenchably cheerful nature sang as she scoured.

Thirza and Mrs Randall were standing at the table with flour to their elbows, working amongst loaves of sugar and bowls of spices, white raisins, almonds and lemon peel. Baking trays lined with brown paper stood laden with macaroons, wigs, little-cakes and jumbles and three wooden hoops were filled with plum cake. Both women were beating a further mixture each but on hearing the boys they abandoned their tasks and came forward to Beatrice.

'Mamma.'

'My love.'

'Bea, dearest.'

'Thirza.'

Again there was a clasping and kissing but this time Beatrice was drawn to a stool and disentangled from her nephews who were shooed to a board where pastry-cutters, currants and ginger-dough were waiting for them.

Mrs Randall held her daughter's face in her hands.

'You look well, my dear, but tired.' She watched Beatrice's eyes, wondering how much she could ask this secretive girl, but today all she saw was a relief painful in its intensity. 'How do you keep at the mill? Is Daniel . . .' She searched for some innocent question that would bring her the truth but found none and in the pause Beatrice heard her husband's voice, loud and with an increased gentility, in the yard.

'I live,' said Beatrice, 'and think of the future.'

Her mother took her hand away and, raising her apron, softly brushed the flour from her daughter's face.

'I'm so glad to have you here, Bea,' said Thirza, 'it seems so long since you stayed.'

Beatrice smiled. 'A good deal has happened since then. Yes, it does seem long ago.'

It added to Beatrice's sense of holiday that Daniel felt an hour's stay would be long enough to demonstrate his goodwill to the Lamfords. Thirza and Mrs Randall left their mixing to join Henry in entertaining him in the drawing-room, where he accepted hot brandy and told them at length of the presumption of his men. It was not to his satisfaction that Henry, while trying to preserve a mild tone, was in agreement that renovation should take place and when Beatrice eventually came down from her room it was to find him in no mood to extend his visit. The sight of him remounting the trap and driving out of her life for a fortnight gladdened her heart and that evening she sang her old songs at the pianoforte with a cheerfulness that delighted her family.

The following morning the house was full of laughter and anticipation. The great baking was over and the invitations to the supper to be held the next day were written and answers received. Now the decorations were to be arranged and the mistletoe-bough hung in the hall. The branches of yew and holly and bundle of laurel that George Lamford brought from his garden were garlanded about the drawing- and dining-rooms and the trail of leaves on the stairs showed how the boys thought the nursery could be improved. The last of the Christmas letters arrived and Beatrice and Thirza sat amongst the baskets, with Charlotte crawling about their feet, and read the news of friends and second-cousins twice removed.

The warmth and happy nonsense were so unlike her long hours at the mill that, when Beatrice left the house on an errand she would not disclose to the children, she felt that it must be make-believe and would not be waiting for her when she returned.

The wide street was more crowded than ever and the stallholders cried their goods with a vigour that rang in the cold air. The frost had melted where it had been most exposed to the wan sunlight but where the shadows had just fled it glistened as it died. Farmers had brought their families and there was an atmosphere of festival for those who had not come to beg.

Beatrice moved from stall to stall. She had persuaded Daniel that Henry would think him mean if she could not give the children gifts and she had money in her purse as she strolled amongst the crowd. The pleasure of choice would be spoiled if she bought too soon and so she walked the length of the street until her view of Colmer's Hill with its plume of firs was unimpeded. Her breath showed in the air and the trees on the hillsides were pale with winter as she stood between the country and the town. The stillness to one side of her and the stir to the other made life seem full of possibilities and when she turned back and began to look in earnest she felt excited and possessed of a benign inheritance for her child.

A box of soldiers, a spinning-top and a wooden doll were bargained for and bought and she made her way slowly to where she had seen the violet lozenges that Thirza liked. There was a stall selling lace between her and her object and she had paused absently to finger the wares when a voice arrested her.

A woman close by was saying regretfully, 'It's too dear.' Her words were low and full; the tones compelling.

A man answered. 'If you want it, love, you shall have it.'

The lace she held fell from Beatrice's hand and the movement, small though it was, attracted the attention of the speaker. He glanced towards it and he and Beatrice looked at one another. The woman noticed the man's sudden silence and turned to see what had distracted him.

'Boaz?' she said.

Beatrice's gaze went from her lover to his companion. She saw the white face and fervid eyes that had struck Isaac and it gave her a jealousy and sadness that exhausted her. Her hand supported her weight on the stall.

'Mistress,' Boaz bowed slightly. The pity he had felt for her was present again now that he could do nothing to protect her. 'Esther,' he said, 'this is Mrs Fayerdon, the miller's . . . Mrs Fayerdon – my wife.'

The women bent their heads to each other. Beatrice smiled. The plainness of the speech scourged and revived her. Her cloak had been thrown back from her shoulders and she drew it about her.

'Are you quite well, ma'am?' Esther asked.

Beatrice received the scrutiny of those searching eyes. She saw no suspicion in them.

'I'm not myself,' she said, 'but my sister's house is very near.' She looked again at Boaz but this time more composedly. 'I'm come to spend two weeks with Thirza. It will be a change from the mill.'

'Can I give you my arm to her door,' he said. 'If you're faint . . .'

She shook her head. 'Thank you, no. I can walk well enough.' She addressed herself to Esther. 'Your husband is generous to my family, ma'am. He carved a horse for my nephew when he was near to dying. I forget nothing of the goodness shown this summer.'

In church the following morning, rising and sitting, kneeling and singing, staring unseeing at the altar where she had sworn herself to Daniel, Beatrice began to revive. The alarm she had felt on encountering Boaz had subsided and the hours she had spent in the night considering her reaction had brought her to a rational attitude to their meeting.

It was natural, she thought, in her situation to have her spirits depressed by hearing the father of her child talk tenderly to the woman he had preferred to herself but she was already honest in her admission of mere liking for him. What she had interpreted as jealousy had only been a painful envy, an emotion without bitterness or spite and born from her yearning for the affection she had had a right to expect from her own husband. There had been a flicker of guilt when in the presence of the wife that the world would say she had wronged but it did not survive examination. Esther had left Boaz of her free will and had refused his pleas for her return. What right had she then to lament if he took his comfort elsewhere? No, she had feared discovery but not because she dreaded Esther's censure. The consequences of exposure would bring such harm to her child that, when the first shock had died down, their meeting strengthened her in her false role. Daniel, Boaz and Esther were those most nearly affected by her conspiracy; she had faced them all and drawn no accusations upon her conduct. She sat in the cold pew amongst her family, believing that she had guarded her young one well, and there was great warmth in the thought.

It was only the family party that came to table for dinner that afternoon. There were Yule logs burning in the dining- and drawing-rooms and candles lit the early dusk. The spiced beef, that Thirza had prepared for a fortnight, was carved and no-one came to grief with the snapdragon. The women in their silks, the silver, the wines, the hands reaching for the flaming raisins and, above all, the friendship that made the laughter easy, reassured and invigorated Beatrice further, so that when the guests began to come with the evening she looked more like her real self than any but Boaz had seen her for years.

George Lamford was the first to arrive. Thirza was upstairs, where the sound of Charlotte crying told its own tale of the day, and it was Beatrice who greeted him. He kissed her hand and then her cheek.

'My dear,' he said, 'it does me good to see you.' He looked at her with pleasure and she, holding her rustling sea-green skirts, turned solemnly around for him to admire as she had done as she grew. He took her arm and they walked into the drawing-room together.

'I'm early,' he said, 'but Susannah fancies the wind, as she left church this morning, has given her a chill and has taken to her bed.'

Beatrice nodded. It was long since his wife had accompanied him to an assembly and she was neither expected nor missed. She helped him to a glass of punch and they stood before the fire. The mention of his wife had put George in mind of Beatrice's absent husband.

'Will you see Daniel before he fetches you?' he asked.

'No,' said Beatrice. 'It's not likely.'

'Then I'll write. The new will is drawn up and he can sign it when he comes.'

'What will?' Beatrice had been trimming a guttering candle on the mantelpiece and now she stopped and turned an anxious face to his.

George was conscious of an annoyance with his client. He had had no wish to remind Beatrice of how little she was consulted by her husband and the fear in her eyes told him how much must occur in the mill that was never told to the Lamfords.

'Nothing to disturb you, my dear,' he said. 'But now that there'll be another generation Daniel wanted to make sure there'd be no problem about the property for any son you may have. He's appointed Henry and myself as the child's guardians if he should die. We thought you knew.'

'Knew?' said Beatrice. 'When am I told anything by him? And why should I not have care of my own child?'

'The law doesn't allow you. Suppose one of

222

Daniel's relations – of the family his father refused to see – claimed the boy? The nearest male kin would have the right.'

'And if it's a girl?'

'She would be loved by all those who love you but, I think, of less interest to the Fayerdons – although as something of an heiress there would still be the danger of interference.'

Beatrice stared across the room. George took her hand.

'Dear Bea,' he said. 'I look on you as a daughter – the years let me say that – and you're Henry's sister. We value you more than some others do. We'd be here to advise you and see to your business but we wouldn't challenge your choices for your child. Believe me, you'd have more freedom this way.'

She smiled and returned the pressure of his fingers.

'I know,' she said. 'I've no objection to you; I would just have liked to have been asked.'

There was a sound of voices and Thirza and her mother came into the room. On seeing Mrs Randall, George's hand again clasped Beatrice's, and she, looking up at him, saw first his momentarily unguarded expression and then her mother's. Her eyes went to Thirza and she, reading Beatrice's surprise, shook her head slightly in warning. George went forward to greet the women and Beatrice, alone at the hearth, felt closer to her mother than she had ever done and knew that her child was safe in George's keeping.

The room quickly filled. Guests collected and climbed volubly to adjust their dress upstairs or congregated before the fire to recover from the seasonal weather. It was not a business gathering, only friends had been invited, and there being no conversational ice to break the evening was warm in the happy intercourse of long acquaintance. It was as Beatrice was sitting on the sofa, having grown tired and refreshing herself with orange wine, that she noticed an exception to the rule of old neighbours.

Isaac Belton had come into the room and was talking to Henry in the doorway. Catching her eye, he bowed to her but being introduced to the Kayes, who were standing close by, was not able to go to her at once. As she sat, exchanging gossip with those who came to sit or stand next to her, Beatrice found that her reaction to seeing him reminded her of the meeting of George and her mother. There had been an instant lift in her spirits and an idea that all was well. She could not justify this notion and it was a new sensation to feel that she was her mother's daughter.

Some time passed before it chanced that the rising of her partner on the sofa coincided with Isaac being able to excuse himself from his company and join her. He took his place beside her with purpose and without embarrassment and it seemed to Beatrice that he had the air of a man who felt he had a right to be there. For a moment he said nothing but merely relaxed as a husband does with a wife he trusts to know his thoughts. Then, without greeting, he said, 'You look more hearty than when I saw you last.'

His accent seemed more foreign than Beatrice had remembered and she liked the sound it made.

'I'm in good health,' she said.

'So I've heard. It suits you well. And how is Fayerdon? Has he forgiven me for my opinions of his mill? We weren't polite to one another in our discussion.'

Beatrice laughed. 'He has not. He was in a rare taking after it, and still is. The men have got up a round robin petitioning for the repairs and Daniel . . . ! Of course, it was Garth behind it. There was none of this courage before he came.'

'If I were Garth,' said Isaac, 'I'd be seeking employ elsewhere.'

'What of your business?' Beatrice took a macaroon from a plate that was offered her. 'Thirza tells me you're much in demand.'

'I'm thankful to say that she's right, and you may repeat the news to your husband with my regards.' He applied himself to two of the macaroons with good appetite. The dinner at the Bull Inn, where he lodged, had been substantial but some hours ago. His severe face surveyed the crowded room as he ate. He had come ready to enjoy himself and it was not in his character to deny that the knowledge that Beatrice would be present had added to his anticipation. The district, the people and the trade he had found were all to his liking and it had been a particular pleasure to have formed a bond with the Lamfords, at whose home he had spent several agreeable evenings. He did not forget that it had been Beatrice who had promoted their meeting and owned honestly to himself that he would have preferred her to be unmarried. It seemed to him a destructive waste that she should be in Daniel's hands and did not doubt that she was a woman who would flourish with a man who appreciated her.

'But, serious,' he said, 'I heard of the accident with the pulley. You should try to bend Fayerdon to make changes or it'll not only be those two who're hurt.'

'What can I do? You saw my position.'

'It's changed. You may have a son. There're some investments which may take long to mature but are worth the waiting. If your husband's mother had said buy an engine he would have bought. Why should it not be the same for you? The Jesuits say: give me a child until he's seven years old and he's mine for the rest of his life. You're a clever woman. Secure your influence from the cradle.' He looked down from her eyes to her lap. 'You're crumbling that fancy on your gown. Is there nothing more substantial to eat?'

Beatrice brushed the fragments of the macaroon into her palm and dropped them into a dish on the side-table. She was unused to such plain speaking and, though shaken, admitted its sound advice. It was not what she wanted from life but it was the best that she could do.

'There's supper in the dining-room,' she said.

'Then, shall we go?' He rose and offered her his arm and they made their way through the other guests. The hall was empty; conversation filtered from rooms to each side but here it seemed quiet and dusky, despite the branches of candles at the walls. Isaac glanced at the mistletoe-bough that was tied in the centre and drew her towards it. She hung back a little but followed him.

'I think,' she said, as they stood beneath the white berries, 'that this is for the family not for any gentleman.'

'But,' said Isaac, 'I've never been a gentleman.' He looked enquiring. 'Do you say no?'

'I don't,' she said.

He bent and kissed her. She found the diversion

226

firm and brief and not at all unpleasing. Straightening, he took her arm back into his.

'You must be an excellent business woman,' he said, 'for I find that I'm in your debt.'

Beyond the dark hills, in the woods beneath Tarrendon, a faint light was to be seen in an upper room of the old house where Boaz now lived with his wife. Towards midnight, the reddish glow that shone from the window was obscured by a figure looking out into the copse.

It was a still night. There was a half-moon but its brightness did not dim the brilliancy of stars that pricked a sky free of any cloud. The cold was bitter and a frost that had lingered all day was white on the branches of the leafless trees. Inside, the room was warm. The fire that he had built hours before was now only smouldering but, though a chill coming from the glass touched his chest, Boaz could stand naked at the window without discomfort.

He was at peace with the quietness on which he looked. Behind him, against linen as white as the frost, Esther lay in their bed. She watched him as he stood with the glimmer of the dying fire on his skin and her eyes had more softness in them than was usual for her. She had committed herself to him and was content.

Their day had not been social; they had not gone to church or paid visits; no-one had come to their house. It had been as they intended, a day for themselves alone. They had walked in the crisp meadows, arm within arm; they had dined with Esther's hair black against the lace of the collar he had bought for her in Bridport. It was a day of

227

expectation and in its evening he had taken her hand to lead her to this room and they had lain together for the first time since her return.

For two months, as rumours of her presence spread about the country and tradesmen found excuse to come to the farm to see her for themselves, she and Boaz had lived as if he were her brother. At first they had spoken with a scrupulous courtesy and paid a delicate deference to each other's wishes. Esther's love and need of him had not been diminished by their reunion but she was shy of the pain her desertion had caused and of the desire for his affection that was as urgent as if she had never been his wife. Boaz could not be open with her. His want for her to stay was barbed with resentment and guilt. He believed that he had not dealt fairly with Beatrice and that in his use of her both he and Esther were to blame. He was not a man to wear disgrace lightly and he could not look in Esther's starving eyes without seeing the part her flight had played in making him shameful.

It seemed in those early weeks that they were too separate to be joined but gradually, as they went about the ordinary business of the days, the impatient humour and small criticisms of those who trust their friends grew into their behaviour and this familiarity unlocked their tenderness. As Boaz watched the ice glitter on the sun-dial in the hidden garden, where his wife would grow her herbs, he felt there was not space enough in that cold sky to hold their love.

He turned back into the room and piled new logs on the soft wood-ash in the hearth. Crossing to the bed, he lifted the cider that stood on the oak floor, offering it to Esther. When she shook her head, he drank before returning to her. She held back the covers for him and he lay, half-sitting, one arm about her as she leant her shoulder against his chest. Her hair was unbound and he drew out a strand, pulling and releasing its natural spring.

Esther felt the warmth come back into him as she rested against him. She wondered whether she would conceive and thought of the life they and their children could have together. Events of the past days went through her mind and she said, 'The miller's wife. She's not a happy woman.'

There was a silence before Boaz replied. 'No,' he said, 'I think she isn't.'

'And I believe she's interested by you.' Esther raised her hand and brushed her knuckles against his cheek. He took her fingers and held them to his lips. She moved her head in the hollow of his neck. 'But she'll soon have other things to think on,' she said. 'I hope she'll be less lonely then. Her eyes . . .'

Boaz moved the hand that he held. 'What will she have?' he asked.

Esther laughed softly in the darkened room. 'Boaz! She's with child. Didn't you see?'

Her talk roved on, touching on this and that, a drowsy discourse spoken out of the comfort of their connection. Soon she slept but Boaz did not sleep and long before the dawn he rose so that she would not see him when she woke.

CHAPTER FIFTEEN

The season of goodwill was a source of pleasure to Daniel, as well as to his wife, for not only were he and his mother able to celebrate with the parsimony they thought proper to the festival but his plans to become a maltster began to take root.

He had heard that a certain Jos Dalby, the owner of a small brewery in Charminster, wanted to expand his business and, unable to compete alone with the Dorchester brewers, had hopes of a fellow investor. On 27 December Daniel called at Dalby's home and before he had retrieved Beatrice from her family a project had been provisionally agreed upon, although neither participant was yet willing to be asked for a signature.

The prospect was so absorbing that Daniel wrote delaying Beatrice's return and on New Year's Eve rode out towards the Sydlings in pursuit of his fortune. The day was somewhat milder than the previous weeks had been and the icy wind that cut through travellers had dropped but it was not an easy journey that he undertook. His route lay along the narrow lanes and sharp descents that crossed the downs to Cerne Abbas and here his horse's hooves slipped on the frozen surfaces of shaded ruts and there were pulled by the clinging mud of thaw. The ford beneath Cowdown Hill was running high between edges of ice cracked by the passage of carts and he could persuade his mare through it only by the use of his whip.

He passed three men cleaning turnips for cattle and in the fields bedraggled figures, made sexless by indiscriminate layers of clothing, spread dung and picked stones but beyond this he was solitary and, hunched within his great-coat, he had nothing to divert his thoughts from his object.

There was an inn on the west side of Cerne whose landlord had died in the autumn. His wife had continued the business herself but word had reached Dalby that she disliked the responsibility and although not actively seeking a buyer, would be glad enough to sell if an offer were made. If they found the property promising it was the intention of Daniel and his partner to take on the inn and use it as a tied house for Dalby's ales. Daniel was to provide half the capital and to have the monopoly of selling malt to the brewer when his proposed maltings were in operation. It was a plan which combined mutual benefit with certain unformed designs in Daniel's mind upon the eventual ownership of the brewery. Novelty, he had discovered, was a stimulant.

He found Dalby wrapped in a rug in a hooded gig some distance from the inn. They had agreed to enter the premises together as if they were ordinary wayfarers so that Daniel, who had never had cause to enter the Three Bells, could take its measure without encouragement from its mistress. Dalby was a sharp-featured man of middle years who, although always well-kempt, was given a slightly unsavoury appearance by the harsh tufts of hair that grew in his nose and ears. He considered himself in his prime and did not regret exchanging the unregulated enthusiasm of youth for the steady energy of maturity. He had married late a matter-of-fact young woman who admired his abilities and had given him a son and two daughters in rapid succession. A common desire to improve their offspring's inheritance united the two men, although neither was likely to become eloquent upon the subject.

He had been waiting in the gig for twenty minutes and the cold had brought out a pattern of thread veins upon his bleached face. Flexing his fingers in his dog-skin gloves, he beat his hands together as Daniel rode up.

'Fayerdon,' he said. 'A hard ride today.'

'I've known worse,' Daniel checked his mare who was delicately touching the quarters of Dalby's cob with a steaming muzzle. 'Is all well with you?'

'It is. And your wife?'

'I hear she's in health. Shall we go in?'

Daniel turned about and together they approached the inn. It was a decently sized and moderately tended building of stone and thatch standing beside its small stable-yard between two dwelling-houses. It was the first hostelry that Daniel had passed since the Sydlings and, despite its position on the edge of Cerne, it was not so far from the main street that it would not gain custom if it built a reputation for fine ale.

A pinched lad emerged from an outbuilding at the sound of hooves and having read his customers' faces and decided that there would be no tip in the transaction, took charge of the horses without eagerness. Daniel and Dalby entered the inn by a side-door. A passage whose walls had been yellowed by tobacco smoke led them into a parlour where a fire was burning and the small windows were blurred with condensation. An X had been drawn in the moisture on one pane but the seat beside it was empty and the signatory not apparent.

The parlour was not crowded but there were five or six men sitting at tables, talking desultorily, with an air of being settled in for the afternoon. They were not labourers, looking more like small tradesmen, and this and the fact that there were two newspapers amongst them was an encouragement to the potential buyers who did not want impoverished clients. The room was shabby but warm and welcoming in a public way and through its open door they could see across the hall into another room from which smoke and voices eddied.

A woman coming out of the other room with a tray of glasses caught sight of the strangers standing in the parlour and came in to take their order. Daniel and Dalby had previously agreed upon a bowl of punch as a drink that would give them ample excuse to linger in comfort and the instruction was given.

'We'll take it through there,' Daniel nodded at the larger room.

The maid was leaving when Dalby stopped her with a word.

'It'll be heavy work for you tonight, girl,' he said, 'if you're alone. Does your mistress serve?'

'She does, sir, when she be able. She's lying down now. She don't have the strength she used to.'

The two men exchanged a satisfied glance and crossed the hall into the second room. This chamber was longer than the first and was more full. They took chairs at an empty table and observed the company.

The customers here were rather younger than in the parlour and had the look of being the sons of comfortable farmers. From the noise and number of empty jugs they had apparently been celebrating the new year for some time and were in a mood to be entertained by mocking the misfortunes of others. They were now directing their attention to a figure in a dirty, green apron who was squatting on a low stool, ineffectually cleaning the brass fender and fire-dogs. This man was obviously something of a side-show to the drinkers and was being urged to talk by a seemingly friendly solicitude whilst winks passed amongst his audience whenever he looked down at his task.

It was another good indication of the landlady's loss of control that morning work should have drifted to past noon and it was this that first fixed Daniel's eyes on the servant but, having begun to watch he could not help overhearing, and for lack of other diversion, let his concentration rest on the action about the hearth.

'So,' said a fleshy young man, leaning back in the settle, 'if I told you I'd a mind to get wed what would you advise me?'

The serving-man raised a sour, weasel face to the speaker and shook his head.

'That you'd do better to nurse a viper in your bosom, sir, that you would, for womenkind are as scheming and ungrateful as ever was a dog that did bite your hand when you gave it meat.'

'And are they faithful, Nat? Could I trust my bride if I turned my back?'

'That you couldn't. Females are as like as peas in a pod and a bitch on heat is nothing to 'em.'

The fleshy youth sighed and his neighbour on the settle pulled down a striped waistcoat that had ridden up as he slumped and lifted a flagon. Nat stared at the jug with parted lips.

'You were married yourself,' said the waistcoat. 'A sorry business. Will you take another glass of gin and tell us of your troubles?'

Nat held up a tumbler that had been sitting at his feet and watched it being filled. The third youth poured in water and Nat drank half in a draught.

'Aye,' he said, 'I married a maid years a-gone, as idle and shiftless a red-headed—'

The door which Dalby had closed was pushed open and the woman came in with a punch-bowl, ladle and cups. In the setting out of the table and talk with Dalby, Daniel lost the conversation around the fire. When he was free to listen again the fleshy youth was saying sorrowfully, '—and so you thought you'd be well rid of her and you sold her like the beast she was?'

'That I did. I—'

Here Nat's reminiscence was interrupted by a shout of 'Thomas-a-Didymus, hard of belief'. The reciter beat time on a table with his tankard and the rest of the group began to stamp their feet and chant with him.

'Sold his wife for a pound of beef.
When the beef was eaten, good lack,
Thomas-a-Didymus wished her back.'

As they came to an end a voice from the corner began:

'Nebuchadnezzar, the King of the Jews,
Sold his wife for a pair of shoes,
When the—'

But a stronger tongue interrupted and drove him out:

'Little Dicky Dilver,
Had a wife of silver,
He took a stock and broke her back,
And sold her to the miller.
The miller wouldn't have her—'

It paused and, with a roar, the company joined in:

'So he threw her in the river!'

Nat, oblivious to the ridicule, finished his glass and wiped his mouth with the back of his hand.

'But,' he said, a mordant self-pity in his tones, ''tweren't she that got thrown. I was swindled and threatened and when I tried to forgive her her fancy-man sets about me. Miller! It's the miller I did ought to have sold her to not the miller's man. River's the best place for her.'

The maid returned to the room. Two of the youths whispered together as they looked at her and laughed with bared teeth.

'Nat,' the woman spoke to him as if it were only because she had been ordered, 'missus wants to know why the water bain't drawn. She d'say you've been in here long enough.'

She turned on her heel before he could reply and, muttering to himself, he collected his pots and rags and followed her, leaving the brass no cleaner than when he had begun.

The drinkers relapsed into gossip amongst themselves and were joined by others of their kind, who entered with loud comments on the weather. The landlady did not appear and Daniel and Dalby sat and took their punch, considering her absence, the free spending of the young men – who from their familiarity seemed to meet as regulars – and the slackness of the service. When their bowl was drained, they went out into the yard and looked into the stables while their horses were brought. Daniel rode beside Dalby's gig to the main street where a brief exchange of views found them in agreement. They were to meet at the brewery two days hence to discuss their offer and approach the mistress of the inn.

Dalby, well wrapped in his rug, drove away towards Charminster and Daniel rode back along the road towards the Sydlings but when he came to the inn he did not pass it. Instead, he turned into the yard and once more gave his mare into the lad's keeping. He found the maid in the small parlour, wiping the tables. One of the tradesmen had gone and the others had gathered round the fire to play cards. Thinking he must have forgotten something, the woman dried her hands on her apron and came up to Daniel.

'That odd-job man,' he said, 'Nat. Fetch him to me.'

The maid nodded. 'Will you take anything more, sir?'

'What does this Nat drink?'

She laughed shortly. 'It d'just have to be wet.'

'I saw him with gin. Bring that and two glasses.'

He seated himself at the window, beneath the cross

that was now misted over, and waited. An excitement was stirring in him as it does in a huntsman who sees the stag begin to falter and be gained upon by the hounds. A red-headed . . . The miller's man. He remembered his mother urging him to discover why Garth had left his old employ to take a lower wage; he thought of no mention of Garth's wife by his previous master; he thought of Canader, helping Beatrice in his house, her red hair gleaming. There was a sound in the passage and Nat came in, looking sly. He held the tray of gin in his hands. Daniel indicated the chair beside him and Nat sat down. The sight of this paltry figure, so plainly a wastrel, filled Daniel with a malicious glee. If he held information that could hurt Garth it would be a simple matter to obtain it and worth the expense. He filled the glasses and pushed one to Nat.

'Your health,' he said.

CHAPTER SIXTEEN

Beatrice was brought home by Daniel on a cheerless afternoon of squalling rain in mid-January. She had been invigorated by her stay with the Lamfords and, although beginning to be slower and more stately in her movements, was feeling stronger than she had been before. At first it was a relief to her to find that Daniel had recovered from the agitation of spirits caused by the round robin but as she settled back into the mill she became uneasy.

There was something in Daniel's manner that smacked of a secret triumph and she could not guess the reason. Learning that he and Dalby were bargaining with the landlady of the Three Bells and were confident of achieving their end, she hoped that it was this that was causing his excitement but there was a furtive satisfaction colouring his mood that seemed not to belong to a simple business deal and to be more sinister. It was natural that she should immediately suspect that he had discovered her deception and was storing his knowledge to use against her when he thought her most vulnerable but his concern for his coming son had hardly diminished and there was definitely an expected pleasure involved in this puzzle that did not accord with finding himself a cuckold.

Daniel himself was suffering no uneasiness. The inn alone would have been enough to cheer him but to find that its investigation should have put him in a position to carry out an act of supreme malice against the man who had become the thorn in his flesh gave him an unnatural elation that was not quite sane. He had always believed that God was on his side and now it seemed to him that it was Providence that had caused Nat Brinsley to fall into his path.

The afternoon that Daniel had arrived looked to prove profitable to them both. A gentleman inviting him to drink was to Nat a signal for business best spoken of quietly and his intuition was that Daniel was approaching him on matters that would interest the excise-men. It had been a considerable but agreeable surprise to have a man of Daniel's obvious calibre probing him, with a sympathetic concern, for details of his unfortunate marriage. The attention was flattering and during the course of that after-noon, as the early dusk closed in and the wind rose, he told the stranger every detail of the affair. He spoke of the day he had taken Canader to Coker Mill for her health and Garth had seen her; he spoke of the clandestine meetings between his wife and her lover; he spoke of the loss of his job and the advantage Garth had taken of his fear of poverty; he spoke of the sale on Tarrendon Hill where he was persuaded out of the woman who could have still been his – and with each revelation he watched the blood come into the gentleman's face and a light into his eyes.

It had alarmed Nat at last to discover who Daniel was but consolation was at hand. It appeared that he and Daniel were in accord on the subject of Matthew's villainy and, as Daniel poured their spirits and ordered cold beef, they agreed on the need for punishment. Nat found his new friend curiously insistent upon whether there had been witnesses to the sale and, feeling that his honesty was in question, put a hand to his heart beneath its dirty linen and swore that, though the place had been lonely, the circumstances had been as he recounted them.

It was then that Daniel had begun to tell him of the law.

Her husband's preoccupation was an advantage to Beatrice for had his mind been free to concentrate upon her it was unlikely that he would have allowed her to resume her solitary drives. Her condition was so much more obvious in January than it had been the month before that it was with some trepidation that she slipped to the stable to order the trap but Daniel had ridden out on an unexplained errand, without learning of her intention, and only the mutterings of old Mrs Fayerdon followed her from the house.

The hours spent with her sister refreshed the fortitude that had begun to flag in the week she had now endured at the mill and she was able to begin her return journey with resolution. Thirza, anxious for her safety, had urged her to leave in time to arrive before darkness fell but twilight was advancing upon the hills as she left the town behind. The cold that had begun to decrease at New Year had grown again and the lanes were hard and ringing beneath the pony's hooves. An indeterminate sky that was neither grey nor white but had a faint red flush in the west hung over a landscape that was still and frozen in its winter sleep. The silence of the season made the road seem more than usually isolated and its separateness from mankind seemed so poignantly to underline her own position that, for once, Beatrice found it to prey upon her nerves. That part of her route that led to Tarrendon always made her heart beat with more force and today, as she drove the high sweep of the downs, she felt Esther's presence more keenly than before they had met. She looked out over the drop to the coombe and, though her eyes saw the far hills, misty and one-dimensional in the pale colours of dusk, her imaginings were in the house in the copse far beneath her where her child had had its beginning.

So absorbed was she in picturing the life in which she had no place that she did not notice the horseman waiting beside the track until she was almost upon him. It startled her to see Boaz on this road. He knew the habits of her travel and she had expected him to avoid any chance of their meeting, yet he sat his cob in the opening of the green lane to the fort and it was plain that he did so with purpose.

He did not ride into the road but stirred and became alert in a manner that told her that he had been waiting for her and she drew in the trap when she came abreast of him. They looked at one another without greeting and then he encouraged the cob and it moved with the reluctance of one who has been standing long in the cold and came up to her side. She was glad to see him. After practising such deception upon Daniel she was ashamed of how clearly she had revealed her feelings when she had met Boaz with Esther. She wanted to show that she was composed when near him and no danger to his marriage. Her hands tightened on the reins so that the thin leather of her gloves was taut and strained but although there was emotion in her face it gave away no secrets.

Boaz tried to read her expression. She was wrapped in her cloak and its folds made it impossible for him to tell how far she was from her time. Pity had always been part of his tenderness for her and it and admiration moved him strongly now. What was the origin of the child she carried? Had she begun to suffer bearing the family of a man who had only contempt for her or was this the result of the day he had told her he would see her no more? In either case she must believe herself abused yet she went about her daily life with the hidden courage that excites no remark from its neighbours. If he himself were the father she must have realized her plight in the same weeks that news of Esther had begun to spread abroad. Had she intended to come to him and been prevented by word of his wife? Had she lain awake in the dark hours as he had done since Esther had casually laughed at his lack of observation? Had her mind chased its guilt?

'I was waiting for you,' he said.

'Yes.'

She found it hard to speak. Now that they were again alone she was afraid of the power of her desire to confide in him. She wanted to cry out – this is yours, ours – are you pleased? Are you proud? What harm could one brief moment of his interest and sympathy do?

'My . . . I've been told that you're with child.' His cob shifted slightly beneath him but he did not move his eyes from hers.

'Yes,' she said.

'Is it mine?'

243

His voice was calm and soft. She thought how much threat could have been put into those words to women such as she, in lonely places with night closing round. In the wood below, his wife moved about his house and here she was near him, without passion, with knowledge in her heart, and was not sorry for the consequence of what they had done.

'No,' she said.

The silence on the hills seemed to intensify as she waited for him to speak, then small sounds broke and increased it, a sheep-bell clanged on the hillside, a wind in the valley moaned and died. He took her hand.

'Can I believe you?' he asked.

She closed her fingers on his. 'Do you think I wouldn't rather it was yours? You've kept one secret of mine. Couldn't I have trusted you with another?'

'If you had needed me I would have been there for you whatever the cost to us all.'

They were so close that their breath mingled as it hung in the air. She held fast to his hand and was grateful for her capacity for lies.

'This last year has been hard on you,' he said.

She smiled. 'I am no coward.'

'No, love, that you're not.'

She wanted to be sure that this sacrifice, which was so painful to her, was to good cause. 'You and your wife,' she said, 'are you happy together?'

'Yes,' he did not want to hurt her by evasion, 'as much as we're able. I think Esther wasn't formed for happiness, but you were. God give you joy of your child.'

He lifted the hand that he held and pressed it to his lips and in the shadows of the lane, a furze-cutter

244

walking slowly home saw them together, occupied and earnest, and remembered a summer's day when a shepherd had told him that the miller's wife had taken a wrong turning and driven to Holt's farm alone.

CHAPTER SEVENTEEN

Throughout the next months Beatrice waited. Frosts came and thickened the windows of the house with ice, as the mill thickened its own with dust, and she thought that next year she would heat a penny on the fire and press it to the pane to make a peep-hole for her child, as her mother had done for her. Thaws came, the river rose and one morning the cellar where Boaz had carried her wine was deep in water to its first shelf. The blackthorn budded and the birds returned.

She moved more slowly and spoke little now but she was not down-hearted. As she had told her lover, she was no coward and she did not regret this change in her circumstance. She remembered Isaac's plain-spoken advice and her determination to forge her own pattern of life for the child did not waver. Quietly and stubbornly, she lived with her secret, ignoring her mother-in-law and being civil to her husband. She was less troubled by Daniel's interest in her condition than she had been before Christmas. He was as triumphant over the advent of his son as he had been but was more used to the idea and had other matters to distract him. She constantly feared that he would put an end to her drives but nothing was said by him beyond the remark that it would be best to stay at home when she was near her time and to this she vaguely assented in order to deflect discussion.

Those who considered themselves her real family did not grow less concerned by her plight as the months progressed and, despite their knowledge of her dislike of them seeing her at the mill, Thirza and Mrs Randall drove out one late February morning when the snowdrops were wet beneath the dripping trees to call on her. The experiment was not a success. Beatrice, afraid that if this became a habit Daniel would think there was no need for her to go to Bridport, sat stiff and uncomfortable in the chilly drawing-room while old Mrs Fayerdon sat in a corner, knitting in a pointed manner and complaining of the price of tea. After the visit, Henry looked at his timetable and arranged that his men should be passing through Wynford Tarrent on the days of Beatrice's drives, so that there should always be one who could be left at the mill to ride with her.

It was a decision which would have irked Beatrice if Daniel had ordered it but to have the matter so settled out of love for her put a different face upon it. She gave up her solitude and as she drove the high road above the farm, where Esther sang as she waited for Boaz to come in, towards the house where her sister waited and Isaac often called to ask how Mrs Fayerdon did, she found she enjoyed the companionship of men who shared her goodwill for the Lamfords.

This uneventful passing of the weeks was not shared by Daniel. For him, life was bright with activity and enterprise. The elation that Beatrice had recognized in him when she returned in January was still present but was better hidden by the zeal with which he pursued his new business venture and by the complacency that was growing upon him as the world seemed to turn his way.

There was great bustle in the yard now. The purchase of the inn was progressing well and the maltings were being built within the mill, just as Daniel had planned. Not a man to hire two workmen where one could manage nor to let an opportunity for spite to escape him, he had taken advantage of Matthew's knowledge of carpentry and given his foreman the extra duties of managing the alterations without any increase of wages. He was encouraged by Matthew's acquiescence and by the absence of any reaction to his ignoring of the round robin and told his wife that he had taught Garth a lesson by standing firm. In truth, what Matthew had learnt was that the millhands were too spiritless and defeated to make any further attempts to improve their own lives. He and Canader were now completely decided that there was no future for them here and he was merely biding his time until spring before he searched for better employ.

Had the inn and maltings been Daniel's only occupation he would have been a busy man but they were not. He had Matthew and Canader's secret safely in his keeping and because he had not yet moved against them did not mean that he felt more kindly towards Matthew. On the contrary, the knowledge that he could deal Garth a devastating blow fanned the flames of his malice and he cherished his ill will, feeding the rancour that festered within him and holding this cruelty in abeyance until he had completed his professional transactions, as he would keep back a jar of fine brandy to savour at leisure.

His anticipation was not idle. He had no illusions that Nat was an honest man and he did not want his actions to leave him seeming foolish. He wrote again to Matthew's old master at Coker Mill, asking particularly whether there had been a Mrs Garth at the time of the foreman's departure and received the answer that there had not. He rode to the Yeovil church where Nat claimed that he had married Canader and consulted the records that confirmed this was so. Unwilling to justify his enquiries to George Lamford, he went to a shabby lawyer in a run-down street in Dorchester and heard for himself what he had already impressed on Nat – that a man who has carnal relations with another's wife has committed an offence and may have a civil action taken against him to claim damages but that a wife-sale protected the buyer from being prosecuted because it was proof of the husband's agreement to adultery. Nat swore that he had invented the sale to prevent himself looking small and Daniel, knowing Tarrendon Farm to have been deserted in April and genuinely incensed by Canader, who had injured his deeply-felt views on a wife's subservience and loyalty to her husband, agreed to provide the money to bring a case against Garth. As the final week of March drew to a close the decision was made that the time was ripe.

At a quarter to seven in the morning on the last Friday in March an unusual procession was to be seen approaching the Garths' cottage. It consisted of Daniel Fayerdon on horseback, Mr Bryant, the Dorchester solicitor in an unwieldy and old-fashioned closed carriage, two muscular and badly-shaven men, whom Bryant found useful on these occasions, mounted on hired nags and Nat Brinsley and the parish constable on foot. The sun had begun to rise an hour before and in its cold light it was noticeable that very different expressions were to be found on the participants' faces.

A look that could only be described as unholy triumph was evident not only on Daniel's features but in the very hold of his body as he rode at the head of the group. It was repeated in Nat's eyes, as he straggled behind the carriage, blowing on his hands, but was as often replaced by a shifty diffidence that did not make the constable any happier about the duty he was to perform. Boredom was the only state of mind apparent in the two henchmen and, if a passerby had been able to see inside the conveyance, he would have seen on their master's face the bland acceptance of one who, while glad to have a profitable occupation, would have preferred not to be about it so early.

Drawing in before the cottage, the riding horses were tied quietly to the rear of the carriage and the driven mare to the hedge. Daniel gave a nod and strode down the path with the others, displaying varying degrees of briskness, behind him. Reaching the door, he did not knock but thrust it open and advanced into the room.

Inside, Matthew, who had heard footsteps and was rising from the table to answer the door, was taken by surprise. It angered him to have anyone enter his house so unceremoniously but seeing that it was Daniel, who had never yet felt that courtesy should be shown to his workmen, he bridled his tongue. The influx of these strangers, the constable and Nat warned him that this was no ordinary visit and he kept silent from policy. He glanced at Canader, who had been fetching hot water from the fire, and she, dressed but her hair still loose, laid the kettle on the hob and came close to him.

'Matthew Garth,' said Daniel, 'you are charged with holding criminal conversation with Canader, the wife of Nathanial Brinsley, and with assault upon Brinsley when he called to retrieve the woman. We have a warrant for your arrest. You will be held in Dorchester gaol until you come to trial.' Up to this moment he had preserved a severe countenance but now he allowed himself a smile that was more the baring of a hyena's teeth than a sign of amusement. 'A prison sentence for the assault, I think, and a pretty compensation for the destruction of your trollop's virtue. Can you pay for your pleasure or will you wait long in a debtor's cell?'

Matthew was rigid with anger. He expected no justice from this motley collection of men and there was a sinking in his heart as he thought what this could mean for Canader but he was determined to show no fear.

'There was no adultery,' he said. 'I bought my wife from this man,' he pointed at Nat, who had taken care to remain near the wall, sheltered by the constable, 'for five sovereigns. 'Twas on Tarrendon Hill in plain sight.'

'Lying!' Nat's voice was excited, 'there weren't no-one.' Daniel directed a sudden, venomous glance at him so that he stepped back until his shoddy, checked suit rubbed the whitewash. 'There weren't no sale. So I d'swear. No sale at all.'

Canader, her hand on Matthew's arm and a sickness within her, could not bear to hear Nat's words.

'How can you say that?' she cried. 'You dragged me to that hill with a rope about my neck. You sold me. Like a beast . . . a beast of the field! You were glad enough of the gold. Tell the truth, you wastrel!'

'There weren't no sale. No—' Nat protested again but Mr Bryant, in contemptuous tones, interrupted him and addressed Matthew.

'You have your story,' he said, 'but do you have witnesses? I think not.'

A bitter regret mingled with Matthew's anger. He had wanted to spare Canader the pain of notoriety a wife-sale could bring; he had thought to protect her by the loneliness of the hill. God, that he had insisted on the old customs – the crowded market-place, the wearing of the halter on the road to the sale, the public auction. Too late, too late to be sorry now.

Daniel and Bryant exchanged a look and Bryant nodded sharply at his escorts. The two men leapt forward and grappled Matthew, bending him over the breakfast table to tie his hands. A cup rolled to the edge and fell, splashing Canader's skirts as it smashed. Realizing how futile it would be, Matthew did not struggle but as Canader leant over him, protecting his face from the board, he said hurriedly, 'Dear heart, I'll find you. Trust me. However long . . .' before he was dragged to the door and down the path to the carriage.

Canader tried to follow. Bryant and the constable went out after the captive but Daniel blocked the doorway as she struggled to run through.

She pushed against him and he took her by the throat and held her against the wall.

'And you,' he said, viciously, 'whore! Polluting my house! A whipping is what you should have.' Still

252

holding her by the neck he shook her as he heard the carriage-wheels move away, banging her head against the wall so that flakes of the whitewash dropped to the floor. Nat, standing by, watched with a smile. 'Go back to your husband and make what amends you can. And don't think to run away. I've helped him take out an order to have his rights restored to him and, by heaven, I'll have you stay. You're vile, loathsome. A woman with no respect for her duties. I can't abide it.' He threw her towards Nat, with a gesture of disgust, and she stumbled against a stool. 'Here,' he said to Nat, who grabbed at her as she half-fell, 'take her. Shameless, a harlot. Make her know her place.'

He went from the house, eager to accompany the prisoner to the gaol. Nat, holding Canader by the arms, watched him go. He had enjoyed seeing her made wretched. It made him feel lascivious. She was a handsome woman and must obey him now. He stroked her hair that had fallen forward over her shoulders and wound it about his finger.

'Don't touch me!'

He was startled by her voice. There was no subjection in it. It was strong and full of hatred. He looked at her face and her eyes made him free her.

'Do you think I don't know why you d'want me back?' she said. 'To earn for 'ee, what else?' She wanted to snatch up a knife from the table and plunge it into him but her mind was working rationally. If I run from him I must keep hidden and then how will Matthew find me if he's released? Better to stay until the trial. Discover the outcome. If it's debtors' prison, then I'll run. Away from here,

253

Nottingham. Make lace and save every penny to buy him out. Wait my time. 'Well,' she said, 'well? That's it, bain't it? I'll work for 'ee, right enough. You'll get your money's worth. But touch me – make one move to touch me – and there the work ends. Understand? I'll let us both starve. Why didn't I do it before? Better to be dead from hunger than in your hands. Believe me.'

CHAPTER EIGHTEEN

It was a surprised clerk who opened the door to
Beatrice at George Lamford's offices the next morning. Mr Moorehead had noticed a junior, standing at
a desk by the window, look into the street with
interest and, on following his gaze, had seen Beatrice
driving her trap in a reckless manner through the
other traffic towards them. She had called out to a
boy as she drew in and, as he held her pony's head,
she had lowered herself to the road and hurried to the
office door with an agitation that was not suitable to
her advanced condition.

For the greater part of his sixty years Mr Moorehead
had worked for the present and previous George
Lamfords and was well acquainted with his master's
relations. Like George, he had a fondness for
Beatrice, who had been such a friendly and vivacious
girl, and it alarmed him to see her in obvious distress.
He reached the door in time to open it as she put her
hand to the knocker and supported her against his
shoulder as she clutched at him. Her face had lost all
colour and she was breathing rapidly. The two
juniors had come from their desks and Moorehead
looked at one of them.

'Call Mr Lamford,' he said. 'And, Powell,' he
spoke to the one who had first noticed Beatrice, 'take
Mrs Fayerdon's other arm. Help her through.' The
young man put his arm about her waist and, grasping

her free hand in his, began to walk her to the inner office from which George now emerged.

'No need, no need,' protested Beatrice but, on seeing George's expression, she felt overwhelmed by the concern being shown for her and allowed herself to be drawn into the master's sanctum and placed in a chair.

At a signal, the juniors left the room. George filled a glass with water from a jug on the sill and handed it to her while Moorehead took down three volumes of legal reference and placed them beneath her feet, with such serious and portly attention that she could not help but smile.

'I'm not ill,' she said, though her voice did not verify her claim. 'A little giddy – I drove so fast. I was upset, out of breath.'

She drank half of the water and George replaced the glass with a smaller one of port.

'My dear,' he said, 'what brings you here like this? How can I help you?'

'Will you take off your cloak, Mrs Fayerdon?' Moorehead asked. 'And let the warmth reach you?' He moved another chair that stood between her and the fire.

George took her wine while she untied the cloak and let it fall back around her seat. As a second thought she took off her hat and George laid it on his desk.

'I'm not cold,' she said. 'I hardly know what I am. I need—' Her face contracted as if she was about to cry but, instead, she raised her gloved hand and made an angry gesture with her fist. 'This must be in confidence,' she went on. 'It's very personal.'

Moorehead looked at George and glanced at the

door with raised eyebrows. George nodded. When his clerk had gone, he pulled the moved chair close to Beatrice and took her hand. She had finished her wine and was twirling the glass by its stem between finger and thumb as she tried to decide how to approach the matter.

'You may trust me,' said George. 'And don't be afraid of anything you have to say. In my profession, nothing will be new to me.'

She placed the glass on his desk and took a deep and shuddering breath.

'Daniel doesn't know I'm here,' she said. 'He musn't know. I'll have been visiting Thirza – a sudden need.'

'That's where you will have been,' said George. 'None of us will have seen you here.'

She pressed his hand as she had often done as a child when he had brought her a sweetmeat to soothe her troubles but when she spoke it was with a bitter irony that he had not heard before.

'My husband is a brave and victorious man,' she said. 'He's exerted a moral influence and right has prevailed. A good man lies in gaol and a good woman is forced back to a rogue but the work of the Lord is done. "Wives submit yourselves to your husbands." Oh, yes.' She looked out of the window at a square of lawn and laurels. 'He told me last night. He has a foreman, Matthew Garth – you know, I've spoken of him – his wife, Canader, was to have been at the house yesterday but she didn't come. Daniel was away until late. When he was back he said – but, I haven't told you. Last April Canader was sold to Matthew by her husband – a scoundrel, good-for-nothing. He sold her with a rope about her neck for five sovereigns on Tarrendon Hill. No-one knew of it but Daniel found it out – he found the husband. Daniel has a grudge against Garth. He'd do all that he could to hurt him and he hates a wife who doesn't obey her lawful man. He has much cruelty in him.'

She paused, struggling to contain her excitement. George thought: surely I could get her an ecclesiastical separation from Fayerdon, but the child. Would she bear to give it up? It would be the father's. No, she wouldn't.

'He went early last morning,' Beatrice went on, 'with Brinsley – Canader's husband – and the constable and a lawyer from Dorchester. Brinsley says the story of the wife-sale was a lie. Garth has been arrested for criminal conversation and for throwing Brinsley in a ditch when he came trying to force more money out of them. He can never pay the compensation if he's prosecuted and Daniel knows it. And this is the worst – Canader has been taken away by Brinsley, forced to go back to a man who's treated her like an animal. She loves Garth and he loves her. Daniel's paying for all this – the first thing he's ever paid for willingly in his life – and he laughs about it.'

She turned her face to look directly at George. 'Do you remember a day last spring when we met at Thirza's? I sang a ballad of a wife-sale and asked you about divorce?'

'I do.'

'That was the first time I'd driven here alone. I was late. I made a diversion on the way. I stopped and walked on Tarrendon. I saw Brinsley sell his wife to Garth. I didn't know who they were then and I kept silence afterwards, for I'd have no woman in the power of a man she hates – then I grew to like the

Garths. They didn't see me there but I *saw* the sale as clearly as I see you. I was a witness. Brinsley and Daniel thought there was none. That must make a difference in the case?'

'It makes a great difference.' George straightened slightly as he considered. 'There can be no prosecution for crim. con. if there was a sale. A husband's connivance at adultery destroys the action. You give me your word that you truly witnessed the sale and haven't turned a glimpse into a conviction because you like this girl?'

'I do and will swear to it in court, but God help me when Daniel discovers what I've done.'

A ribbon of Beatrice's hat was hanging over the edge of the desk. George ran a finger down it.

'Has he ever been violent towards you?' he asked.

The colour that was returning to her face came faster now.

'Yes,' she said, 'he has.'

If things had been otherwise, thought George, her mother would be my wife and she my step-daughter. I could have prevented the marriage.

'When I first saw Daniel at Thirza's,' Beatrice said bitterly, 'I thought him so fine. You tried to warn me. I wouldn't listen. I'm listening now but it's too late. I don't want it to be too late for Canader.'

His face was more grim than she could recall having seen it.

'A Dorchester lawyer,' he said. 'Did you hear his name?'

She thought for a moment. 'It was Bryant.'

'Good. If Daniel felt himself on entirely solid ground he wouldn't have chosen that one. Why

259

didn't he come to me? No, I think it likely your name need not be mentioned. Would you be prepared to tell what you saw on the hill in detail to Moorehead and myself? His discretion is complete.'

'I would. To what purpose?'

'He and I will call on Bryant with signed statements that we've heard the testimony of a witness who can be brought forward if the case goes to trial. It'll shake him. He knows my reputation. I think it probable the charges will be dropped – and Daniel no wiser about the identity of the witness.'

She pressed his hand again. 'And the assault?'

'Of that I can give no assurance. But if Daniel thinks it worth his while to press the charge you need have no great fears. Skirmishes between men of their class are rarely treated with severity if there's no theft involved – and I'll visit Garth to see what may be done in his defence.'

The story of what Fayerdon had caused to be done to the Garths was quick to spread through Wynford Tarrent. If Daniel had thought to gain respect as well as satisfaction from this deed he was sorely mistaken for the mood of the inhabitants was much against him. It is one thing to enjoy disapproving of your neighbours' morals but it is quite another to cast them into gaol for their strayings. Although Matthew and Canader had not mixed greatly with the other villagers during their spare time, no-one who had known them had anything but good to say of them, whereas the miller was known for a mean and vindictive man. An account of the wife-sale was told by one who had heard Nat boast of it and, as well as being widely believed, this was held to vindicate the

Garths – for such sales were agreed to be legal and binding.

In the contemptuous discussion of Daniel's character the accusation by his wife that he was a eunuch – which had been so repeated and relished at the time of its saying – was recalled and brought out against him. The strangeness of Beatrice's words when she must have already suspected she was with child was commented upon and conclusions that were not flattering to Daniel were drawn. In the alehouse where Nat had spent the night after being thrown out of the cottage by Matthew, the furze-cutter, who had seen Beatrice and Boaz together on the road by Tarrendon, told of how they had held hands and how the shepherd had seen her drive to Holt's farm alone one summer's day. Her solitary drives and the absence of Esther were remembered; opportunity, inclination and accusation were married together and a vicious rumour of the parentage of Beatrice's coming child spread like fire and gratified all those who had reason to dislike Daniel. On Sunday morning, leaving church with his mother – Beatrice having declared herself too unwell to join them – Daniel found himself to be looked at askance and to hear sniggers in his wake.

It was shortly before noon on the Monday following Beatrice's applying to George for help that Daniel received a message from Bryant asking him to call at the lawyer's office to hear of a complication in the case brought against Garth. The matter was of such strong interest to Daniel that he rode at once to Dorchester to discover what had arisen. The shock it gave him to find that his plans had been thrown into disarray by George could not be adequately described.

It was his immediate intention to continue to press the charge of adultery and attempt to outface the mysterious witness but Bryant was not prepared to act for him, on the grounds that the Lamford firm would not have involved themselves if they did not feel sure of their man and – though he did not say this to Daniel – he did not feel his own professional reputation would be benefited by many more lost cases.

Reflecting upon the subject, Daniel was compelled to agree that it would be unwise to proceed and his fury at being thus made foolish was unbounded. He was convinced that Nat must have known of the witness and concealed it from him and, despite it going to his heart to have Garth released without punishment, he could not resist withdrawing his promise to pay for the action for assault. It was left in Bryant's hands to inform the gaol of the development and Daniel rode away pondering upon who the witness could be and how he could take out his spite against Nat.

Beatrice lived in fear that night. Daniel had not trusted himself to see Nat the same day and sat brooding in the dark parlour with such ferocity that even his mother did not dare go near him. Beatrice, lying alone in the room where he had so hurt her for insulting him, felt the child stirring and prayed that her part in this business would not be revealed. He did not join her in their bed but slept fitfully, with violent dreams, in his chair and early in the morning rode out to Cerne Abbas. It was not yet clear in his mind how he would make Nat regret having ever been born but he was not to be cheated of his vengeance. As he rode in the sunlight and birdsong that welcomed April, he thought that a man such as Nat could not be expected to work at an inn without falling into some form of pilfering. It was only for him to ask sly questions of the other servants or, if necessary, put temptation in Nat's way for the thief to be detected and placed more securely in his power than Garth had ever been. The courts could yet be his instrument and the gaol hold the object of his wrath. It would not serve his purpose to frighten Nat into fleeing from the inn and so, to achieve his end, he disguised his anger and tempered his severity with a readiness to forgive and even promote the interests of Nat if an undertaking to remain in his place were given. Nat, puzzled by the appearance of the witness, flattered by Daniel's attitude and with Canader, oblivious to the developments, scrubbing the back kitchen accepted this tribute to his worth and gave his word to stay. After privately arranging with the barmaid to have warning sent to him if Nat tried to leave, Daniel set out upon his return journey, his thoughts busy.

The repression of his rage had called for the utmost exertion of his will-power and, as he travelled the lonely lanes, the relaxation of the need for pretence left him in a state of mental and physical excitement. He shook as if he were feverish; his palms were wet, his temples felt congested with hard-driven blood. He was ready, in his hatred and disgust for the world, to harm whoever came near him and had he known that Matthew, newly released and with a bitterness to rival his own, was walking the road parallel to his in search of the mill and Canader, he would have altered his course to waylay him and there would have been murder done.

It was Daniel, however, who was waylaid. Samways, who he had turned off after the accident at the mill, was waiting for him where the road ran steeply down into Wynford Tarrent. The arm that had been broken by the winch had taken long to heal and had never fully recovered its strength. There had been bleak months through the winter for Samways and his family as they sold their possessions and searched for work that was not there to find and in them Samways had coveted a means to serve Daniel as Daniel had served him.

The misfortune of a neighbour had prevented the family from entering the workhouse and given Samways the freedom to have his desire today. That February the old woman who took in most of the washing in the village had suddenly been struck with a stroke. It was not so serious that she lost all power of movement and speech but she could no longer continue her business alone and because she was fond of the kind-hearted Mrs Samways, who had always been ready to lend a hand in flurried times, she arranged that the Samways should move in with her. They saved on their rent and had most of the work and profits, and she had a family to tend her. It was an arrangement which had been successful so far and it allowed Samways, who fetched and delivered the laundry, to hear the gossip of the village as he passed from one kitchen to another.

He did not have the money needed to spend his Saturday evenings at an alehouse and had not attended church, where he would have been obliged to see Daniel, since his accident and so it happened that he did not hear the rumours about Beatrice until he called at his first house on Monday. It had seemed to him that his wife had been unlike herself when she had come home from morning service the day before but her explanation of having a toothache had accounted for her strangeness. Now, as he sat before range after range, welcomed as one who would have reason to take special delight in hearing scandal against the miller, he understood what had affected her and why she had not told him of it.

He was not an overly intelligent man and it flattered him that his wife should think the news might propel him into some incautious action. The thought of Boaz cuckolding Daniel was greeted by him with indecent enthusiasm and, in his joy at having such a tale to fling at his old master, he did not think of any consequences for Beatrice. He returned to his cottage in a state of unnatural elation and, leaving the hand-cart still loaded, entered the steamy yard where his wife was boiling sheets. Seeing his excitement, she left the dolly that she had been plunging in the water and wiped her bare arms on her apron.

'Jane,' he said, 'had you the story? You had! Don't 'ee deny it.'

'I heard un,' she said, without eagerness. 'Don't put yourself in a fret. 'Twill all come to nothing.'

'Will it? Will it?' Samways thrust another stick into the fire beneath the cauldron and a scatter of sparks fell on to the brick surround. 'It's talked on all over. Every house I bin in. By God, the master's been riding for a fall and here 'tis.'

'He may never know. Who's to tell him such tittle-tattle?'

'I'll tell him myself. He can't do me no more harm than he's done. I'll go now afore anyone gets there first.'

His wife caught hold of his arm. She knew him to be a fool when in this mood and hoped to delay him long enough to recover his reason.

'You won't find him today,' she said, 'he's rid into Dorchester on his law business. I had it in the shop when I were buying cheese. He won't be back till the morning.'

Her husband was not inclined to believe her but she was adamant in her assertion and persuaded him that going to the mill would have no purpose. She thought that the interval would cool him but she had not reckoned on the extent of his spite against Daniel nor the temptation the choiceness of the rumour offered. It was rare that a man of Samways's class had the opportunity to injure one above him and he could see nothing but this single chance to have his revenge upon Daniel.

His eagerness to impart the scandal was so great that he went to the mill on Tuesday morning in the hope of finding Daniel but, on being told where the master had gone, he took himself to a place that Daniel must pass on his return and prepared to wait. He considered himself cunning in his choice of position. He was in the open country where they would not be overheard and yet was close enough to the village to run to the houses if he were pursued; he was within yards of the lane but was on a footpath in a meadow protected from the road by a hedge. He sat on the grassy bank that faced the lane and thought of the satisfaction to come.

It was early afternoon before Daniel was to be seen riding down the hill. Samways let him draw level and then stood up.

'Mr Fayerdon!' he called.

Daniel reined in but, noticing who had hailed him, moved on without speaking. Samways ran a few paces along the path so that he was beyond Daniel.

'Ye'd better hear me,' he said. 'Or you'll hear it from another and maybe it'll be too public to suit 'ee.'

The journey had not soothed Daniel. He drew in his mare again and turned a face that was stiff with imprisoned anger on his accoster.

'What can you have to say to me?' he said.

'Only that your wife's a whore,' said Samways, 'and the child that's coming naught to do with 'ee.' He had planned a hundred teasing ways to lengthen the telling of his tale but now he wanted only to shock. 'Another man's been fishing your pond, master, bain't you heard? 'Tis all about the village.'

With a savage pull at the reins, Daniel turned his mare's head and was brought close to the bushes. Samways, safely out of reach, went on.

'Why d'you let her go driving alone? A neat little maid like she? All down the lonely roads and in the hot summer days? 'Taint no wonder she were taunting 'ee. Eunuch, she called 'ee. No better nor a gelding. Didn't you never get to wondering?'

Hardly knowing what he was doing, Daniel rose in his stirrups but he was helpless to touch Samways.

'Does she love 'ee, master?' Samways jeered. 'Does she true? Those be lonely roads up-along and Farmer Holt were a lonely man afore his wife come home. You ask he if 'twas only his own land he was a-sowing.'

CHAPTER NINETEEN

He expected some threatening retort but none came. The claim was an abomination to Daniel but memories and suspicions were rearranging themselves in his mind, sliding unbidden into a new and wholly noxious order. There was more than thwarted malice in his heart now – there was a real hurt such as he had never imagined could exist. His pride was ruined. His son; his cherished boy . . . He did not speak or move and Samways, who had expected to triumph, saw on his old master's face an expression that made him back quietly away in dread of what he had done.

Daniel did not notice him go. The world contracted for him and there was nothing in it but the fraud that was being played upon him. Until this moment he had not realized how much he hated Beatrice. Above all other things he loathed the adulteress and the disobedient wife and she, who had been so carefully chosen to enhance his name, was both of these and mocked at him behind his back. The wheres and hows of her debauchery furnished his imagination and his belly moved with his disgust. There was not punishment enough that could be dealt her and her lustfulness. He did not mourn his son as a living boy who would not now have being; he could not yet spare his mind to dwell on what part Boaz had acted in this depravity; he saw only a wife who had fouled his bed and the justice there would be in taking revenge with his own hands. He turned his mare towards the village and, as he rode slowly through its streets, those who saw him knew what he had heard.

He dropped to the ground as he reached the yard and threw open the house door. His mother was fussing about the parlour but, seeing his face, drew back as he passed up the stairs. He stood an instant with his hand on the latch of the drawing-room and then went in.

Beatrice was sitting in a chair that looked on to the river, startled by the sudden sight of him. A shaft of sunlight had found its way into this dark house and lit up her hair as she sat with her sewing falling from her lap. The water was high and the noise of the great wheel turning outside the wall had masked all other sounds.

Daniel took a few steps towards her and stopped. Behind him a shadow moved as old Mrs Fayerdon crept up the stairs and hid herself on the landing. Beatrice stared at him and the fear that had laid waste her night returned to her. He knows, she thought, oh, God, he knows I was the witness. Her heartbeat quickened and bile burnt her throat.

The guilt in her eyes was enough for Daniel. To have been played false in this way, to have been cheated of the son who was to have carried on his name. The balking of the hopes that had roused his arrogance and set him on the path of such changes was a raging disappointment in his incensed mind. He had never used reason in his dealings with Beatrice but now he looked at her and it was as if he had discovered his accounts to have been altered and all his profits filched away. He shouted to her, 'Holt!

Harlot, harlot! They say you've Holt's bastard!'

She stood up, bulky and awkward, her feet catching on the sewing she had dropped. There was terror in her now; he would kill her for this. Deny it; deny it. Any chance to protect her child.

'What rumour?' she said. 'Who would say such—? Daniel! Do you listen to evil lies?' Her voice was weak and husky. She knew herself to be trapped and unable to make a defence against him.

He let out a moan and came across the room to her. She made herself stay still as if she were innocent and unafraid but he had abandoned all trust in what she might do. He took her face in his hands, squeezing her features out of shape.

'You bitch!' he said and there was a strange, caressing tone to his words. 'Admit, admit your guilt!'

'The child is yours!'

He pressed her head harder between his hands. 'Oh,' he said, 'you ensnared me. Always like Eve. So vile!'

He took his hands from her face and she ran towards the stairs but he caught her arm in the middle of the room and, drawing her back by it, he punched her beneath the breasts. She fell backwards with the force of the blow, gagging. Still holding her arm, so that her upper body was raised from the floor, he kicked her in the side of the belly. The movement made him lose his grip on her arm and she rolled on to her side, trying to reach the poker in the hearth. She was sick and faint but she would say nothing that could be held against her child. If it should survive there would be no proof from her to harm it. Daniel stood on her gown and, with all his weight behind his foot, he kicked her again in the small of her back. The pain and a sensation she had never experienced before overwhelmed her. She could not move from where her skirts were fast but she gathered herself on her knees, her head near the floor, protecting the baby as best she could. The roar of the wheel was loud but there were men in the mill. Daniel was pulling his foot back to aim again. She lifted her head and screamed.

Outside in the yard, Matthew saw the untied mare and open door. He was looking for Daniel and his temper was grim. He had been treated in the gaol as no man should be treated and his release had not caused him to pardon Daniel for his imprisonment. The stigma of his confinement marked him more deeply for its injustice than for the physical humiliations it had encompassed. That a man such as Daniel should have the power to treat him as a felon was wormwood to him. The unfairness of his detention had made a criminal of him. The law that bound Canader to Nat was not worth his consideration. He would find her and they would run and run again until they had found refuge. He had come now in search of Canader. As he had lain awake the night before there had been no offence or injury that might be done to her that had not been in his thoughts. His release had removed his helplessness but not his wrath and neither Daniel nor Nat was safe from him. He had walked from Dorchester with vengeance in his heart and if he had followed Daniel slowly to the mill it was from fear of doing too much violence when they met.

The door being open, he went in without

ceremony. He glanced into the rooms to the sides of the hall but they were empty and he thought he heard, above the rumble of the wheel, sounds from the upper floor. A woman screamed as he mounted the stairs and he ran to the landing. Old Mrs Fayerdon, her face maddened with excitement, had seen him and was doing a queer, dithering dance in the doorway of the drawing-room to prevent him entering. He pushed her aside.

Beatrice was lying towards the door now. Her legs were hunched up and her arms clasped about her belly. She was retching and there was blood on her hands. Daniel was reaching down to her hair when her sudden, hopeful glance made him look behind him. He saw Matthew.

'Leave her be!'

The disgust that was in Matthew at this sight was beyond anger. Contempt and scorn were plain upon him and Daniel, straightening and turning, saw a man who was not afraid of him.

'You're a fine hand at hurting women,' said Matthew. 'How are you with men?'

He came a step closer. Daniel moved back and stumbled against a small table that fell and rolled sideways. The interruption to his assault exhausted him. He did not want to grapple with Matthew. His pleasure was in hurting the weak not in brawling with strong men. It was unfair that he should be faced with one who had a grudge against him when he was tired from chastising his wife.

'Where's Canader?' Matthew began to walk slowly towards Daniel. What had been done to Beatrice so consumed him with rage that he dared not reach the perpetrator before he had governed himself.

Daniel made a shuffling movement to the right. He looked about stupidly for some weapon or method of escape. He could not believe he was trapped – he was master here and was treated thus. Images of injury and pain that might be inflicted upon him flickered in his mind.

'Where's my wife?' Matthew's voice was heavy with menace. Daniel retreated. His men – his men were in the mill. There would be protection. He turned and ran the few paces to the door to the bridge; the key was in its lock and it swung open easily. The tumult of the waters drove into the room, swelling to the walls that confined it. Daniel glanced back over his shoulder. Matthew was leaping towards him. He fled out on to the bridge. The mill and safety were so close. His feet struck at the thin wood. The planks were green and slippery, giving him no hold. He grasped at the rail to keep his balance but the post, from which Beatrice had dislodged the nail, had rotted and came away in his hand. He looked down at the planks and the sight of the dazzling spray flung from the moving wheel dizzied him and he lost his balance, falling forward on to the mouldering wood. There was a soft breaking, a dropping, a sound that might have been a cry and the planks gave way. He fell hard upon the waiting rungs and the wheel beat him down deep into the race.

CHAPTER TWENTY

Daniel's body was recovered from the river the following day and it could truly be said that he was mourned by no-one but his mother. This judgement on his life was hard for Beatrice to bear, for though she did not want his return she had not wished his departure to be so harsh and, despite his treatment of her, she was afflicted by the memory of the man she had thought she was marrying those years before. It was the gentle Thirza, who, though diplomatic, always spoke the truth, who disabused her sister of any sentimental regrets for her husband and delivered the verdict that Daniel had been a cruel and selfish man, worth no-one's tears.

Both Thirza and Mrs Randall were summoned to the mill on the day of Daniel's death and remained to aid the widow, for bereavement was not the only misfortune that Beatrice had to suffer. She had been too stunned to appreciate her state as Daniel ran out on to the bridge but Matthew had realized that her pain was not only that of a beating and, carrying her to her bed, had called for the necessary assistance for a birth. While Daniel still lay lodged in the depths of the race, Beatrice was delivered of a son and, though her labour was short, it was made terrifying to her by the knowledge that she was four weeks before her time.

The initial concern for the boy, with his spindly

legs and over-large head, was soon despatched. He had his father's endurance and mother's spirit and, with Beatrice's own zest for living pulsing strongly in his small veins, he prospered and flourished. Each time his aunt or grandmother looked into the cradle that rocked by Beatrice's bed, his face was fuller and his eyes more good-humoured and knowing. He was his mother's joy and when she fed him, in the days of spring sunlight or dark hours amongst the candle-flames, she began to feel peace and comfort and understand that now she need fight no-one to bring him up as she chose. She had never expected to be consulted in naming him and to prove her freedom and declare his family she called him Randall and watched her mother smile.

There was little stillness in the house for her apart from the times of her nursing. She hardly noticed the hurry of the search for Daniel's body but when the funeral was over it was no less busy at the mill. As executors of Daniel's will and guardians of Randall, George and Henry Lamford came more quickly to her bedside than they would have done in normal circumstances. It was revealed that, in keeping with his character, Daniel had not provided for his mother and old Mrs Fayerdon was, to all effects, destitute. She was almost broken by her grief but had not discarded her spite against her daughter-in-law. Blaming Beatrice for Daniel's death, she clung to her son's opinions as if they were written in letters of fire. He had accused Beatrice in her presence of carrying a by-blow and she believed him, trying alone to raise scandal against the mother and child. She had no success; the violence Daniel had done to his wife in her condition so horrified those who heard of it that it was held to vindicate Beatrice and harm was spoken only of her husband. An annuity was arranged by George to be paid to old Mrs Fayerdon and she was seen leaving the village to live with a Somerset cousin – vilifying Beatrice to the last – and exchanging the inside ticket bought for her on the coach for one outside for the sake of economy.

Beatrice had been eager for George to arrange more for her than the riddance of her mother-in-law. The dropping of the charges against Matthew made no difference to the order binding Canader to Nat and she felt it imperative to do all that she could to help the Garths avoid the law. She had money enough to give to the pair to hide themselves from discovery but merely to travel to a part of the country where they were not known, without sure plans of employment, was unsatisfactory and she needed advice on this and on the preliminary task of finding Canader.

The former was an awkward question for a lawyer to be asked to give counsel upon but the latter was easily dealt with. Matthew considered that Canader would have remained with Nat while waiting for the result of his case. George remembered that during his interview with Bryant, the solicitor had mentioned that Nat was working at Daniel's inn. A message was sent privately to the relieved Canader informing her that all was well with Matthew and that she must be ready to leave secretly at a moment's notice.

There was still the problem of where the Garths should go and Henry was brooding on this in his drawing-room one evening shortly after Randall's birth. He was a man who liked to have his family about him and, in feeling the lack of his wife, was the more ready to sympathize with the Garths upon their separation. It was early dusk and the candles had not yet been brought in. Henry was sitting in the wing-chair from which he could usually see Thirza, turning over the pages of a book and occasionally poking the fire unnecessarily.

A tap at the window roused him and, on looking up, he saw Isaac in the street outside. A short mime between the men resulted in Henry going to the door to let his friend in without waiting for the maid to perform her duty. Isaac had continued to call upon the Lamfords and had become regarded as a companion with whom personal matters could be discussed. His easy presence and direct informality fitted comfortably into the life of the house and he was doubly welcome at this time of disruption and anxiety.

Together they entered the drawing-room and Isaac took Thirza's chair. There was wine already at Henry's side and he filled a glass. Isaac noticed that his friend was preoccupied and his own mind flew to a matter which had recently much concerned it.

'I hope,' he said, 'you've no bad news of Mrs Fayerdon.'

'No, none.' Henry did not alter his expression but a thought that Thirza had given him began to provoke questions. 'She and the boy do bravely but she worries over the Garths and she has enough to trouble her.'

He had no need to explain the situation to Isaac nor to fear that he would side with the law. Isaac was himself a proud and independent man and the idea of binding an unwilling wife to him or, if he were in Matthew's position, of standing meekly by while Nat reclaimed Canader was equally repugnant. He had admired Matthew both as a man and a craftsman and, when he had taken supper with the Garths, he had found Canader likeable and strong-minded. It occurred to him now that he could assist the couple in their plight and, in doing so, gain the good opinion of one he wished to think kindly of him.

'It seems to me,' he said, 'that there can be no doubt that Garth and his wife – for what else is she? – should be reunited regardless of the legal ruling. Escaping from one such as this Brinsley appears to be can surely not be too much for them. The difficulty must lie in establishing themselves elsewhere.' He paused and thought briefly of his own decision to remain in what was proving to be a profitable and promising locality. 'If I wrote a letter of introduction I'm certain my parents would offer the Garths the hospitality of their mill. Garth would be in the midst of his profession, in an area of burgeoning trade and able to look about him without fear of homelessness. If you think this would be acceptable and can provide me with pen and paper, I'll write at once.'

His own wife's intelligence had Henry's admiration as he listened.

'You'd have your family do so much for the Garths?' he said, with a smile.

'I'd have them do a great deal to prosper my intentions,' said Isaac. 'They've always done so in the past and it's possible the future may bring a change that's much to my benefit. Do you think approval will be general?'

Henry was aware that with Daniel so recently buried most would call this conversation precipitate but he was not prepared to injure Beatrice's prospects for

278

the sake of misplaced delicacy. His disgust for Daniel did not allow him to be tender for the man's memory.

'I'd say,' he replied, 'that it would be falsely sentimental for anyone not to be pleased by this change. Especially those most closely related to the ones involved. It would be a happy day if all lovers were together – and I would certainly promote it.'

'And so,' said Thirza, 'they're safely away and you may set your mind at rest. George was at the inn this morning and found Canader gone and Brinsley very sorry for himself and sodden with gin well before noon. It was a fine opportunity to turn him off and George didn't hesitate.'

Beatrice, lying back amongst her pillows, looked at her sister who sat at the foot of the bed. The news should have gladdened her but the accidents of the past days had made her fearful.

'How can we be sure they're together?' she asked anxiously. 'If Canader grew tired of waiting and hid herself?'

Thirza came nearer to the head of the bed and took Beatrice's hand. 'She knew she was to be there ready to leave with Garth. He was near, watching for an opportunity and it came last night. The stable-lad was to let him know when Brinsley was dead drunk – and he did. They had until morning to begin their journey. No doubt we'll have word from them soon.'

Beatrice raised her eyes to the ceiling. There was sunlight on it and the familiar corn-dust made the air cloudy and dense. She was not easy in her mind. Her inability to be cheered by the news disquieted her. She was assured by her family that a lowness was natural to one who has experienced events of such moment and has not yet recovered from the effects of child-bed and assault but she felt that her dullness was more than that. The mill oppressed her. It was haunted by too many disappointments and degradations and she believed that she would not regain her spirits until she left it.

'I envy them,' she said. 'I envy Randall. All three have a new life beginning while I've only the end of an old one. I envy you, Thirza.'

Her sister still held the hand that she had taken. She had long drawn her own conclusions as to the remedy that would restore Beatrice to the brightness that had been present in her before she had met Daniel and a restlessness and envy of such as the Garths and herself seemed to point to a willingness to entertain thoughts of change. A withdrawn and depressed widowhood devoted to an only child would not serve to make Beatrice happy as the sharing of an enterprising and vivacious manner of life would. She knew nothing of Isaac's overtures at Christmas but they would now have met with her commendation if she had.

'The Garths have much to thank Mr Belton's kindness for,' she said. 'It must be a relief to them to be welcomed into his parents' home instead of having the worry of searching for lodgings in a strange place.'

She waited for Beatrice to comment.

'It was kind,' Beatrice said. 'It's fortunate he was told of them. I've been glad of his evenings in your house, Thirza, his work must be a lonely way of living.'

It was an innocent reply but the hesitation and consciousness with which it was spoken encouraged

Thirza to enlarge on the friendship now established.

'We're glad he chooses to be with us,' she said, 'he's a good-humoured man and I think a pleasant temper is the sweetest asset in a husband or friend. Daniel never fitted into our home but Mr Belton is as if he's one of us.'

Downstairs, in the strange silence since the great wheel had been stilled, they could hear Mrs Randall come in from the yard where she had been walking to and fro in the sunlight with her grandson.

'He asks of you continually,' said Thirza. 'Your old life has ended in a way that need not hamper you with any weeping. I think you've only to put out your hand to take a new one.'

There were footsteps on the stairs and their mother entered with Randall, heavily swaddled in shawls, in her arms. Her eyes were alive and shining with the first hour she had spent without uneasiness since her daughter's confinement and she brought with her the freshness of the spring day. She came to Beatrice and laid the boy in his mother's lap as she disentangled him from his outdoor garb.

'He's hungry,' she said. 'He wants his nursing more and more. We'll have a strong man of him yet.'

Knowing her preference, Thirza and Mrs Randall left Beatrice alone to feed him. He hurt her as he suckled but she had rarely experienced love without pain and it did not surprise her. She sat against her pillows with her son at her breast and thought of what had been said. It was Thirza's love only that had never injured her and Thirza's circumstances that had given her warmth. Now it was Thirza who was opening a door and pulling her out of a darkened room into a garden where one waited who was 'as if he is one of us'. Could she believe that there was happiness in store for her or accept that she, so recently widowed, was free to dwell on its promise? Her mind rested on Boaz. It would be hypocrisy for her, holding her guilt in her arms, to be coy with Isaac because she was newly bereaved of a husband he had judged to be worthless. She had withheld nothing of herself from Boaz; she had willingly allowed the desire for love to deceive her – how wrong it would be not to be open to the interest of a man who lifted her heart as Isaac did on each occasion that they met. If what Thirza had told her was true the warmth of Christmas could be hers always. Yet she would not come to him unsullied – at this moment the poison of the rumour of her adultery might be seeping towards Tarrendon – with what results for Boaz and herself she dared not think. The hope she had been given was so precious that she did not know how to face Issac if he came to her. It was not in her character to be passive but she was tired and, for once, she would rest and await events.

It was on a clear morning with warm, buffeting breezes, two days after her rising, that Isaac, having received word from Thirza that Beatrice was downstairs, rode over to the mill. He brought with him a paper of sugared almonds and the sheet-music of several ballads that had nothing of the lament about them. There was more confidence in his manner than he felt. He had come courting Beatrice with the approval of her family and the knowledge that he had her liking but the peculiarity of her situation was such that he could not tell what obstacles might

282

prevent his reaching her heart. It was no time for fervent declarations of love nor for any emotion which might drain her energies from her recovery. He wanted to demand that she accept him and join him in a life which could have so much of enjoyment for them both but there must be no demanding before she was strong enough to laugh at him.

He was shown into the kitchen at the mill. The parlour and drawing-room had too many associations for Beatrice and the life of the house now took place about the range. She was sitting with her mother and sister when he came in. He felt that his eyes must speak his errand for him but her fears prevented her from reading them aright. Suspecting that he had heard the scandal about her she flushed but she was so pale that this only restored her natural colour. He noticed the bruises on her face and hands and did not express his views on Daniel. They all took wine and cake together and there was a little conversation but, shortly, both Thirza and Mrs Randall felt that they were needed elsewhere and Beatrice and Isaac were alone.

Isaac had not troubled to console her for her loss and did not do so now. He had wondered whether entering the dead man's home might arouse some pity for him but the marks of violence that Beatrice bore answered 'no'.

'I was afraid to find you much worse than you are,' he said.

'I begin to recover but I won't have my health until I leave here.'

Beatrice felt herself confused in speaking to him. She believed that where this man loved he would not offer the tenderness of Boaz but would give the

283

steadfast, joyful fidelity for which she hungered. Was it being entrusted to her and if it were could she, in honesty, accept it without making her past known to him?

'Your brother-in-law says that you'll return to your sister's house,' said Isaac. He saw her embarrassment and was glad of it; she could have kept her countenance before a visitor to whom she was indifferent.

'Yes, at first. Henry will find a foreman for the mill.'

'I was thinking of taking a residence in the town myself. Lodgings are one thing . . .' He made a gesture with his hand.

She felt her spirits lift. 'Your business prospers so well?' she asked. 'All that you need is here?'

'Everything I desire is close at reach.' He watched her face and the hectic colour that rose in it encouraged his hopes and reminded him to treat softly one who had suffered so much. 'You won't want to stay with your sister for ever,' he said. 'You'll be wanting to find a home of your own where you can act as you wish.'

'I suppose that I shall.'

She was sitting at the head of the old table and he at the side with the gifts he had brought her spread among the glasses and plates on the white cloth. He leant across and took her hand.

'There's no need for you to hurry,' he told her. 'Let me have the trials of seeking out property and if I should find what I hope may suit you I can tell you of it. Who knows what household you may decide to have charge of? It will be your choice.'

She fingered the music he had brought with her

free hand. Protestations of love would have been too much for her state of mind but he was making the way easy for her.

'I think that will do very well,' she said. 'It's a pleasure that you think of me.'

He smiled. 'Yes, it is a pleasure. Always.'

She laid the music aside and put her hand on his sleeve.

'There's things,' she said with difficulty, 'that you don't know of me.' She wanted to confess her guilt and rest in his acceptance of her as she was but there was too much at stake and she could not speak out.

'I know that you're generous, loving and strong,' he said. 'What more should I know? That's enough.'

She looked up suddenly as if she thought his words hid an awareness of her sin but she could see that they did not.

'You must remember,' she said, 'that it won't only be myself. There is my son.' It was the most that she could do. She could not risk so many people's happiness for the truth; she had lied to Boaz to protect them all and it was better that she should live her lie.

'A boy,' said Isaac, amiably, 'who I've not yet seen.'

'He sleeps upstairs. Will you come?'

He drew back his chair and stood beside her.

'Take my arm,' he said, 'and we will go together.'

THE END

BRIEF SHINING
by Kathleen Rowntree

Willow Dasset was the most wonderful place in the world to Sally and Anne, a place of sun, and hay-making, and poppy fields, and Grandpa Ludbury striding across the farmyard to welcome them. Everything was perfect at Willow Dasset – everything except Meg and Henry, their parents. Meg and Henry brought all their tensions and resentments with them, and a pervading sense of restlessness that somehow damaged the enchantment of Willow Dasset.

As Sally, the eldest, changed from a child into a young girl, she began to realize that the tension came from her mother. Meg was a Ludbury, and possessed all the strangeness, all the greeds and longings of that curious clan. But now Meg's dislike and resentment was centred on her daughter. Sally, reaching out for a life of her own, realized that if she wanted happiness, any kind of happiness, she had to fight her mother any way she could. And the one thing she never forgot was the memory of her Grandmother – for Rebecca too had had to fight the Ludburys – and Rebecca had won.

0 552 13557 7

THE QUIET WAR OF REBECCA SHELDON
by Kathleen Rowntree

THE LUDBURYS WERE A CLANNISH AND DOMINATING FARMING FAMILY – REBECCA WAS THE NEW YOUNG BRIDE THEY DIDN'T LIKE.

Rebecca first met George Ludbury when she was eleven years old. Her mother had died that morning and George was the only one to give her comfort. She loved him from that moment on.

But George's family were a different matter. The Ludbury's – an affluent Midlands farming family – were snobbish, possessive, malicious, and in the case of Pip, downright mad. The matriarchal Mrs Harold Ludbury was enraged when George – for whom she had planned better things – insisted on marrying Rebecca. From that moment on the family did their best to wreck the marriage, win George back to the family farm, and alienate Rebecca's children from her.

It took thirty years of gentle compliance and evasive pleasantness before Rebecca won her private war and achieved exactly what she wanted.

0 552 13413 9

A SELECTION OF FINE TITLES
AVAILABLE FROM CORGI BOOKS

THE PRICES SHOWN BELOW WERE CORRECT AT THE TIME OF GOING TO PRESS.
HOWEVER TRANSWORLD PUBLISHERS RESERVE THE RIGHT TO SHOW NEW
RETAIL PRICES ON COVERS WHICH MAY DIFFER FROM THOSE PREVIOUSLY
ADVERTISED IN THE TEXT OR ELSEWHERE.

All Corgi/Bantam Books are available at your bookshop or newsagent, or can be ordered from the following address:

Corgi/Bantam Books,
Cash Sales Department,
P.O. Box 11, Falmouth, Cornwall TR10 9EN

UK and B.F.P.O. customers please send a cheque or postal order (no currency) and allow £1.00 for postage and packing for the first book plus 50p for the second book and 30p for each additional book to a maximum charge of £3.00 (7 books plus).

Overseas customers, including Eire, please allow £2.00 for postage and packing for the first book plus £1.00 for the second book and 50p for each subsequent title ordered.

NAME (Block Letters) ....

ADDRESS ....

....